"YOU REM ...
TERI WH ...

"I told you I'd ... n
replied, grinn... ...urned to
Ireland, and throughout the years I've cared for it
and added the other plants. It's an arbutus tree. Do
you like it?"

"Like it?" Automatically her hands reached around
Kevin's neck, and in response his arms slipped
around her waist. "I don't know what to say." She
glanced at the flowering tree again. "It's so
beautiful." Facing him, she saw the excitement
shining in his eyes. "You didn't forget me, did
you?"

His voice became as warm as the sunlight that shone
over them in the hillside hideaway. "How could I
have forgotten you? You're the only woman I've ever
really loved...."

ABOUT THE AUTHOR

Kelly Walsh grew up hearing stories about Ireland
from grandparents who were born in County
Cork and County Kerry. A Florida-based author,
Kelly tells us there are palm trees in the south of
Ireland, too! Unfortunately Florida can't boast
many lush, unspoiled forests, hauntingly beautiful
moors or mysterious boglands, all of which are
featured in *A Place for Us*, Kelly's third
Superromance, set on the Emerald Isle.

Books by Kelly Walsh

HARLEQUIN SUPERROMANCE
248—CHERISHED HARBOR
286—OF TIME AND TENDERNESS

Kelly Walsh

A PLACE FOR US

Harlequin Books

TORONTO • NEW YORK • LONDON
AMSTERDAM • PARIS • SYDNEY • HAMBURG
STOCKHOLM • ATHENS • TOKYO • MILAN

Published December 1988

First printing October 1988

ISBN 0-373-70336-8

Printed in U.S.A.

PROLOGUE

Manhattan, 1976...

THE RAYS of the late afternoon sun slanted off the clean white snow in Central Park as Teri ambled along the pathway. Even the shrill sounds of the sparrows and starlings in the leafless branches overhead failed to break her deep concentration. She was too busy weighing the pros and cons of the decision she had come to during her sleepless night.

She glanced at her watch, knowing that Kevin would be arriving from Boston in just a few hours—only to return to Ireland in the morning. *Kevin O'Shea.* Even his name conjured up an enticing image: a tall, smiling young man with vibrant blue-green eyes, a ruddy complexion and wavy, burnished-blond hair.

A well-wrapped jogger huffing steamy breaths nodded as he passed her, but Teri was too preoccupied to notice. She was engrossed in trying to sort out her feelings about the halcyon evenings she and Kevin had spent together the past week. It had all started with a chance meeting on a train from Washington, D.C. Then there was the awesome impact of their first kiss as they had stood in the falling snow outside her apartment building, and then the lovely nightly dinners together in intimate restaurants.

How had she, Teresa Rosario, a shy nineteen-year-old, fallen in love so quickly? she wondered. She stopped suddenly, telling herself it didn't matter how it had happened, only that it had, and tonight would be the last time she and Kevin would be together. Her decision reaffirmed, she turned and hurried back to her Upper West Side apartment, two blocks from the park.

TERI HAD JUST FASTENED the clasp of her single strand of pearls when the buzzer sounded. Tense, she hesitated and took a deep breath before opening the door.

"Welcome back, Kevin," she said with a smile, her heart hammering in her chest. He made no motion to enter, and she knew it was because she was usually ready to leave with him the moment he arrived. "Please come in," she said, a gentle softness in her tone. But as he crossed the threshold, an uncertainty gripped her and she wanted to grab for her coat immediately. However, another, more powerful emotion—love—forced a false calmness to take over.

After closing the door, she asked, "How was your trip?"

He turned and silently filled his eyes with her youthful loveliness: her warm sable-brown eyes, her delicate features and her dark brown hair, which fell in soft waves to the shoulders of the silky white dress she wore.

"Your trip to Boston," she reminded him in a wisp of a voice, stepping directly in front of him, seeing that there were gray shadows under his restless eyes.

"God! I've missed you," he blurted out in his melodic Irish brogue.

In the next instant she felt his arms around her waist, pulling her up against him with such force that she lost her breath momentarily. She wasn't sure who had kissed whom; she didn't care. The sensations were too overwhelming and too beautiful for such thoughts. Dizziness threatened to overtake her when his lips became more demanding and his arms tightened around her. For a long while he held her, tempering urgent kisses with tender ones and sighing her name. Needing air, Teri drew back her head and glanced up at him with sparkling eyes, easing from his embrace.

She ran unsteady fingers through her hair, and in a whisper she told him, "I missed you, too."

She wasn't at all surprised by her own nervousness, but his became apparent when he regarded her quizzically, then looked away.

His words were throaty when he asked, "Are you ready? I've made reservations at the—"

"Kevin," she interrupted, "I thought it would be nice if we had dinner here this evening."

He faced her, his eyes sharp and assessing, then she saw him glance at the small table by the window. She had wanted to please him, had wanted everything to look perfect. She'd taken special care to polish the single silver candlestick until it shone, and she'd rearranged the small vase of flowers several times. Yet he didn't seem pleased. Why wasn't he saying something? She went to him and slowly slipped the green-and-blue plaid scarf from around his neck.

"Teri, I—"

"Please, Kevin, this is the last time we'll be together."

Hesitantly he let her slip his overcoat off.

"May as well let me have your jacket, too," she suggested, smiling lightly. "I keep it pretty warm in here." On the way to the hall closet, she asked, "Would you like something to drink? I bought a bottle of Irish whiskey today."

"Yes," he said quickly, looking around for the liquor cabinet. "How about you?"

"With ginger ale, please. Everything's set up on the kitchen counter."

As he left the room, Teri touched her cheeks with unsteady fingertips. She guessed that her face, like Kevin's, was flushed. She heard the sound of ice clinking into a glass, then the snap of the ginger ale cap. Instantly she realized how keen all her senses were.

Kevin returned to the living room, and she accepted the glass he offered. Glancing at the bubbles in it, she said quietly, "I guess this is a welcome-back and a goodbye drink." Her dark eyes lingered on his for a seemingly endless moment. "Do you really have to leave tomorrow?"

The anxiety she had previously noted in his eyes was still there, and his voice sounded even more strained to her when he said, "I wish I didn't have to."

Forcing a not-too-convincing smile, she set her glass down on the end table by the sofa and murmured, "So do I."

After a healthy swallow of his drink, Kevin placed his glass next to hers. "There's something you should know—something I haven't told you."

Instinctively feeling she didn't want to hear whatever it was he was about to say, she told him in a rush, "There's something *you* should know, Kevin. I've fallen in love with you." She turned away, wondering what his response would be—dreading what it might be. Would he be embarrassed? Would he laugh? Would he just be polite and tell her she would soon forget him? She knew she wouldn't, knew she couldn't.

For a long while it was so quiet in the room that Teri thought she would scream if he didn't say something. Her heart was beating so rapidly, she had trouble breathing. But then Kevin was in back of her, his arms around her. His warmth was comforting, and she closed her eyes, feeling his cheek press against her hair.

Softly he said, "Please, don't make it any harder for me to leave than it already is."

"Will it really be difficult for you?" she asked hopefully.

"It will probably be the most difficult thing I'll ever have to do in my life."

Turning, she slipped her arms around his waist and rested her head on his shoulder, basking in his closeness. After an almost silent sigh, she admitted, "That shouldn't make me happy, but it does." She nestled in the curve of his neck and inhaled deeply, wanting to memorize the spicy fragrance that blended so pleasantly with his manly aroma. Her fingertips tingled as she trailed them up and down his back. Quietly she asked, "Does it bother you that I love you?"

She could feel his heart pound against her chest as she waited for his response. Anxiously she searched for the reason behind his silence, but found none. Again she asked, "Does it?"

"Teri," he pleaded, "we don't want to do anything foolhardy."

Knowing that her composure was just a fragile, protective shell, she pressed her hands more forcefully against his back, wishing she could hold him forever. In as steady a voice as she could manage, she told him, "I've never done anything foolhardy in my life. Maybe it's time I did."

When he tilted her chin up with a gentle finger to gaze down at her, she looked up into his glistening eyes. For her, happiness and all the goodness and kindness in the world were centered in his handsome features.

"Are you sure?" he asked gravely.

"I'm sure," she whispered back, then took his hand in hers and led him to the bedroom.

Without switching on the light, she began to undress, unable even to glance his way. The rustling sounds she heard told her he was doing the same. She could feel the pulse at her temples throb when she laid her final garment over the chair in the corner of the room. With effort, she lifted her eyes and gazed at him.

Moonlight streamed through sheer yellow drapery panels and cast his youthful, athletic body in a golden-amber glow. He held out his arms to her, but she couldn't move. Warring emotions of love, fear and uncertainty rioted in her brain, immobilizing her. She thought she had come to terms with her decision, but now, in the room's semidarkness, she wasn't at all sure she was doing the wise thing.

"Luv," he whispered, "come to me."

At the sound of Kevin's imploring voice, her doubts dissipated like snow in sunlight. With steady and graceful steps she walked over to him, put her palms on his chest and rested her head against his bare shoulder. When his arms folded around her and he gently pulled her closer, a thrilling sensation heated her skin. His warmth curled about her, enveloping her in a lovely cocoon of tranquillity. Tenderly she kissed his shoulder, then the side of his neck, and was surprised at the strength of the pulse there. As her hand slid upward over his chest, her fingers touched a small object on a chain. Drawing her head back, she saw a small gold cross with a circle at its juncture.

"It's a Celtic cross," he said quietly, and kissed her forehead.

She felt his hands slide slowly down her slender arms and take hold of her fingers. When he clasped his hands around hers and began backing away, Teri was struck with sudden embarrassment.

His shimmering gaze wandered over her in silent adoration, and in a husky voice he whispered, "You're even more beautiful than I'd imagined."

She followed the movement of his hand to her face, but closed her eyes as his fingers traced the smooth curve of her chin, brushed over her lips and gently threaded their way through her hair. When he stepped away she opened her eyes, and saw him go to the bed and swoop back the coverlet and the rose-colored top sheet. Moments later she felt him brace her back with one arm and reach under her knees with the other. In one powerful motion she was swept off her feet.

"This will be our night, yours and mine," he whispered as he carried her to the bed and set her down with great care. "We won't think of anything or anyone else."

Slowly and with great gentleness, Kevin led Teri through an unfamiliar passage into a world of voluptuous sensation. His kisses were soft yet enticing, his probings tender yet intense. The momentary stinging pain she ultimately felt was quickly replaced by a blissful joy and contentment as his deep sigh and endearing words wafted against her ear. Cradled securely in his arms afterward, she experienced a peace more complete than she had ever dreamed possible.

Later, still luxuriating in her newly discovered essence, she felt Kevin move, and she opened her eyes. He was leaning on his arm, smiling down at her.

"You're a bit of a witch," he murmured. "You've cast some kind of spell over me. But it's a wondrous spell. I've never felt so happy and content before... not with anyone."

She tightened her arms around him and gave herself over totally to the exquisite feeling of oneness with him, delighting in the tender kisses he dotted on her shoulder and face. "I do love you so," she said softly.

He nuzzled the side of her throat, and his voice was low and filled with infinite emotion when he said in Irish, *"Mo ghrá thú."* Then he slowly lifted his head and gazed at her moonlit face. For silent moments he struggled with the realization of what he had just admitted.

Kevin had tried desperately not to fall in love with the enchanting young American, but during the past week, as they had talked and laughed together, he hadn't been able to think of anything or anyone but her. Captivated by her sweet innocence and endearing charm, he had felt himself being drawn closer and closer to her, as though he had been destined to lose his heart to her. And indeed he had.

But now, gazing down at her, he could only feel joyful. "Yes, it's true...I do love you."

At his words Teri's heartbeat quickened, but then a terrible reality forced its way into her thoughts, and she asked, "When will you be coming back to the States?"

The sparkle in his eyes dimmed. "Not for a while—if ever."

Despite the sharp pain that jolted her heart, Teri was sure of one thing: she would never regret this time with Kevin. She had told him she loved him, and he had said he loved her. She knew she had no claim on him. She had asked nothing, and he had promised nothing. But she had to wonder how long her heart would ache as it was doing now. Remembering that he had tried to tell her something earlier, she asked, "Kevin, what was it you wanted me to know?"

An awesome silence hovered over the room, then he sat up and leaned back against the headboard, his features somber. "Nothing, luv," he said. "Nothing that could change anything."

His response was offered softly, but something in his tone made her lift herself onto her arm. When she looked up at him, she saw the pain in his eyes. "Yes, there is. Be honest with me."

"Teri . . . I—"

She watched as he threaded his fingers through his tousled hair, and she was chilled by his obvious torment.

"When I get home," he said quietly, "I'm to be married."

For Teri, all sensation stopped for long, wordless moments. She felt that she had no past, no present and no future. She had nothing. Then, slowly and mechanically, she sat up, raised her knees and clasped them tightly.

"You see," he explained with difficulty, "Moira and I grew up together. I'm promised to her, and she's waiting for me to come home to her." He cupped the back of his neck and squeezed the tightened muscles. "She was everything I ever wanted . . . until I met you."

Hardly able to speak, still staring straight ahead through the semidarkness, Teri managed with great anguish, "But . . . you're still going to . . . marry her."

"I have to! I've given my word, and a man's word is his promise . . . his honor. I've got to have that, or I'm not a man." Gently he tilted her face up to his. "And I have to go back home, luv. It's been said that only the past lives in Ireland, unforgotten and unforgiven, that there is no future for the country, only the past happening over and over. I need to help change that. At least I have to try."

CHAPTER ONE

Dublin, the present...

KEVIN RUSHED out of his office at the Department of Foreign Affairs, too angry even to notice the brilliant rainbow that arched over the valley city bordering the Irish Sea. Seamus McFadden had just called to notify him of an emergency meeting of the National Museum's board of directors.

Knowing the unfortunate reason for the meeting, Kevin hurried down Kildare Street toward the museum entrance. As he entered the building, he checked his watch. It was almost three. His pace slowed as he passed the rows of ivory-colored display cases. As he always did when he viewed the antiquities, he felt a deep kinship with the ancient artisans whose work represented millennia of Irish history. For him, the feeling was almost religious.

When he crossed the huge circular floor depicting the signs of the zodiac, his eyes swept over the exquisitely tooled silver pendants that had been found with the Viking-Age silver hoard and the Celtic gold collar that had been discovered in County Westmeath recently. His stride slowed even more when he reached the new Treasure Room, and a definite pride shone in his blue-green eyes as he gazed at the splendid gold crosiers, chalices and the beautifully decorated book shrines that had made Ireland one of the great centers of religious art in the early centuries of European Christianity.

His attention shifted when he heard Seamus call his name. He joined the man, and the two started up the stairway toward the meeting room on the second floor.

"Any news yet?" Kevin asked.

"The police found the truck."

"And the artifacts?"

Seamus shook his head. "Gone."

"What about the driver?"

"He's in the hospital . . . in a coma."

"And the guards?"

"Died before they reached the hospital."

"Damn!" Kevin stopped at the top of the stairs, slumped back against one of the Corinthian columns and crossed his arms. "How many pieces were in the shipment?"

"Nineteen, including the two gold Celtic torques and the fifth-century bronze harness plaque."

Kevin glanced down over the white wrought-iron railing to the exhibit room below. "It galls me even to think that an Irishman might be in back of this. It's a great way to celebrate Dublin's millennium, isn't it?"

Seamus's gray eyebrows arched. "Unfortunately there's a great deal of money to be made in the illegal trade of antiquities, if they can be gotten out of the country."

Facing him, Kevin said, "Whoever planned the hijacking had to have someone on the inside. Only a few people knew when they were to be transported from County Tipperary to the museum here."

"More than a few, really, if you consider Denis Fitzgerald and the workmen who crated the pieces."

At the mention of Fitzgerald's name, a muscle in Kevin's jaw twitched. "The workmen weren't to be told when the shipment was scheduled."

"Maybe they weren't, but there's still the entire board of directors here at the museum. We all knew."

Kevin's eyes narrowed. "You don't seriously believe any of the board members could be involved in this, do you?"

"Frankly, I don't know what to think. All I know is that a great deal of Irish history may be on its way to someone's private collection in London, Japan, or God knows where by now."

"All because there was a weak link in our security. I can't help but think it was at Fitzgerald's end."

"Perhaps," Seamus said, knowing that Kevin and Denis were usually at odds. "But, the antiquities *were* found buried in the bogs near his turf plant. I thought he behaved rather well in offering them to the museum."

"What else could he have done after the workmen who uncovered them bragged about their achievement in every pub in County Tipperary? Besides, Fitzgerald doesn't own the bogs. The state does."

Seeing that Kevin was becoming more upset, Seamus changed the subject. "Will you be at the CRC meeting tomorrow morning?"

Kevin nodded. As assistant to the minister of foreign affairs, he chaired the meetings of the Cultural Relations Committee and was involved in everything from arranging theater and opera company tours to promoting Irish exports, which was the business Seamus was in.

"Will you be attending?" Kevin asked.

"Oh, yes, but I'd like to talk to you about export potentials after we're through here, if you have the time."

Kevin placed a hand on the older man's shoulder. "I'll make the time. Thanks to businessmen like you, Irish exports are up again this year."

Seamus grinned. "So are my profits."

"Some of which I hope you're planning to invest in the new financial center at the Custom House when it's operational," Kevin said, smiling.

His eyes twinkling, Seamus asked, "Would you give me a moment's peace if I didn't?"

"Seamus," a young woman called from down the corridor, "the meeting's about to begin."

"We'll be right there, Fiona," he shouted back to his assistant. Then he asked Kevin, "Have you had any luck in getting Fitzgerald to back it?"

"No, he still pours his investments into the London Stock Exchange instead of Ireland, but I'm going to give it one more try when I see him next week."

"So, our white knight is going to seek out the black knight right in his own castle, eh?"

"Right after my meeting in Cork."

"By the way, how are Moira and Patrick?"

"She's fine," Kevin said noncommittally, but his face brightened when he added, "and Patrick is great. You should see how he's grown. I can't believe he'll be eight years old in just a few months."

"Seamus," Fiona called again, and the two men started toward the conference room as Kevin continued to brag about the boy's skill at the sport of hurling....

IT WAS MIDMORNING at the Irish Import Boutique on Columbus Avenue in Manhattan. Teri leaned into the display window to replace a white silk-and-mohair sweater jacket similar to the one she had just sold. After making a final adjustment, she ran her fingertips over the soft material and again marveled at the work-manship of Irish craftspeople. Standing erect, she brushed back a wayward strand of her dark brown hair and glanced down at the Galway crystal pieces spar-kling in the June sunlight. She made a mental note to stick with the clear crystal and not reorder the emerald pattern; it wasn't moving as well.

"Do we still have the damask tablecloth and napkins in the Celtic design, Teri?"

She turned and saw her partner, Colleen, holding a hand over the mouthpiece of the phone. "Just one left," she told her, smiling when Colleen made a circle with her thumb and index finger to indicate a hefty sale was in progress.

As Colleen's pen scribbled over the order pad, Teri thought how fortunate she was to have such a good friend. The two of them had been close ever since they had met at City College in New York more than a de-cade ago. They had been able to depend on each other through good and bad times over the years. Sadly, Colleen had been experiencing more bad than good re-cently.

After adjusting the belt on her yellow shirtdress, Teri picked up her clipboard and continued the inventory check she was working on between customers, but her mind was only half on her task. She was thinking how important it was that their business venture be a finan-cial success. Things were still touch and go, as she and Colleen had been in operation only a little more than a year and a half. Finally, though, the net results of their hard work were being recorded in black ink rather than red. *Thank goodness,* she exclaimed silently, beginning to count the tweed picnic rugs.

"Teri," Colleen said as she put the receiver down, "make sure we add several more sets of the Celtic design in the Irish linen to our list. Mrs. Donovan told me she saw the set we sold Mrs. McCarthy last week and just has to have one herself." She crossed her fingers. "Maybe she'll show hers to somebody else."

"That's right, think positively." As she put her clipboard down, Teri asked playfully, "Has it ever occurred to you how few customers we have with names like Garibaldi, Montaldo or Alfieri?"

Colleen flicked her straight, shoulder-length blond hair away from her neck, and began rubbing her nape. "Right, Mrs. Manzoni, as soon as our landlord gives us the okay on the vacant shop next door, we'll knock a hole in the wall and open up a pizza parlor."

"Irish jig music here mixed with a tarantella there, huh?"

"That would be a little much, wouldn't it?"

Concern gripped Teri as Colleen's smile disappeared and she sat down on the green leather stool in front of the jewelry counter. "Are you all right?" she asked worriedly, laying her hand on her friend's shoulder. "Is it the baby?"

Colleen forced a halfhearted smile. "If you're going to coddle me, how about getting two of those crackers from the box I stashed on the shelf under the cash register?"

Teri started behind the counter, shaking her head. "I worry about you. I really do, and I don't think it's a good idea for me to be taking off for three weeks right now."

"Better now than later. Besides, if I look as green as a shamrock every now and then, it's only because I envy you the trip to Ireland."

As she handed Colleen the crackers, Teri furrowed her brows. "You know, I still can't get over Seamus McFadden's concern for us. After all, we're just one small shop."

Munching on a cracker, Colleen said, "That's the Irish for you...all heart."

Teri mulled that over. In the past year and a half, she'd corresponded quite a bit with Seamus Mc-Fadden, who headed the export firm in Dublin she and Colleen did business with. And she had spoken to his assistant, Fiona Riain, last month. Fiona had called to tell her a box of merchandise had been shipped to her store in error. She had asked Teri to hold it when it arrived; she would arrange to have it picked up. It was in that phone call that Seamus's assistant had told her about the new Irish Craft Center in County Cork, an eight-thousand-square-foot showroom in a gallery setting that exhibited the best of Ireland's craftwork and was staffed by top-notch sales and marketing personnel.

At first Fiona's suggestion that Teri visit it and several other craft manufacturers in Ireland seemed out of the question. But when Fiona explained that she herself would order what Teri selected, thereby receiving a discount, and see to the shipping of the merchandise at a minimal fee, Teri and Colleen began to take the offer seriously.

"I don't know," Teri remarked. "We're all in business to make money, but McFadden's got to be making less than he would if we bought from him instead of direct from the manufacturers."

"Maybe he's trying to cut down on his own buyers' expenses."

"Speaking of expenses, we need to talk about your not wanting to hire temporary help while I'm gone."

"We already have. Besides, Charlie said he would help out."

That didn't quite convince Teri; she wasn't certain just how reliable Charlie would be. He was basically a great guy, and she knew he loved Colleen dearly, but he had a sickness—alcoholism. It had finally cost him his job with a prestigious Madison Avenue advertising agency. He was trying, however, Teri reminded herself. He had even begun attending AA meetings after finding out that Colleen was pregnant again. Teri prayed that the sessions would help, for Colleen's sake and that of Betsy, their five-year-old daughter.

Colleen stood and patted her stomach. "There, that was all I needed. The little fellow must have been hungry." She noted the troubled look on Teri's face. "Don't be such a worrier, and remember, it's not just a business trip. You haven't had a vacation since we opened this place."

"And you have?"

"Just wait until after the baby's born and it keeps Charlie and me up all night. That's the way it was with Betsy. That little pixie knew exactly when our eyes shut, and she would have none of it." She smoothed her palm over her stomach and gave it a pat. "Maybe this one will be a sleeper. And speaking of Betsy, she adores the dollhouse you gave her for her birthday. But you're spoiling her, you know."

With a teasing glint in her eye, Teri said, "Be honest. You're just jealous because she won't let you play with it."

Colleen smiled and narrowed her eyes. "Who says I don't?" After a thoughtful pause, she added, "Rick stopped by the house last night and asked about you again. He wanted to know what your favorite flowers were. I guess he's not a man who takes no for an answer."

Teri's eyes lowered, as did her voice. "The thought of dating someone else doesn't have great appeal for me yet."

"Will it ever? It's been two years now." Teri didn't respond, so Colleen said, "You know, friend, you may not want to hear this, but you let Angelo make just about all of the important decisions for both of you...where you two would live, what kind of a job you could have, even whether you'd have children. Isn't it about time you became the heroine of your own life, spread your wings and soared a little?"

Coming from anyone else, Colleen's remarks would have hurt, but Teri knew they had been said with affection and concern. And quite a bit of truth. Yet the habit of not facing up to that truth was deeply ingrained. She glanced at the wedding band she still wore and the engagement ring she had accepted from Angelo—much to her parents' joy—in her junior year at City College. "Such a nice Italian boy," her mother had said time and time again, and even today Teri had to wonder if she hadn't married Angelo as much to please her parents as herself.

"Well," Colleen asked, breaking into Teri's reflections, "don't you think it's about time you tried your wings?"

Not wanting to discuss the matter any further, Teri tried to put her friend's inquiry to rest by explaining, "Right or wrong, I still feel a sense of loyalty to Angelo."

"Teri," Colleen said impatiently, "loyalty is one thing, but you're too nice and too darn attractive not to be getting on with your life. Angelo would have wanted you to."

In her heart Teri knew that Colleen was right. Who was she saving herself for? The answer came instantly, but he was in Ireland, married, and he probably had three or four children by now.

The bell over the shop door tinkled, and a man entered. "You go on with the inventory," Colleen suggested. "I'll take care of him." She put on her brightest smile and greeted the man pleasantly.

As Teri started to count the plaid pleated skirts on a rack at the rear of the shop, her eyes lingered on the adjacent display of matching scarves. Smiling softly, she set down her clipboard and pen on the countertop, picked up a scarf and slowly ran her fingertips over the fleecy material. As she gazed at it, another scarf, very similar to it, came to mind, the one Kevin had worn that winter's evening twelve years ago—the last time she had ever seen him. *So many years have passed and so much has happened,* she chided herself silently, *and you still think about him.* She wondered if Kevin ever thought of her....

Teri's attention was drawn to the shop door once more as three chatty women came in, and she was forced to chase the subject of Kevin from her mind.

The morning passed quickly, and when the wall clock chimed twice Teri gathered up the lists she and Colleen had made and retrieved her purse from under the counter.

"You're going to love Ireland," Colleen told her. "Just make sure you come back. You may think the Italians are the world's greatest lovers, but you've never come up against an Irishman who's kissed the Blarney stone.''

Teri avoided Colleen's eyes and began to place the lists in a file folder, wondering if her friend had noticed the smile of remembrance that had bloomed too quickly to hide. She had never told Colleen about Kevin; she had wanted to keep that cherished memory tucked away in her heart's most secret place.

''Have a good time . . . promise?''

''I promise,'' Teri assured her, adding, ''and you promise to hire temporary help if you need it.''

''I will, I will. Now remember, don't buy anything with shamrocks on it. Think Celtic patterns.''

With their farewells said, Teri left the boutique and hailed a taxi to take her to her apartment on Riverside Drive that overlooked the Hudson River.

Once there, she finished packing and phoned her parents, who had moved to Naples, Florida, when her father had retired from the Long Island Railroad. Her mother told her how excited they were about Teri's upcoming trip and that they were looking forward to visiting her in New York when she returned. They wanted to hear all about the Emerald Isle. Teri also called Mr. and Mrs. Manzoni, Angelo's parents, who still lived in Brooklyn. Ever since their son's death, they had been more caring than ever, treating Teri as though she were one of their own daughters.

After giving the apartment a final check, she set her luggage by the door and was just about to leave, when a sudden thought brought a faint smile to her lips. She went to the dresser in her bedroom, opened the top drawer and searched for a few seconds, finally locating a small blue velvet box. Carefully she opened it and withdrew the gold chain with the small Celtic cross on it.

The day she had accepted the engagement ring from Angelo, she had taken the chain off and set it aside. She had tried to set aside her memories of Kevin, but the chain had proved easier to forget than him. Quickly she placed it around her neck, tucked the cross under her blouse and started out for her seven-thirty flight from JFK Airport.

Traffic was heavy as the taxi skirted the south side of Central Park and crossed the Queensboro Bridge to Long Island, and because of an accident on the road leading to the terminal, Teri barely had time to check in her luggage before boarding the Aer Lingus jet.

A five-and-a-half-hour plane trip over endless water wasn't exactly Teri's idea of a good time. She smiled pensively, remembering how Angelo had had to cajole her into going to the Bahamas for their fifth wedding anniversary.

Angelo. Their eight years of marriage had been nice; maybe the correct word would be "comfortable," she amended. But she had been disappointed upon discovering early on in the marriage that he wasn't as supportive of her career goals as she'd thought he would be. She had dreamed of eventually opening up her own accounting firm, but he had complained that such an ambitious project would take too much of her time. So Teri had settled for a nine-to-five job in the purchasing department at Lord & Taylor's. There had been no children; that, also, had caused her much regret. Angelo had wanted to wait until he became more established as a construction engineer. But they had waited too long. She could hardly believe two years had passed since a partially constructed cement overhang had fallen on him and killed him instantly.

Teri had settled into grieving, but Colleen hadn't let her continue for very long, telling her she had a great idea—an Irish import shop. The two women pooled their financial resources and work experience, and the Irish Import Boutique was established. The problems and long hours involved in starting a new business did indeed get Teri's mind off her personal tragedy, and she soon convinced herself that in spite of the disappointments she'd experienced with Angelo, she had been happy, and there were enough good memories to last the rest of her life.

The flight attendant broke into Teri's reflections, asking if she would care for a cocktail before dinner. Teri declined, then wondered if she'd be able to sleep later. That was doubtful; she was too excited. Anyway, she told herself, it would be early morning, Ireland time, when the plane landed, and she could sleep after she checked into the Royal Dublin Hotel.

After dinner, her eyes drifted from the movie screen to the darkness outside the plane window, and her thoughts wandered again, this time to Kevin. She recalled, as she had many times in the past, how excited and happy she had been when he had taken her into his arms in front of her apartment building the night they had first met.

She also thought of the Italian dinner they had shared, during which he had told her how beautiful the rainbows in Ireland were: he had described them as lovely ribbons of pastel colors that arced over the land from the Irish Sea to the Atlantic. And she'd been surprised to learn that there were palm trees in the south of the country. "Trees," she murmured, peering out the airplane window into the dark night, and suddenly she could hear that Irish brogue of his again....

"Do you know what the first thing is that I'm going to do when I get back home? I'm going to have a tree planted in your name. There's a program underway to help restore the forests of Ireland...."

Teri closed her eyes and clutched at the little gold cross under her blouse. She wondered if Kevin had remembered to plant her tree.

DRIVING ON THE LEFT SIDE of the road in her rental car was nerve-racking at first, but Teri soon adjusted. As she scanned the landscape, she instantly knew why Ireland was called the Emerald Isle: the grass, trees and shrubbery were brilliantly green and velvety.

The sprawling city of Dublin, only six miles south of the airport, was situated in a valley and appeared to be a bustling metropolis. She passed numerous well-kept parks and gardens and decided Dublin certainly had enough small bridges over what were either narrow rivers or canals. After driving by a square high-rise building along the River Liffey twice, Teri realized she wasn't doing too well with the directions the clerk at the car rental office had given her, so she pulled over and asked a couple the way to the Royal Dublin Hotel on Upper O'Connell Street.

After she had finally located it, she drove into the underground car park, checked in and was surprised to find a message from Seamus McFadden, asking her to phone him either at his office or his home when she arrived. Teri glanced at her watch. It was almost 9:00 a.m. Since it was Friday, she guessed he would be at his office. When she was settled in her elegant room, complete with a blue velvet headboard on the bed, matching drapes and an emerald green carpet, she returned his call and waited for his secretary to get him on the line.

"Mrs. Manzoni," he said in an animated tone, "Seamus McFadden here. Welcome to Ireland. How was your trip?"

"Very enjoyable." She smiled into the receiver. "I want you to know how much Mrs. Parnell and I appreciate your helpfulness."

"How nice of you to say so. You'll find that the Irish are a people who like nothing better than to be liked by everyone."

"I have a proposed itinerary I'd like to discuss with you," she said.

"Of course, but we'll talk business later. The reason I left a message for you is that my wife and I would like you to join us in a little midsummer madness."

"Excuse me?" she said, perplexed.

"Bonfire Night," he explained. "June 27. We're entertaining a few friends at home. I thought you might enjoy seeing a bit of Irish folklore in action and meeting some Dubliners—all quite respectable, of course."

Again Teri smiled. "I'm sure they are, but I've just checked in, and I am rather tired."

"Oh, yes, the time difference. But the celebration doesn't begin until dusk this evening, and Margaret will be severely disappointed if you don't let her extend you a warm and proper welcome to Dublin."

"Well," she said quietly, having planned to spend the evening alone, "you'll have to give me directions. And is it formal?"

"No, not at all. Just dress comfortably and don't worry about directions. I'll send my car for you. Will eight-thirty this evening be all right?"

"That will be fine."

"Wonderful. See you then, Mrs. Manzoni."

"Yes. Goodbye."

Teri put down the receiver, annoyed at herself for not having been more assertive. As she removed several outfits from her garment bag, she wondered what "not formal" meant in Dublin, and she finally decided on her mauve jacket dress; it was simple but sophisticated. Yawning, she decided she was indeed tired, so she postponed a bath in favor of some sleep first. Her instinct proved true, for no sooner did she rest her head on the pillow than she dozed off, thinking it hard to believe she was actually in Ireland.

Hours later, a groggy Teri rolled over, peered at her travel alarm clock and saw that it was ten past four in the afternoon; she had slept almost seven hours. After a leisurely bath, she switched on the television and began to dress, half listening to the newscast.

"Unsure exactly what artifacts have been hijacked. With me now is Terence McKenna, spokesman for the National Museum."

The words "National Museum" caught Teri's attention, since Colleen had made her promise to visit it while in Dublin.

"Mr. McKenna," the interviewer said, "do you think the police are doing all they can to find out who is responsible for the hijacking?"

"I'm certain they're doing their best, considering that the driver of the truck is still in a coma."

"Then there are no leads?"

"Unfortunately, no."

Teri shrugged into her dress, saddened at the reminder that even Ireland had its share of crime. She listened more intently as the interviewer continued.

"Just how valuable are the artifacts?"

"There's no way of setting a sum on them in pounds. The real loss is in the way of our national heritage. No amount of money can replace that."

"Mr. McKenna, do you believe the theft could have been planned without the help of someone inside the museum?"

"At this stage I imagine that as far as the police are concerned, no one is beyond suspicion."

"Yourself included?"

Rather stoically, he responded, "You would have to ask the authorities that."

"Yesterday Seamus McFadden—" hearing the man's name, Teri's eyes darted back to the television "—told us that an armored car would be used to transport further shipments to the museum. Can you tell us what precautions are being taken to ensure that the artifacts already hijacked aren't taken out of the country?"

"Everything possible is being done. Customs has been notified, and the police are doing spot checks at all ferry ports to England and France."

As she switched off the TV, Teri wondered what Seamus McFadden's connection to the museum was. Then, after a final glance in the mirror, she set out for the hotel dining room for an early dinner.

THE CAR that Seamus McFadden sent over to Teri's hotel was a chauffeur-driven limousine, and she found that the McFadden home was a mansion. A butler opened the massive carved door and led her through carpeted rooms luxuriously appointed with furniture of richly finished woods, exquisite embroidery and sparkling chandeliers. She followed him onto a back terrace, deciding then and there that the Irish export business was alive and well—at least for Seamus McFadden.

Teri looked down over the expansive sloping lawn, and in the distance she noted several small groups of people by the bonfire, a low, sprawling one rather than the kind with flames leaping high in the air. A moment later she saw a man turn and start up the steps toward her; her host, she assumed.

He was short and appeared to be somewhere in his late fifties. His eyes were pale green, and he had a prominent aquiline nose and bushy gray hair, strands of which defied gravity. All in all he was the nearest thing to a leprechaun Teri could imagine. There was an easy charm in the wide smile that greeted her.

"Seamus McFadden," he announced, shaking her proffered hand enthusiastically. "How lovely you look."

"It was kind of you to invite me, Mr. McFadden." She glanced around at the fashionably dressed women in view and was happy she had bypassed slacks and a pullover.

"Let's make it 'Seamus' and 'Teresa,'" he suggested, his eyes twinkling. "How are you enjoying Dublin so far?"

"I really haven't seen much other than the hotel, but I'm looking forward to viewing the crafts at the Enterprise Tower tomorrow. Then on Sunday I'll be just another American tourist."

"Wonderful. Fiona told me this was to be a combined business trip and vacation for you." He glanced around. "She's here somewhere." Focusing on Teri again he asked, "Are you going to Cork first or to Killarney?"

"Cork, then on to Killarney and Galway. I've changed my mind about visiting Waterford. We've been doing very well with the Galway crystal, and the profit margin is higher."

He tilted his head a little and looked at her with admiring eyes. "You American businesspeople amaze me. You do everything with such precision. From your agenda, though, I'm wondering just how much time you'll have for pleasure."

"I took the fly-drive package Aer Lingus offers, so I have a car at my disposal. It will be a pleasure just to take my time while I'm driving."

"Just make certain you top up your tank before starting out. You won't find as many petrol stations along our country roads as you do on your wonderful highways in America."

"I will."

"Are you acquainted with the south of Ireland, Teresa?"

"Uh, no—" her eyes sparkled with the remembrance of what Kevin had told her about Ireland "—but I once knew someone who made it sound like the most beautiful place on earth."

"Well, your friend wasn't all that wrong, and this is a nice time of year to see the countryside. The view changes so quickly."

"I'm looking forward to it very much."

"I'll have the order forms Fiona told you about delivered to your hotel in the morning. After you decide just what you want from each of the manufacturers you visit, let me have the forms. Fiona will do the ordering, and I'll make sure that everything is packed securely and shipped to you in New York."

"Seamus—" Teri tried to minimize her curiosity "—when Fiona explained that this roundabout way of ordering would save us money in the long run, Colleen and I were . . . well, we were surprised at your willingness to go to so much trouble for us. After all, we must be one of the smaller shops you deal with in the States."

"Ah, but you'll grow." He arched his fuzzy, gray brows and smiled mischievously. "Then you'll order even more merchandise through us, and we'll all make out like bandits. Come now, Margaret is looking forward to meeting you."

With a gentle tug on her arm, he led her down the stone steps onto the lawn and toward a lantern-lit table set under a canopy of aged oaks. There he introduced her to his wife, Margaret, a fair-complected, svelte woman who was just as charming as her husband, Teri decided.

As her hostess handed her a glass of punch, a man's voice close to Teri's ear said, "Be careful. Margaret's punch could wear a hole through steel."

Teri turned abruptly and instantly recognized him as the man she had seen interviewed on television. Sure enough, Seamus introduced him as Terence McKenna, spokesman for the National Museum in Dublin, and added that he himself was on the board of directors.

Holding out her hand, Teri smiled and said, "I saw you on a newscast earlier today, Mr. McKenna. You were being interviewed about the theft of Irish artifacts."

"Irish treasures," he corrected. "The hijacking is causing quite a stir throughout the entire Republic."

"And in Northern Ireland, too," Seamus said. "Although they certainly have other things to worry about."

"Ah, the Troubles," Margaret commented. "Will they never end?" She faced Teri. "Fiona has a married sister living in Belfast. Brenda...uh...Quinn, isn't it, Seamus? She has a baby girl, and Fiona worries about them constantly. Imagine living in a city patrolled by armed men and shopping at stores surrounded by barbed wire fences."

"Don't carry on so, dear," Seamus said. "Statistics on terrorism show Northern Ireland to be safer than London." His eyes shifted, and he called out, "Fiona!" Then he beckoned to an elegantly dressed young woman across the lawn. When she joined them, he introduced her to Teri.

"I've been looking forward to meeting you, Mrs. Manzoni."

Teri responded appropriately, taking time to assess the woman. Her auburn hair was beautifully coiffed, and she had a face Teri wouldn't have been surprised to see on the cover of a fashion magazine. The striped burgundy wool suit she wore could have come from the pages of *Vogue*, and even in the semidarkness the sculpted gold chains she wore glittered.

Fiona said pleasantly, "We have really enjoyed doing business with you and Mrs. Parnell."

"Your firm's service has been exemplary," Teri assured her, silently recalling the order that had been shipped to her by mistake.

"We do have a good track record," Seamus remarked, "and it's largely due to Fiona here. She just about runs the place, particularly the shipping department. I don't know what I'd do without her."

"Nonsense, Seamus. I only follow your instructions."

"No more business talk," Margaret said. "This is Bonfire Night." With that she spirited Teri away to refill her punch glass.

"Exactly what is Bonfire Night?" Teri asked as Margaret ladled the aromatic drink into Teri's glass.

"Well, in the west of Ireland they party on June 23, but here in the east we celebrate on June 27, the eve of the feast day of Saints Peter and Paul. For hundreds of years it's been a Christian celebration, but it supposedly had its origins in pre-Christian times . . . some sort of fertility rite." She laughed, then added, "Nowadays, though, you'll find most people at home watching *Dynasty* or *Dallas*. I do love that J.R. He's so deliciously evil."

Smiling, Teri sipped some punch and thought that after a few more swallows she'd be jumping over the bonfire right alongside some of the more adventurous souls who were doing so now. As she watched with interest, she said to Margaret, "I'm sure there's a point to what they're doing, but isn't it dangerous?"

"That is the point," Margaret answered, adding secretively, "actually, some people believe that jumping over the bonfire enhances your luck in love. Shall we go watch?"

Teri set her glass down on the table and walked with her hostess toward the orange-blue flames. Away from the terrace and buffet table, the fire was the only light source other than the pale rays emanating from a half-moon. The sound of mirthful laughter brought a soft smile to Teri's face, and she watched as a young man leaped high and wide across the tallest lick of flame, then fell to the ground, rolling and laughing at the same time.

He must have had quite a bit of Margaret's punch, Teri thought, her smile widening. She continued to look on with interest as another man on the opposite side of the fire took several steps backward and charged toward the flames. As he leaped, the fire's yellow-gold light illuminated his face.

Teri's heart stopped, and she gasped, "Kevin!"

CHAPTER TWO

PAST YEARS MELTED AWAY and Teri stood immobile, her eyes fixed on Kevin as he sauntered toward her and Margaret. She saw that time had only made him more attractive, if that was possible. Her mind's eye flashed her a vision of a lean young man standing naked, his arms held out to her. And yes, the man coming toward them was the same person: tall, with wavy blond hair and a still athletically trim body—the snug fit of his maroon sweater and brown corduroys proved that. But his once angular features were now finely honed to manly perfection.

"Wonderful fun, Margaret," he said, smiling, "but each year it gets a little harder to—" he glanced at the woman a few feet away "—to...make the...jump." His smile evaporated, giving way to inquiry, then recognition, then utter disbelief. "Teri?" he muttered, the word cloaked in strained emotion.

He moved toward her, staring at her, and Teri fought the lump in her throat. She felt as though a heavy weight were pressing against her chest. After a long and excruciating silence, she managed to whisper, "Kevin."

Just then Seamus joined them, having overheard Teri. Surprise colored his comment. "Apparently you and Mrs. Manzoni are acquainted, Kevin."

His disbelieving eyes riveted on her, Kevin explained, "We met briefly many years ago in New York."

Seeing that Teri had paled suddenly and appeared unsteady, Margaret asked, "You're not ill, are you, dear?"

She shook her head. "No...no." Conquering the vertigo she briefly experienced, Teri forced what she hoped would pass for a smile. "I imagine I'm just experiencing a little jet lag."

"Would you like a glass of water?" Kevin asked.

Casting him a troubled expression, she shook her head again. To Margaret she said, "I would like to freshen up, though."

"Certainly, dear. Come along with me." After turning to her husband and saying, "Seamus, our guests have hardly touched the buffet," a concerned Margaret led Teri into the house.

Alone in the spacious bathroom upstairs, Teri doused her face with water, her breath still coming in gasps. Staring into the mirror over the sink, she saw that her face was quite pale. Earlier she had pinned her hair back into a twist, but several strands now hung askew. As she tucked them in place, she tried to organize her whirling thoughts.

The shock of seeing Kevin again had sent her emotions into a spin; surprise mingled with joy, confusion with hope, reality with cherished memories. Resting her palms on the edge of the sink for support, she looked at her reflection in the mirror again and muttered, "Teri, you've made a complete fool of yourself!"

She retrieved a small kit from her purse and began to repair her makeup, wondering what Kevin was thinking. *Why did you just stand there like a mute?* she berated herself. *Why couldn't you just have smiled like an old friend and said how nice it was to see him after all these years?* She tossed her compact back into the kit and asked herself why she had accepted Seamus's invitation... and why she had come to Ireland in the first place.

"Why?" she said, groaning. Moira was probably downstairs with Kevin at this very moment. What was going on in *her* mind? Had Kevin told his wife about her? She doubted it. No man in his right mind would have. She gripped her purse more firmly and tried to think of a good excuse for leaving the minute she saw her hosts, but she realized that would be extremely impolite.

She started down the blue-carpeted stairway and saw Kevin waiting in the entry hall below. He turned and stared up at her, then moved slowly toward the bottom of the steps. For years he had doubted his recollections of the young woman he had met and made love to. He had thought then that she was the sweetest and loveliest thing he had ever seen. She'd had an innocence and a vulnerability that had captivated him completely and unmercifully. But the woman coming down the steps toward him now was totally sophisticated and more than lovely. She was magnificent!

That very assessment—magnificent—was the same one he had made when Teri had opened the door to her apartment that evening, wearing that silky white dress. Then her dark hair had hung in soft waves; now it was stylishly drawn back, but still soft looking and lustrous.

Extending his hand to her, he said quietly, "It's good to see you again... so very good."

As she held out her hand, she saw that Kevin's eyes had not changed. They were still vibrant and glistened with silver lights that enlivened their lovely blue-green hue. His warm hand clasped hers firmly, and his mere touch was electrifying, bringing to life a troubling resurgence of the longing and desire she'd thought she had laid to rest.

The little speech she had rehearsed upstairs was forgotten; the only words that came from her lips were nervously spoken. "I . . . didn't think I'd ever see you again. I mean, I . . . yes, it's good to see you, too."

Still holding her hand, he asked, "Are you feeling up to more of Bonfire Night, or would you rather I take you back to your hotel? Seamus told me you were staying at the Royal Dublin."

Forcing the most pleasant expression she could muster, she said, "I'm fine, really. In fact, I'd like another glass of Margaret's punch."

Kevin took hold of her arm, and they returned to the candlelit tables under the oak trees, where he got each of them a glass of the potent concoction. Teri glanced around, expecting to see his wife approach them. Of course, she thought, it was possible that something had kept Moira from attending—children, perhaps.

When he handed her the glass of punch, Teri thought his expression was strained. Then she realized he had to be as surprised as she was. In the next moment, though, she was totally disarmed by his charming smile.

Raising his glass, he made a toast. "To the ticket agents of the Pennsylvania Railroad for getting us on the same train that night."

His lively eyes held her dark ones for long, quiet moments, and when he saw her look down, he took a healthy swallow, never breaking his penetrating gaze.

For Teri, his toast instantly brought back memories of the glorious week they had shared—and the months of agony she had lived through after he had left.

Seeing that she was pensive, Kevin said, "Seamus mentioned you were here on business."

"Yes, a shopping trip for our Irish import shop."

"Yours and your husband's?"

Teri glanced down at the wedding band she still wore. "No," she said, unable to look up at him. "I'm in a partnership with a friend, Colleen Parnell."

"I see," he commented quietly, but his insides were in a state of upheaval. He wondered if the twelve years that had passed had completely washed away her memories of the closeness, the intimacy and the joy they had experienced together. He felt a painful and silent laugh ripple through his chest, and he told himself that if the years hadn't made her forget, Mr. Manzoni would have. He wondered what her husband looked like, and his stomach twisted when he visualized a faceless man taking her into his arms, holding her close and—

Needing to obliterate the mental image, Kevin drained his glass, then refilled it. When he turned to Teri again, he saw that she was watching the younger men and women jumping over the bonfire. He studied her face, concerned; it was almost drained of color. "Are you sure you're all right?" he asked anxiously.

"Certainly," she said, brightening her expression. "Why do you ask?"

"When you first saw me I thought you were going to faint."

Her eyelids flickered nervously, then she raised her glass a little and told him, "Margaret's punch, most likely. I suppose it was foolhardy of me to have drunk it so quickly."

The muscles in Kevin's face became taut, his eyes restless. He still couldn't believe she was there in front of him. His voice was soulfully soft when he said, "I remember you once told me you'd never done a fool-hardy thing in your life."

Kevin's words rioted in her ears, and she experienced a sharp thrust in her heart, as though a knife had pierced it. Why was he reminding her of that night? Had he lost all feeling about it? Did he expect her to laugh and admit how capricious and inexperienced she had been?

As she stared out over the grounds, barely seeing the partying guests, a bitterness replaced the ache in her heart, and she felt that she wanted to hurt Kevin the way he had hurt her so long ago. *No,* she decided. *What good would that do? It wouldn't change a thing.*

She looked directly at him, and her voice was edgy when she said, "I was foolhardy only once, Kevin. Actually, a better word is 'naive.'"

"Yes," he said, setting his attention on the glass he held. "We were both much younger then...both naive...and trusting." He lifted his eyes abruptly. "Did you...regret it afterward?"

Teri's breathing was becoming more difficult by the second. She was also becoming more confused. Who was she talking to: the young man she had fallen in love with or a man interrogating her about something best forgotten?

"Did you?" he repeated.

She searched his eyes in vain for some hint of compassion, then responded in a thread of a voice, "No, I never did. You see, you were very special to me. You were the first man I ever loved, the first man I ever made love with." Her faint, low chuckle was bittersweet and shattered him. "I didn't really know how much loving someone could hurt, until after you left New York."

She put down her glass and took several steps toward the massive trunk of a nearby oak tree. He followed.

Without looking at him, she said calmly, "I remember that night you said goodbye. It was snowing. I watched from the window and saw you get into the taxi. It was so cold, Kevin, so very cold." She felt strong hands take hold of her shoulders and turn her around gently.

"I didn't want to leave you. You *knew* that."

She gazed at him with dewy eyes. "Yes," she said softly, "I really believed you didn't want to leave. I told myself just that over and over again. I thought it would help, but it didn't."

"Teresa," Seamus called from a distance, "there's someone here I want you to meet . . . an American."

Kevin and Teri joined Seamus, and after a brief conversation with him and the man from Texas, she told Seamus she wanted to get an early start in the morning. She asked if he could call her a cab to take her back to her hotel.

"Nonsense," he told her, "my driver will take you back."

"That's not necessary," Kevin said. "I'll drive her into Dublin. I have to leave, too."

"No," she said quickly, not wanting to be alone with him. "A taxi will be fine, really."

But he only grasped her upper arm and said, "Let's say good-night to Margaret." Then he started toward the terrace, where their hostess was chatting with a small group of guests.

Once they were in his car, Kevin regarded Teri with intense eyes before switching on the ignition and taking off. A nervous Teri stared straight ahead, trying to think of safe topics of conversation. Finally she asked, "Are you still trying to interest Irish-Americans in buying vacation or retirement homes in Ireland?" She was referring to the job he had held when she had first met him.

"No," he said, and glanced over at her elegant profile, which had an amber glow from the light coming from the dashboard. "I gave that up soon after I...left you. Now I work for the Department of Foreign Affairs here in Dublin, mainly as liaison with the IDA, the Industrial Development Authority."

He didn't want to talk about his job—not now. He needed desperately to know if she had ever thought about him or the last evening they had spent together. But his eyes swept down to the wedding band on her finger, and he forced himself to continue their damnably mundane conversation.

"Right now there are two projects I'm putting a lot of time into," he said dully. "One involves developing stronger commercial links between Ireland and the United States. We need an increase in the number of American firms set up here, high growth sectors like electronics, pharmaceuticals and consumer products. The other project is the development of an international finance center here in Dublin."

Teri sat rigidly, Kevin's words sounding hollow to her ears, as though he were speaking from a great distance. If only her heartbeat would stop thudding for just a while, she thought. Then she would be able to pull herself together.

Her silence weighing heavily on him, Kevin tried to get Teri to speak by saying, "Seamus mentioned you were a customer of his."

"Yes," she said, and during the remainder of the drive into Dublin, they talked about Seamus's export business and how Teri had come to know him.

A half hour later, when he turned off Clonliffe Road and parked in front of a town house, Teri said, "This isn't my hotel."

"I know. The bar at the Royal Dublin is far too noisy for us to be able to talk."

"Talk?" Just when she had regained a modicum of composure, she felt it slip away. "Kevin," she said with determination in her tone, "it's late, and I have a busy day tomorrow. I'd appreciate it if you took me to my hotel."

After sighing deeply, he said, "I know it's late," and he placed a gentle hand on her shoulder. "Twelve years is a long time. Surely we have something to talk about."

It's not fair! she screamed silently. Her feelings for Kevin O'Shea were a thing of the past. They were behind her, only memories. But his hand seemed to burn through her jacket, belying her silent protest. Pressing a thumbnail into the strap of her purse, she looked over at the building. "Where are we now?"

"This is where I live when I'm not traveling."

And Moira isn't here just now, I imagine, she added mentally.

"Please," he requested, "just for a short while."

Lifting her chin a little, she looked at him. A warning voice told her to run; a stronger one—curiosity, she imagined—forced her to stay. "A short while," she agreed finally.

As Teri entered Kevin's town house, she was immediately struck by the charm and order of the spacious living room—except for the large desk by the window on which were scattered numerous papers and folders. The walls were paneled in a polished reddish brown wood. Window shades matched the blue-and-maroon plaid of the two wing chairs placed near the screened fireplace. The same blue was repeated in the sofa that sat on a large hand-woven rug with a Celtic design. Along one wall was a floor-to-ceiling bookcase, and behind the desk, in the center of a trio of windows, luxuriant ivy leaves cascaded from a hanging basket. She glanced around, looking for signs of a woman's touch. There were none.

Closing the door behind him, Kevin asked, "Can I get you something?"

"No, thank you."

"Make yourself comfortable," he said, gesturing toward the sofa.

Teri sat down and watched him walk to a bar cart at the far corner of the room, where he poured himself a drink in a short crystal glass. She looked away, finding it hard to believe she was in the same room with him. And she had to wonder just why she *was* there. Kevin's movement caught her attention and she looked back at him as he walked to the wing chair across from her and leaned an arm on it.

"If it's possible," he said, "you're even more beautiful now than the last time I saw you."

Dismayed by his intimate tone, she rose quickly. "Kevin, I'm tired and I do have a lot of things to do. Would you—"

She was startled when he set down his drink and began to move toward her, and then she saw his eyes fo-

cus on the vee of her mauve jacket. In the next instant
she felt his warm fingers brush her neck as he lifted the
gold chain from under the collar of her dress.

Kevin stared at the little Celtic cross he had given her
that night in her apartment. He slowly lifted his aston-
ished eyes and held her alarmed ones. "You've kept
this? You still wear it?"

Feeling her neck warm suddenly, she eased the cross
from his fingers and said in hushed tones, "Only for
this trip. It's Irish, and I thought —"

"Teri," he whispered, placing his arms around her
and rocking her gently, "I've thought about you so
often, wondered how you were and what you were
doing." He closed his eyes and swallowed hard before
continuing. "When all the weeks of my life are over, the
one I'll remember with the most happiness will be the
one we spent together. I wish we could relive that time
we had together, forget everything else and everyone
else, just the way we did then."

The sincerity in his deep voice was a balm to Teri's
aching heart, yet as she nestled against him, supported
by his manly strength, she knew it was wrong. She had
no right to be in Kevin's arms, and he had no right to
hold her, but she had no strength left to judge herself or
him. And she had to face the truth: the attraction she
once felt for him was as strong now, if not stronger.

The evening had drained her emotionally and physically, and that which she had fantasized about so many
times in the past was actually happening. Kevin was
holding her, surrounding her with his protective
warmth. How could something so wrong feel so right?
she asked herself. Despite herself, her trembling hand
rose, and her fingertips lightly touched his cheek, then

slowly moved over his lips. Garnering all her strength, she forced herself back from him and turned away.

"So, Kevin," she said, her voice tremulous, "we've had our little talk. There's no need for you to drive me to the hotel. I'm sure I can find a taxi now."

"Just like that?" he asked. "After all this time we just chat for a few minutes and you walk out the door? That strikes me as a little bizarre. After all, as I recall we didn't exactly have a casual acquaintanceship."

"No," she whispered, "it wasn't casual." Then she spun around and commanded her voice to be steady. "That was a long time ago, only a few days of your life and of mine."

"I remember every minute of it."

"We hardly knew each other," she insisted. "And people change."

"Then we do have something to talk about. You've changed. I've changed. It might be pleasant to learn more about the new us."

"Why, for heaven's sake?"

"Call me a sentimental ol' Irishman."

"Please, Kevin, I—"

Taking hold of her shoulders, he searched her eyes and scrutinized her pained features, trying to see through her protests. Then he shook his head slowly. "No, I don't think either of us has changed that much. I know my feelings for you haven't. There's been no one since you, no one who really mattered."

Disbelief shot through her. His wife didn't matter? And Seamus had called Teri "Mrs. Manzoni." Kevin couldn't possibly know there was no longer a Mr. Manzoni. Shrugging from his hold on her, she spoke with as reasonable a voice as she could manage. "If we do have something else to chat about, I think it would be Moira, your wife."

"Moira?" Kevin repeated. "She's not my wife."

Kevin's words echoed in Teri's ears and an overwhelming sense of emptiness drained her of all feeling. Then the full weight of what he had just said struck her unmercifully and she stared at him with dark eyes that mirrored her tortured thoughts. Finally she stammered, "But . . . but you told me."

"I know what I told you, and it was the truth at the time. Moira and I were engaged to be married."

She turned away and nervously fingered the cross under her dress. "You didn't marry her?"

"No." Kevin sat down on the sofa and slumped against it.

Agonizing thoughts of wasted years and regret crashed through Teri's mind: years of a prosaic marriage to Angelo, years of longing for Kevin. The past twelve years could have been so different. It would only have taken one word from him—if he had wanted to speak it. No regrets, she had told him before he left her. No rancor to overcome, she had forced herself to believe. Theirs had been a simple act of loving, an uncomplicated moment in time that had meant much to her but, apparently, very little to him. God! she wanted to get away from him—and now.

Drawing from some inner source of strength, she picked up her purse, composed her features and faced him. "I'm very sorry to hear it didn't work out for you and Moira. You must have been terribly hurt . . . or disappointed, at least." The distorted smile she gave him was at once wry and complimentary. "But you certainly appear to have come through that trick of fortune extremely well."

Kevin looked up at her. "Fortune had nothing to do with it. I just didn't know Moira as well as I thought I did." He jumped up as she started toward the door and reached it before she did. "Teri," he said in a voice that wrenched her heart, "I know now that I put too much faith in the wrong woman."

Slowly she shook her head. "Don't...please don't."

With gentle fingers he raised her chin and saw the moisture glistening in her eyes. "Sweet Teri," he said quietly, "I never meant to hurt you."

She took several steps back into the living room and whirled around. Her voice rose in pitch when she asked, "Why didn't you tell me?"

He went to her, took her purse and set it on the sofa. "I guess I do owe you an explanation." After a deep breath, he said, "I'd like some tea. How about you?" He added apologetically, "I never got in the habit of coffee. Sorry."

Teri didn't know whether to laugh or cry, and she didn't know what good it would do to listen to his explanation, but something kept her from turning her back on him and rushing out the door. Perhaps, she decided, she really did want to hear what he had to say. Or perhaps she just wanted to be with him awhile longer. Settling for a smile she didn't feel, she nodded, followed him into the kitchen and watched as he put a kettle on to boil.

Kevin reached up into a cabinet and withdrew a little box. Glancing down at Teri, who had taken a seat at the small table, he said, "Hope you don't mind tea bags."

"Of course not. It's what I always use."

"Don't let Mary Kate know that."

"Mary Kate?"

"My mother," he said as he put the tea bags into two china cups. "She calls them 'impious things.'"

Her memory jogged, Teri recalled his having told her long ago that his mother and father lived in Glengarriff in County Cork. Mary Kate taught Irish and history in the local school, and Padraig, his father, owned his own boat; he and his crew fished for salmon in the Atlantic off Bantry Bay.

"How are your parents?" Teri asked, still not sure why she was sitting in his kitchen, making casual conversation.

"Mary Kate's as robust as ever," he told her as he reached into the refrigerator and withdrew a plate of sliced beef and some Blarney cheese. "My father died ten years ago."

"Oh, I'm sorry."

While he sliced through brown bread, Kevin said, "I was in the army at the time." His knife paused momentarily. "It still bothers me that I never had a chance to say goodbye to him, to tell him how much I loved him." The kettle began to whistle, and he switched off the burner, asking, "Is butter all right, or would you rather have mayonnaise on your sandwich?"

"I'm not hungry," she told him. "Just tea will be fine."

He looked over at her. "I'm used to having a snack at night when I'm trying to catch up on my work."

Teri smiled weakly, then asked, "How long were you in the army?"

"Two years." He poured the boiling water into their cups. "I joined up the year after we...after I returned home."

"Is that why you didn't marry?" she asked tentatively.

He began fixing his sandwich. "No. When I first returned to Cork, I turned down a high-paying job with the real estate firm I worked for to take a lower-paying government job there. I've always been concerned about the problems we have here in Ireland and felt I had a duty to help make things better. Unemployment is nearing the nineteen percent mark now, and there's an increasing stream of emigration. Thirty thousand people a year. In a country of three and a half million, that's a lot, although I can't really blame our young people." His face clouded over, and a pensiveness shadowed his eyes. "I thought that if I worked hard enough, I could help steer Ireland toward prosperity again, but with so many problems it takes all my strength just to keep trying."

When he became silent, Teri could see little stress lines at the corners of his mouth and eyes, and she decided that Kevin hadn't changed all that much. When she had first met him, he had been enthusiastic about his country, just as he was now. He was, she decided, a man who had held on firmly to his youthful dreams—no matter the cost. She only wished she had been part of his dreams. . . .

"If you don't like your tea strong," he said, breaking into her musings, "you'd best take the tea bag out."

As she did, she said, "I take it Moira didn't approve of your turning down the real estate job."

"To put it mildly. She married Denis Fitzgerald—" his eyes turned cold "—a man of 'substance,' she told me. He owns a dairy farm and a turf plant . . . peat, you'd probably call it. Along with that he invests heavily in foreign enterprises."

Toying with the handle on the china teacup, she asked, "Is that why you joined the army...because Moira married him?"

Kevin sat down across from her. "Actually, I did so to straighten myself out. I went berserk for a while, but army training settled me down, and after that I entered government service here in Dublin...put all my energy into my work at the Department of Foreign Affairs."

Teri wondered why Kevin's explanation didn't make her feel better. She wanted to ask why he hadn't told her he hadn't married Moira, but the answer seemed apparent: he hadn't wanted to.

After a sip of tea, a wry smile spread her lips slightly. In all the years that she had fantasized about seeing Kevin again, she had never once visualized sitting at a kitchen table with him and having tea.

"That was delicious," she said, checking her watch. "But I really have to be going." She rose, asking, "Can I help you straighten up first?"

"No," he told her, and watched as she headed toward the living room. Following, he saw her pick up her purse, turn and smile at him.

"It's been nice seeing you again, Kevin. Perhaps before I return home we can have dinner...my treat."

Reaching for his jacket, he said, "I'll drive you."

"No, I'm sure I can find a taxi, but thanks, anyway."

"You have a penchant for taxis, don't you?"

"I'm a New Yorker, remember?"

"I remember...only too well."

Teri's eyelids flickered a few times, and unconsciously she nipped at the inside of her lower lip.

"How about having that dinner tomorrow night?" he asked.

Her dark eyes pierced the distance between them, and she could feel her heartbeat escalate until she was afraid she was going to shake visibly. At the moment, the last thing she wanted was Kevin in her life again. Had they just been old friends, their reunion could have been pleasurable, but as it was, there were too many somber ghosts haunting Teri.

Straightening her shoulders, she said, "Tomorrow wouldn't really be convenient. Let me phone you before I leave." She turned to head toward the front door.

"Teri!" he called, and she froze.

Seconds later Kevin was in back of her, and she felt his strong hands grasp her shoulders. The warmth of them shot down her arms, tempting her unbearably, but she was determined not to weaken in her resolve.

"I've been doing all the talking tonight," he said in a quiet voice, "but there's so much I want to know about you—your work, your family." After a moment, he asked, "Do you have children?" He felt her shoulders tense. "I'd like to hear about your husband, too."

Teri inhaled deeply and emitted a long, uneven breath before she turned. Unspoken pain was obvious in her eyes when she said softly, "Angelo died two years ago."

Not waiting for Kevin's response, she left quickly, quietly closing the door behind her.

Outside, the Dublin night air was cool. She hurried down the walkway and started for the well-lit street to her right, wishing she had never come to Ireland, wishing she had never met Kevin O'Shea, wishing—that she didn't feel so damn miserable.

Alone in her hotel room Teri paced, trying to salvage what little remained of her lovely but shattered illusions. For most of her adult life she had depended heavily on her memories of that brief encounter with Kevin, but now he had robbed her even of those.

A bitter laugh almost choked her when she thought of the innumerable times she had held to the belief that he had truly loved her. Now she understood that his words had been spoken in a fleeting moment of passion. "Honor!" she blurted out in the silence of the room as she continued pacing. He had been so concerned about protecting his honor that night he had left her in New York. Where was his honor when he had been free to return to her and decided not to?

She went to the window and stared down at the car lights moving along the thoroughfare, realizing that the night ahead would be long.

CHAPTER THREE

IN THE MORNING, true to his word, Seamus had the order forms delivered to Teri at the hotel. After breakfast she found that Irish Cottage Industries, Ltd. on Dawson Street had an interesting and imaginative range of knitwear. At Weir's, she decided on a dozen each of the exquisite Tara brooches, the Claddagh bracelets with two hands clasping a heart and the pins inlaid with green enamel shamrocks—even though Colleen had told her no shamrocks.

Her real finds, however, were at Dublin's Enterprise Tower, a high rise situated near the Grand Canal. There she met and spoke with a number of talented young craftspeople. Some worked at artistic glass creations in brilliant colors; others produced lovely needlework designs on beautiful fabrics, contemporary wall hangings or elegant suede and leather outfits.

Most fascinating was the gentleman who fashioned unique pieces from precious metals using a process he called "granulation," by which minute spheres of gold—over a thousand to the square inch—were fashioned into delicate objects. It was a craft, he told her, hardly practiced in Ireland for the past thousand years.

Teri spent an hour with him, examining the exquisite, tiny gold sculptures. Some of the pieces, he told her, were replicas based on drawings he had made of art treasures now exhibited in the National Museum. When the artisan enthusiastically explained how various past cultures—such as that of the Druids, the Celts, the early Christians, the Vikings and the Normans—influenced his creations, Teri couldn't help but be reminded of Kevin.

Entranced, Teri took out her pocket calculator and played with figures until she had adjusted her spending plans to include a reproduction of the bronze, gold and silver Ardagh Chalice. After leaving the artisan, she decided she didn't dare explore the remainder of the Enterprise Tower, since she had already gone through half the money she and Colleen had allotted for the trip. Besides, she had yet to see the National Craft Center in Cork.

When Teri returned to her hotel, she was given several phone messages from Kevin, asking her to call him, and she entered her room to a ringing phone. She started to reach for it, but then pulled back. The phone continued to ring, and the walls suddenly seemed to be closing in on her. She grabbed her purse and left the room, deciding that during the remainder of the weekend she would become further acquainted with Dublin—alone.

ON MONDAY MORNING, after visiting several shops, Teri lunched on steak-and-kidney pie at a pub near Seamus McFadden's suite of offices. As she sipped her glass of Guinness stout, she wondered if Colleen had gotten the okay from their landlord regarding the vacant shop next to theirs. She recalled the discussion she and her partner had had about enlarging their business. *Think big and dare to dream,* she told herself as she paid her check and walked the two blocks to Seamus's office.

There, his secretary directed her to Fiona's office, where the woman greeted her as though she were an old friend. After explaining that Seamus was in a meeting, Fiona glanced at the large briefcase Teri carried and remarked lightly, "That's quite a satchel you have."

Teri smiled. "It's my travel office. In it are my calculator, business folders, maps, credit cards and zillions of other things I couldn't live without." She set it on Fiona's desk and opened it. "I have the order forms from the craft houses I've visited so far."

"Wonderful." Fiona beamed as she took the papers. "I'll have them typed and make copies for you." After scanning the lists, she said, "We'll ship the merchandise to you in New York as soon as possible, but if there's any problem at all, you will phone me at once, won't you?"

"Of course," Teri agreed, then added, "I would like to see Seamus before I leave. Do you think the meeting will last much longer?"

"I don't really think so. They've been at it for more than an hour. It's been quite a day around here, what with the hijacking yesterday."

"Hijacking?"

"You haven't heard?"

Teri shook her head.

"There's been another one—the second shipment of the artifacts that workmen found buried in the bogs near Denis Fitzgerald's turf plant. They were on their way to the National Museum here in Dublin in an armored car. Seamus said the front end was blown away as though some kind of rocket had hit it. The explosion killed the driver and the guard. Seamus and some of the other museum board members are in there discussing it now. When he first heard about it, I thought he was going to—'' The flashing button on the inter-office phone drew her attention, and she picked up the receiver. After a moment she said, ''Both shipment schedules? Yes, Seamus, I'll bring them right in.''

Fiona went to a file drawer behind her desk, unlocked it and pulled out a folder, then started toward the closed door across the room. Before opening it, she turned to Teri and smiled. ''I'll tell him you're here.''

Moments later Seamus opened the door wide, and Teri caught a glimpse of Kevin and Terence McKenna sitting at an oval table with several other men and women.

''Teresa,'' Seamus said, his smile warm and sincere, ''I hadn't expected to see you until tomorrow. I'm sorry you had to wait—'' his expression darkened ''—but this hijacking business has everyone upset.''

Teri glanced at Kevin, who, upon seeing her, rose from his chair. Facing Seamus, she said, ''Fiona was just telling me about it. I'm so sorry. It's terrible that two men were killed.''

''Yes,'' he said, lifting his bushy gray eyebrows. ''It's the men and their families I feel so bad about. The loss of the antiquities can be borne, but . . . ah, well. Has Fiona taken care of everything for you?''

''Most efficiently. She has the order forms I filled out.''

''Fine. She'll process them right away. Margaret asked if you'd care to come to dinner this week.''

''Thank her for me, but I've decided to leave Dublin today.'' From the corner of her eye, Teri saw Kevin listening to every word.

''Are you leaving for Cork now, then?''

She turned her attention back to Seamus and nodded. ''I thought I'd drive down the eastern coast.''

"Ah, that friend of yours who told you about the south of Ireland must have known the country well."

"Yes," she said quietly, feeling a betraying warmth spread upward over her cheeks, "he did."

Seamus took Teri's hand in his. "Just don't forget the vacation part of your trip. Leave the shipping worries to us."

"I will. Again, thank you for all your help." She started to leave, but Kevin's voice stopped her.

"Teri, wait up, will you?" Going to Seamus, he said, "I have to go now. There's not much we can do until the police recover the artifacts. The museum will just have to go for a different show. Getting the Book of Kells on loan from Trinity College and working an exhibit around it sounds good to me."

Seamus asked, "Will you be at the IDA meeting on Wednesday?"

"No, I have a conference with the Golden Vale Creamery people, then I'm going to try to talk Fitzgerald into supporting the financial center."

"I don't envy you that chore. Frankly, the man's been behaving rather queerly of late."

"When you're as wealthy as he is, it's called being eccentric." After patting Seamus on the shoulder, Kevin went to the hallway door and opened it for Teri, following her with accusing eyes as she walked past him.

Halfway down the stairway, he said, "I tried to reach you at your hotel."

"I know."

"So you did get my messages."

"Yes."

"Why did you decide to go into hiding?"

Teri stopped just outside the entrance to the building and looked directly at him. "Hiding? From what?"

"Not what . . . whom."

"As in Kevin O'Shea?"

"Exactly." He took hold of her arm and started down the street toward the O'Connell Bridge.

"Kevin, I really have a lot to do today."

"One more thing won't hurt, then."

He guided her across the busy two-lane thoroughfare, and when they reached the pathway under the row of trees that bordered the River Liffey, he released his hold on her. After they walked in silence for a while, he asked, "What's this about a vacation?"

"I'm combining business with pleasure."

He strode toward the railing at the water's edge and looked down at the narrow river. He stared at the easy flow of the water, and followed it downstream, then scanned the elegant Doric columns and the pale green dome on the Custom House. His head throbbed, and he had to fight the impulse to take hold of her and shake her until she admitted she wanted to be with him. He knew he had hurt her badly in the past, no matter what she might have said about "no regrets." But on the other hand, she had known how he felt about his country and about duty.

Hadn't she?

He hated the way she was looking at him now. It was almost as though she couldn't stand the sight of him—and that hurt like hell.

As soon as he felt he had his emotions in check, he said, "So, you're mixing business with pleasure. I take it seeing me again hasn't been part of the pleasure."

Teri took slow steps toward the railing and looked across at the double-deck buses moving slowly down the street on the other side of the river. Without facing him, she said, "Seeing you again was a bit of a shock."

"That goes for me, too." He moved nearer. "You weren't even going to try to locate me to say hello, were you?"

"To be honest, I hadn't thought about it." And she was being truthful; she hadn't, not consciously.

The urge to shake her soundly returned, so he pushed back the sides of his brown suit jacket and shoved his hands into his pants pockets. Scrutinizing her expression, he asked, "Why not?"

Lightly she asked, "Why should I have?"

"Because we were in love once."

The flurry of sensation that started at the back of her head shot down her spinal cord, then flared out, tingling each and every nerve end in her body. When her heart started pounding against her rib cage, she lowered her eyes. "Were we?"

He took a moment to mull over her question and had to decide that what they had shared hadn't been all that meaningful to her. True, they had been together for only a week, but through the years he had discovered just how unique Teresa Rosario was. Since leaving her, he had come to realize that without her he was simply existing.

Moments later, his tone was dry when he suggested, "I guess it is safer to have a short memory."

Ah, yes, she agreed silently, *it would be much safer.* Looking up at him, she said calmly, "You took the safe path, didn't you?"

"If you think I wasn't concerned about you when I left New York, you're wrong."

She turned and looked down at the river. "You said you would write."

Hearing the hurt in her voice, he had to rethink his earlier assessment. He placed a hand on her shoulder. "Teri, I—"

Her head jerked toward him. "Not one letter. Not a note, even. Do you have any idea of how that made me feel?" She moved away, letting his hand slip from her shoulder.

"I'm sorry about that, truly sorry, but when I got back here...there were the problems I told you about."

Her lips formed a caustic smile. "Maybe you do have some indication of the way I felt."

"But it turned out well for you. You married."

"After two years of waiting to hear from you, hoping your marriage wouldn't work out." She shook her head. "God, what a silly, naive fool I was."

"Two years," he repeated softly. "That is a long time." He waited until a couple walked by, then his tone became defensive. "What was I supposed to do...run back to you and tell you that since Moira wouldn't have me, you could? What the hell kind of man would do that?"

"Is that your honor talking or your pride?" she asked.

"I hadn't thought you would want a man without both."

Struck by the bitterness in his voice, Teri tried to understand Kevin's reasoning, but she couldn't. She suspected that his attempt to hide behind his grandiose sense of "honor" was merely a convenient excuse. Or at best, he was confused. *She* was certainly having a difficult enough time sorting out her conflicting emotions. All she could see clearly was that this conversation was making both of them miserable. "Kevin, what's the use of dredging up the past? It's done with. A lot has happened since then."

"I suppose you're right," he agreed sadly. "We're different people today—strangers almost."

Softly she said, "Yes," giving in to her instincts that told her to keep a protective barrier firmly in place between Kevin and herself. She'd had to say goodbye to him once, and it had nearly killed her. She wasn't going to let him hurt her that way again, not when he could have saved her from going through all that pain so many years ago.

After glancing at her watch—it was a little after three—she extended her hand to him. "It has been nice seeing you again."

"Where are you going?"

"To find a taxi. Remember, I have business to take care of."

"In Cork, right?"

"Yes."

"Good, we can drive there together." He took hold of her arm again.

"Kevin!" she objected, jerking her arm free, "Don't do that."

"What?"

"Grab hold of me and tell me what I'm going to do. I don't like it."

"Sorry, I thought you might be in a hurry to get started."

"I am, but I can certainly find Cork on my own."

"That doesn't make sense," he said, following her toward the cabstand near the corner.

"You don't think I can?"

He opened the taxi door for her, slipped in quickly and told the driver, "The Royal Dublin."

Shifting cool eyes toward Kevin, she informed him, "Believe me, I'm perfectly capable of driving to Cork alone. Why doesn't that make sense to you?"

"Because I'm going there on business, too. What's the point of both of us driving alone? Ireland's a much nicer country to see when you're with a friend." He paused, sensing he wasn't making much headway. "We are friends, aren't we?"

"Not if you keep up this dictatorial attitude."

He turned sideways in the seat, forced his most charming smile and said, "Mrs. Manzoni, you're going to Cork, and I'm going to Cork. It would please me greatly if we could go together. As we Irish say, *'Giorraíonn beirt bóthar'*—two shorten a trip."

Suddenly it was twelve years ago, and she and Kevin were standing in a near blizzard outside of Penn Station in Manhattan. At that time her brain had tried desperately to find an excuse to keep them together for just a while longer. Kevin had come up with a reason, and they had talked and laughed for hours over Irish coffees. Now he was doing it again. She told herself she was no longer a naive nineteen-year-old starting down the pathway of a first love. She told herself she had gotten over him once, and that even to consider traveling with him was asking for trouble.

"Please, Teri?" he implored, placing his hand over hers.

The warmth of his touch penetrated her skin and shot through her hand, again rekindling an intense desire she thought she'd safely buried. Words like "sensible," "caution" and "danger" couldn't detract from the wonderful feeling of being with him again, and despite her determination, when his fingers tightened around hers she was lost.

Her voice was low when she asked, "You really have business in Cork?"

"I do . . . serious business."

WHILE TERI PACKED, Kevin returned her rental car and dashed home. After phoning his secretary, he threw some things in a suitcase, then picked her up in his car, all in record time. Soon they were driving south on the Naas Road.

Once out of Dublin, the scenery changed quite abruptly. Teri tried to concentrate on the undulating green foothills, stately country houses and gushing springs they passed. And she tried to relax, but she had the uneasy feeling that history was about to repeat itself.

Focusing her attention on the narrow road ahead, she saw that it rose steeply. At the top of the hill, it curved, and she glanced out the car window, looking past ancient trees bent by the wind. Behind them she saw a splendid panorama of the city and Dublin Bay. In the next moment, the road plunged downward and wove between a moorland covered with purple heather and deep green grass. A little farther on, she saw sheep grazing and an occasional deer that would jerk its head up and dart toward a nearby copse.

After glancing furtively at Kevin, Teri turned toward the car window again, trying to quiet her concern by interesting herself in the view. The road rose again before it dipped down into a valley. In the distance, beyond winding lanes and old stone walls, she saw farms backed by rough upland pasture, and more sheep and some cows. But her heart wouldn't permit her to enjoy being a tourist just now; it kept bringing her thoughts back to the man next to her.

Kevin was silent as he drove, and that made her even more nervous. She wondered what was going on in his mind, but she wasn't at all certain she wanted to know. Soon the silence became unbearable, and she asked, "What business do you have in Cork?"

"Cheese."

"Cheese?"

"A meeting of the Golden Vale Creamery officers. We're trying to get tariff numbers for a new cheese they want to export. They sent over four hundred and fifty tons of Blarney cheese to America last year."

Now that they were talking, Teri began to relax a little. "You seem to be working at it from two directions—exporting Irish talent and importing new industry."

"That's about it." A light drizzle speckled the car windows, and Kevin switched on the windshield wipers. Watching the hilly road ahead, he said, "Poor Ireland. She's not had an easy time of it. All through the years, one wave of invaders after another has been hellbent on stripping her of her wealth and her forests and has tried to destroy her heritage, even her language."

Teri recalled that many years ago Kevin had said he loved her in Irish. *Mo ghrá thú.* How many times had she repeated his words to herself? Too many. Softly she said, "It's a beautiful language."

"We have our own Irish-language radio network, and soon we'll have an Irish-language TV station. Since it's now being taught at all school levels, the number of people who know Irish is on the increase. Look," Kevin said, nodding toward his right, "the River Barrow."

She took in the idyllic sight of the clean, sparkling river slipping through the picture-perfect landscape of sloping carpetlike green grass and robust, leafy trees. A little farther down, she saw a cabin cruiser and waved back at the young people who were apparently having an outing.

For a distance they rode in silence, Kevin giving Teri the opportunity to enjoy the scenery. But each time he glanced over at her, he knew he longed to make love to her again, longed to find out if his wonderful memories of the night they had spent together in her Manhattan apartment even approached reality. Those memories had kept him company over the years, but he had always suspected they were too perfect and too exquisite to have been real. He knew it hadn't just been the sex, either. Being with Teri those few days had taught him what it was like to feel whole, to be able to share his hopes and dreams and feel totally accepted. He had never felt that way before or since. Yes, he thought as his eyes drifted her way, he wanted to make love to her again.

They crossed from County Waterford into County Cork a little after nine o'clock. Kevin drove to the coastal town of Crosshaven, a yachting resort on the Irish Sea, and checked them into adjoining rooms at the Grand Hotel. Since they had stopped at Kilkenny for dinner, neither was really hungry, so he ordered only a tray of light fare sent up to them.

Before unpacking, Teri went to the window and scanned the panoramic vista. It was almost dark, and the lights on the yachts and other pleasure boats in the harbor were like slow-moving stars the way they twinkled against the indigo water. But as she searched the shore, she realized that one thing was lacking.

She went to the open door connecting their rooms and asked, "Where are the palm trees?"

From the closet, where he was hanging his garment bag, he laughed and said, "You'll see them soon." Then he faced her and his expression turned serious. "You have a good memory."

"Yes," she whispered, suddenly feeling vulnerable. "I remember many things you told me...about Ireland," she was quick to add. After a strained pause, she said quickly, "I'd better unpack some things, too."

"I'll call you when our snack arrives."

After closing the connecting door, Teri washed up and changed into white slacks and a turquoise sweater. The "snack" that Kevin had ordered turned out to be a mixed seafood grill, oven-fresh brown bread and Murphy's stout, a beer that was somewhat lighter and sweeter than Guinness. After they ate he suggested a walk down by the shore.

The pungent smell of the Irish Sea filled the air, and the cool sea breeze felt good wafting across Teri's face. As they walked, she glanced over at Kevin, thinking how handsome he was. The heavy yellow sweater he wore and the moonlight shining over his wavy blond hair and ruddy complexion gave him a golden-boy look. The young man she had known so long ago had matured beautifully, she thought.

Yet she was also struck with the feeling that the man she had known in New York and the one walking beside her now might as well have been two different people. Twelve years was indeed a long time, and each of them had had life experiences that the other knew nothing about.

Kevin took hold of her hand and said, "You're elegant even in casual clothes."

"Oh, I'm sure I am," she said, a smile blossoming of its own volition. She raised her other hand to brush back the strands of hair that the wind had whipped over her eyes.

As she did, Kevin noticed the silver wedding band that caught a ray of moonlight. A horn from a yacht in the distance moaned, punctuating the unrest he felt. The drive and the evening had all been perfect—yet something was very wrong.

He looked straight ahead as they continued down the rocky shoreline, and his voice was low when he asked, "Why do you still wear your wedding ring?"

In one second the soothingly warm hand Kevin had been holding turned to ice. Teri eased it from his grasp and stared out over the sea. In her heart she knew why she had never removed the silver band. She had married Angelo thinking she would never see Kevin again, but after her husband had died, secret feelings for her young Irishman had bloomed anew. Marrying again had been the last thing she had wanted to do, and she'd used the ring as a protective device.

"Well," Kevin asked, turning her to face him, "why do you?"

Teri studied Kevin's face, and in his expression she saw not only the question he had asked, but more personal ones, as well. Questions like *Were you happy?* and *Did you ever think of me?* Questions she didn't at all feel ready to answer—not yet. She glanced at her ring finger. "Angelo and I were married for eight years. I guess I've just gotten used to wearing the ring he placed on my finger." The wind grew stronger, and she shivered. "Let's go back. I'm getting cold."

She started to move away, but his hand tightened on her shoulder. "Just a minute more," he said. "There's something we both have to acknowledge."

"Please don't say anything," she pleaded, but he went on.

"I can't go on pretending we're just friends." His voice was colored with deep emotion. "The moment I saw you at Seamus's house, it was as though the past twelve years never happened. I wanted to say so many things to you, tell you how often I've thought of you, but I didn't, because you were Mrs. Manzoni. But now—" he moved his arms around her "—there are no barriers between us. We're both free to make the decision we should have made years ago. We belong together. We always have and always will."

She drew back slightly and stared at him. The night wind was blowing his hair, and the moonlight made his eyes shine. She felt a weakness in her legs and a pounding at her temples. Kevin was saying the very words she had wanted so badly to hear that night in her apartment. If only he had said them then! Summoning all her emotional and physical strength, she pushed herself away from him, breaking his hold.

"No!" she said forcefully. "There are barriers between us, solid ones, barriers you built twelve years ago when your so-called honor demanded that you leave me for Moira."

"It was something I had to do," he tried to explain. "I'd given Moira my word, and I had work to do here in Ireland."

"Not only did you neglect to tell me of your promise to Moira, but you placed me—supposedly the love of your life—at the bottom of your list of priorities."

"Don't put it that way. You make me sound so callous."

Teri drew her eyes from his and gazed out over the dark water. "It was a cruel, callous thing you did, Kevin. How can you expect me to just forget it?"

"That was a long time ago. This is now."

She faced him, a dim, wry smile settling on her features. "And again you find it *convenient* to fall in love with me."

"Now who's being cruel and callous?" he asked in an uneven voice. He strode angrily down the shore and leaned back against a small boat that had been pulled up on the beach.

Teri stood quite still, shaking inside. All the resentment that had been festering within her over the years had surged out suddenly, and she had a moment of satisfaction. But now, as she glanced at Kevin's downcast expression, she realized she felt as miserable as he looked.

Slowly she walked to the boat and rested her back against it, next to him. With her eyes on the deserted beach ahead, she said with quiet emphasis, "There are other barriers, too, Kevin. Your life and commitments are here in Ireland. Mine are at home, where I belong. There I have family, friends and a business to run. And how much do we really know about each other? Do you have any idea what goals I've set for myself in life? Do you know the kinds of things I enjoy doing when I'm not working? Do I want children? How many? These are things you don't know about me and questions that I don't have the answers to as far as you're concerned."

Her fingers trembled as she unclasped the gold chain she had around her neck and placed it and the little Celtic cross in the palm of his hand. "If we're to continue this trip together, it will be as friends only."

Teri tried not to be affected by the hurt she saw in Kevin's eyes as he stared at her, but she felt a dull ache where her heart should have been when he looked down at the cross for several quiet moments before slipping it into his pocket.

Unspoken pain dulled his eyes when they met hers. "You're right, of course. There's so much we don't know about each other, but I do know this. Not once have I been as happy as I was when we were together. As for the barriers you mentioned, be honest. Are they real, or are you erecting them because you think you need to?"

Teri stiffened. "That doesn't make any sense to me, Kevin."

"Maybe it will someday."

He started back toward the hotel, and silently she followed, forcing his remark from her mind.

When they reached their adjoining rooms, Teri saw that the door between them was still open. She went over to it, intending to close it, and noticed him standing by the window, peering out into the darkness. She was doing the right thing, she told herself with conviction. But his forlorn demeanor made her feel even more miserable. Softly she said, "Good night, Kevin."

Turning slowly, he sent her a pained grin. "Good night." After a momentary pause he added, "There's no need to lock the door. You're perfectly safe, Mrs. Manzoni."

CHAPTER FOUR

DURING A QUICK and mostly quiet breakfast the next morning, Teri asked Kevin if he would drop her off at the Cork Airport in Ballygarvan so she could pick up another rental car. The look he gave her was less than friendly, but he muttered something she took for assent. Later, as they drove the seventeen miles to Cork and Teri responded to his questions about her shop, Kevin's dour mood lightened somewhat.

"It was pretty rough going at the beginning," she admitted, "long hours and few customers, but we're doing so well now that we're going to expand the boutique."

"How did a nice Italian girl like you decide to open up an Irish import shop?" he asked with a gleam in his eye.

She glared at him. "It was Colleen's idea."

"Oh," he said, and his voice almost sounded chipper when he added, "I thought maybe you had a personal reason."

"Think again," she told him lightly. Now that his mood had improved, Teri could feel the inner tension she'd experienced since last night begin to dissipate.

Her relief was short-lived, though. She soon realized that once they reached the airport, she and Kevin would be saying goodbye again. Disciplining herself, she decided that that was exactly what was best. Not much later she spotted a sign saying the airport was three miles west. He ignored it and continued driving north toward the city.

"Shouldn't we have turned back there?" she asked.

"Why?"

"To get to the airport so I can get a car."

"Why would you want to do that?"

"I thought I explained that at breakfast. What do you expect me to do with my luggage while I'm visiting the craft center...carry it around with me?"

He shot her a boyish grin. "Your luggage is fine right where it is."

"Kevin, I plan to go on to Killarney when I finish here."

"And after my meeting with the members of the Golden Vale Creamery, I'm going to County Limerick. Killarney is on the way."

Teri blinked a few times, then leaned back against the car seat, not knowing whether she should be angry or thrilled at his having changed her original plans. He certainly had a habit of doing that, she thought, sighing. Despite her earnest resolve to be cautious where Kevin O'Shea was concerned, she found she was having a difficult time restraining the smile that wanted to spread over her lips.

CORK CITY, Teri discovered, was actually on an island, just like Manhattan. Yet unlike Manhattan there were no high rises. Instead she saw low Georgian-style buildings and others of blue, green, pink and orange brick. As they drove over steep cobble and winding flagstone streets, she commented on the charm of the stone bridges they passed, and Kevin said there were sixteen in all around the heart of the city.

When he dropped her off at the craft center, he told her he would be back for her in two hours, but remembering how fascinated she had been by the crafts exhibited in Dublin's Enterprise Tower, Teri suggested he give her at least three. Then, armed with Seamus's order forms, her calculator and comfortable shoes, she set out to explore the beautifully arranged eight-thousand-square-foot showroom.

If she had been impressed with what she had seen of Irish craftsmanship thus far, Teri was delighted with the soft leather shoulder bags and jackets, exquisite porcelain sculptures, hand-woven tweeds, laces and Aran handknits she saw now. When she finally tabulated what her selections would cost, she winced, but smiled at a young woman hand-painting a silk scarf and tossed the calculator into her briefcase.

Teri was still gloating about her buying spree as she and Kevin were being served lunch at Lovett's on Churchyard Lane. "Colleen is going to kill me when she finds out how much I've spent," she told him, "and I haven't even been to Killarney yet."

After their young, dark-haired waiter poured their white wine, she glanced around the intimate dining room. The early afternoon sun was streaming through the floor-to-ceiling windows and lent an almost luminescent quality to the cheerful floral draperies.

"It's lovely in here," she remarked.

"It is now," he said, and raised his wineglass. "Welcome to Cork."

Teri held up her glass, and when Kevin touched his to hers, the crystal caught a ray of sunlight. She gazed into his blue-green eyes—they shone so brilliantly that she was momentarily mesmerized by their beauty—and smiled softly. Though his face now boasted strong, manly contours, his eyes were the same expressive eyes of the young man she had fallen in love with so long ago.

For silent moments they held their wineglasses, the rims barely touching; then Teri felt her face flush and she sipped from her glass. Suddenly she was overcome with a feeling of great tranquillity. The ambience? she wondered. Her successful buying trip? She glanced over at Kevin. Neither, she had to admit, suddenly realizing that the attraction she now felt was not solely based on her youthful feelings. The mature man in his own right had awakened new feelings in her, feelings that teased, allured and promised. The sensations were both exciting and disturbing: exciting because she hadn't felt this way in more than a decade; disturbing because she knew she was playing with fire.

The waiter served them their broiled flounder in a sauce of cream and white wine, and as they dined, Teri turned the conversation to Kevin's business in County Limerick.

His expression darkening, he told her, "I have to see Denis Fitzgerald."

Teri paused with her fork just outside her mouth. "Moira's husband?"

"Yes. I'm trying to get him to lend his support to the financial center project in Dublin. The government has approved generous tax incentives to encourage large-scale investors to ante up the two hundred and fifty-eight million pounds needed for development. Denis could take on a good share of that if he wanted to. Right now his money is going to investment firms in London."

She understood that Kevin was upset with the man, but now she wondered if Moira had been a part of

Kevin's life even after she had married Denis Fitzgerald. That thought disturbed her more than she wanted to believe. Before she could stop herself, she asked, "Would Moira be able to help you convince him to back the project?"

Kevin wiped his lips with a napkin and set it beside his plate. "The lady is too busy with her Thoroughbreds and jet-setting to care what Denis does with his money...as long as he has it. They have a seven-year-old son, Patrick, but Moira doesn't seem to have much time even for him. She couldn't wait until he was old enough to pack him off to boarding school." He was pensive for several moments before a smile relaxed his features. "You're looking at the world's most experienced baby-sitter."

"Baby-sitter?"

He nodded. "I spent my vacation last summer at the Fitzgerald estate with Patrick while his parents took off in different directions."

Deciding that the scenario was becoming stranger by the minute, Teri sipped her wine. As she set her glass down, she asked, "Don't they have summer camps in Ireland?"

Kevin frowned. "After the boy's been at boarding school all year, the last thing he needs is to be shuffled off to a camp. What he needs is a sense of place, a home and individual attention."

Hesitantly she asked, "It's none of my business, but why should that responsibility fall on your shoulders?"

"Responsibility? It's something I do because I want to. If you met Patrick, you'd understand. He's starving for love and affection, but unfortunately he's not going to get it from his parents. Denis is too busy with his dairy farm and his turf plant, and when he's not away from home taking care of them, he's in London."

"Sounds as though Denis goes his way and Moira goes hers," Teri suggested, beginning to feel extremely uncomfortable with the topic.

"That's about it, but the lady made her bed, et cetera."

Kevin asked for the check, and once they were in his car again, he asked, "Do you mind if we take a little side trip? Glengarriff is only a little more than an hour's drive from here. There's someone I'd like you to meet."

Teri agreed a little uneasily, realizing he was taking her to meet his mother, Mary Kate. She was pleased, but her pleasure was tinted with caution; she had the disquieting feeling she was being intricately drawn into Kevin's personal life.

As they left the city, she remembered what Seamus had said about how quickly the scenery could change in Ireland. One minute they were driving along a wild seascape; the next, through a hauntingly beautiful moor, then through high and bare mountain passes with tumbling and sparkling waterfalls, only to descend into a peaceful glen strewed with gardens of lush semitropical plants, palm trees and giant hydrangeas.

Mary Kate's cottage rested at the foot of a soft-sloping hill draped with luxuriant blue-green grass and yellow wildflowers. Its roof was slated, its walls white-washed. Teri thought the setting idyllic as she scanned the waist-high stone wall covered with climbing pink roses, which protected the small vegetable garden from the sheep that grazed not too far away.

As soon as Kevin parked alongside the stone wall, the cottage door opened and a slender woman in a pale blue dress with a collar of delicate ruffled lace rushed out to meet them. No words were spoken as she threw her arms around her son's neck and kissed his cheek. When she did turn toward the woman with him, Teri saw that her wavy gray hair, pulled back into a loose twist, was still threaded with blond strands, and there were tell-tale wrinkles at the corners of her lips and her blue eyes—eyes that shone with the same youthful vigor that Kevin's did.

"Mother," he said with respect and love in his voice, "this is Teresa Rosario." In the next breath he corrected himself. "Teresa Manzoni now."

Mary Kate took Teri's hand in both of hers and spent several moments scrutinizing her face. *"Dia dhuit, a Teresa,"* she said, and gave her son an inquisitive sideways glance.

"An Irish welcome," Kevin explained.

"I'm very happy to meet you, Mrs. O'Shea."

"Please, 'Mary Kate,'" his mother requested.

Kevin told her, "Teri's in Ireland on business."

"All the way from New York," she remarked, and Teri was surprised that the woman knew that.

Gesturing toward the cottage, Mary Kate said, "Come inside. We'll have tea."

The house was as charming inside as outside—and larger than Teri had thought. The living room was high ceilinged with cozy, comfortable furniture and richly polished wood. Along the far side of the room was a large stone fireplace, already lit to ward off the chill in the air.

"Make yourself at home, Teresa. I'll be but a minute putting the kettle on." Again Mary Kate sent her son a curious look that Teri couldn't fathom.

As soon as Mrs. O'Shea went into the kitchen, Teri asked Kevin, "How did your mother know I was from New York?"

"She has an excellent memory, that woman," he said as he gestured Teri to the floral-print sofa. "I told her about you when I first returned home."

Startled, she asked, "Everything?"

He grinned. "Not quite."

Relieved, Teri commented, "Your mother's lovely."

Kevin removed his tweed jacket and sat down on the easy chair adjacent to the sofa. "She is, isn't she? I've tried to get her to come live with me in Dublin, but she wants to continue teaching here. Actually, I don't think she wants to leave her home—" his eyes drifted around the room "—or her memories of her life with my father."

Mary Kate returned with a tray of scones and cakes and set it on the low table in front of Teri. "Do you travel much in your business, Teresa?" she asked, handing her a white linen napkin, then giving one to her son.

"No, this is my first trip."

Reaching for a scone, Kevin said, "Teri owns and operates an Irish import shop in New York."

"I have a partner—Colleen Parnell," she added.

"Parnell, is it? That's quite a respected name here in Ireland. During the last century, like so many other Irishmen, Charles Stewart Parnell spent his life working for home rule and the establishment of an independent Irish government." She shook her head. "He would be greatly saddened by the Troubles in Northern Ireland." With that, she served the tea in lovely china cups.

When Teri tasted it, she decided it was the strongest and darkest tea she had ever had. The delicious small cakes were quite another thing. The secret, Mary Kate told her, was the quality of the brandy she used.

Reaching for another scone, Kevin asked, "How is school coming along?"

"As well as can be expected, considering what young people are like nowadays. Their minds are always on the latest rock group or hurling heroes."

"Hurling," Kevin told Teri, "is a game similar to ice hockey, but we play on grass rather than on ice."

As she poured her son more tea, Mary Kate said, "You remember Colm McCarthy, my former student who went on to Trinity College."

He considered a moment, then nodded, "The boy you thought was so brilliant."

"Yes. Well, he graduated this month, and his mother tells me he obtained a visa to go to America. It's probably the last we'll see of him." She sat down on the sofa next to Teri. "Would you like more tea, Teresa?"

"Please," she said, not wanting to refuse her hostess's hospitality. But after Mary Kate poured it, Teri added quite a bit more cream than she usually did. After taking a sip, she asked, "What kind of a visa was he given?"

"Tourist, for all that means," Mary Kate told her, and sighed. "Ireland is losing too many of its well-educated young people and professionals. Within a year after receiving their diplomas, half the university graduates leave the country. The unemployment problem, you know. It turns them into illegal aliens in America."

Kevin put down his cup and looked over at Teri. "Your government estimates there are 150,000 Irish people living illegally in the States, mainly in Boston, New York and Chicago. They enter on tourist visas and find jobs in Irish communities, where they blend in easily and get work using false papers. They can earn six hundred dollars a week there instead of two hundred here, if they can find work. The 'New Irish,' they call themselves, looking to be part of the American Dream."

"It's not all a bed of roses for them, though," Mary Kate said, shaking her head. "They live a life of fear and suspicion. Many times they take on new identities and purchase Social Security numbers, but if they dare a visit home here, they risk detection by customs."

Kevin turned to check the fireplace, then got up and placed two more rectangles of dried, brown turf in it. Blue-gray smoke curled up the chimney, and a yellow-gold flame sent a wave of heat across the room to where Teri sat. She felt the warmth waft over her arms and cheeks.

"I'll bring in some more turf," Kevin told his mother. "We'll need it in the morning."

We'll, Teri repeated silently, realizing too late that she and Kevin would be spending the night at the cottage. She glanced at her watch. It wasn't yet five o'clock, and she wondered why they just didn't drive on to Killarney.

When Kevin returned with a basket of turfs, he told his mother, "The stack is low. I'll cart some more here tomorrow." Then he went out to his car and brought Teri's and his luggage in. "You'll be in that room," he said, nodding to his left. "C'mon, I'll show you."

Teri rose and followed him into a room that was small, but spotless and charmingly furnished. Kevin set her suitcase on the downy comforter folded at the bottom of the bed and hung her garment bag in the hand-carved, wooden armoire.

"Do you have a warm sweater packed?" he asked.

"Yes, why?"

"I'd like to show you something."

She nodded, then said, "I thought we were going on to Killarney."

"We will be—tomorrow, after I haul back some turf for my mother."

"Oh," she said, as though that answered all her questions.

"I'll go tell Mary Kate we'll be gone for a little while."

Wondering at the grin he gave her before he left the room, Teri unpacked a few things, donned her heavy woolen sweater and changed back into her comfortable walking shoes.

Outside, Kevin led her around to the side of the cottage, and Teri studied the neatly piled turfs that looked to her like foot-long hunks of dried dirt. "How often do you collect the peat?"

"I make about four trips a year to the bog. I'll show you tomorrow morning when we go there. You'll be a big help."

She wasn't so sure of that. In the next instant Kevin took hold of her hand and started toward the hillside at a good pace. Gray clouds sailed under the sun, creating pools of dark shadows over the land, and Teri felt the strong, cool wind on her face. It didn't seem to bother Kevin at all; in fact, she noted, he seemed to be invigorated by it. The incline became steeper, and she had to struggle to keep up with him as he tugged her along.

When they neared the trees growing halfway up the hillside, he said, "These hills were bare until the reforestation program. Now they're home to oaks, pines, elms and holly trees.''

He guided her downward on the east side of the hill, and there, shaded by trees and protected from the wind, Teri saw a semitropical oasis that was lovely beyond description. At that moment, the clouds overhead passed, and the sun sent yellow-gold rays streaming through the branches of the tall trees.

A small waterfall cascaded down the far side of the grottolike area and formed a gurgling clear stream that wound down the hillside. On either side of the water Teri saw luxuriant ferns and short, deep-green windmill palms interspersed with what she could only describe as pink and purple daisies and other wildflowers she couldn't name.

"It's beautiful, Kevin!" After taking a few steps nearer the stream, she turned. "But these plants can't be indigenous."

He shook his head. "No, it's all my doing, but they thrive here because of the warm Gulf Stream, which keeps our winters mild and our summers comfortable." Joining her, he took hold of her hand and led her nearer to the waterfall. "Look," he said, pointing to the other side of the stream, "it's the tree I planted for you."

Teri stared over at the twenty-foot-high tree with the reddish-brown bark and the clusters of urn-shaped pink flowers that glowed in the sunlight. She glanced at Kevin, then her eyes returned to *her* tree. "You remembered," she whispered, feeling a lovely warmth radiate from her heart and spread throughout her entire body.

"I told you I'd plant a tree in your name. I did it soon after I returned to Ireland, and through the years I've cared for it and added the other plants. It's an arbutus tree. Do you like it?''

"Like it?" Automatically her hands reached around Kevin's neck, and in response, his arms slipped around her waist. "I don't know what to say." She glanced at the flowering tree again. "It's so beautiful." Facing him, she saw the excitement shining in his eyes. "You didn't forget me, did you?" she said.

His voice became as warm as the sunlight that shone over them in the hillside hideaway. "How could I have forgotten you? You're the only woman I've ever really loved." Tenderly he moved his fingertips across her lips and down over her soft, white neck. "My sweet, lovely Teri."

The movement of his fingers sent a delightful rush of sensation shooting down her neck and over her breasts. Suddenly her body was alive with wanting him. Her hands cupped the back of his head, and she pulled his face toward hers. "Kevin," she murmured, and she touched her lips to his.

Their kiss was at first gentle and tentative, as though they were relearning the feel of each other's lips, but after a deep moan, Kevin crushed Teri in his embrace and kissed her with a hunger too long unsatisfied.

For Teri, years melted away, and once again she was nineteen and Kevin was twenty-four. There was no Angelo, no Moira, no ocean to separate them. She was aware only of the warmth and power of his masculine body pressing hard against the softness of hers, the feel of his strong arms supporting her and the heady intimacy of his kiss. As his fingers dug into the sensitive flesh at her back and moved down her spine, pressing her closer to him, she felt her body awaken to his urgent caress. Now she had to face the truth: Kevin was the man she had been waiting for all her life, the only man she had ever really wanted, the only man she would ever want. The admission became an exhilaration, and she surrendered to the full force of her love and desire.

So enrapt were they in each other's arms, neither noticed that dark clouds had blocked the sun's rays. Nor did they feel the first sprinkles of rain that fell on them. But as the drops came quicker and harder, Kevin drew his lips from hers and looked up at the clouds. Then he gazed down at Teri and smiled at the water trickling down her face. "The famous Irish rains," he said, grinning broadly. "Come on, let's get back."

Hand in hand they ran down the hillside toward the cottage, laughing as the rain soaked their hair and their clothes. Just before they reached the rose-covered wall, Kevin stopped, took Teri in his arms once more and kissed her. Both were oblivious to the strong wind whipping them and the rain streaming down their faces.

"Kevin, Teresa!" Mary Kate called from the doorway, "You'll both catch your death!"

He looked over at his mother standing in the doorway, and told Teri, "I guess we should go in. What do you think?"

Brushing the water from her eyes, she smiled and said, "I think your mother is right."

Inside, Mary Kate rushed Teri to the bathroom and began filling the tub with hot water. "And here I thought it was just the young people acting crazy these days," she mumbled. "Get out of those wet clothes before you come down with pneumonia."

Obediently Teri began to do so.

"That son of mine. I don't know what's come over him—" a knowing smile lit up her face "—but whatever it is, I like it. I haven't seen Kevin this happy for so long."

"Mary Kate—" Teri began.

"Hush now. Take your bath, and we'll talk while you help me with dinner."

When Mary Kate entered the living room, she saw a smiling Kevin still standing by the fireplace, water dripping from his hair down over his forehead. "Are you daft, son?"

"No, Mother . . . I'm in love."

Mary Kate wiped her hands on the towel she held and her eyes narrowed. "And I suppose you'll be emigrating to America, too."

Kevin laughed. "Of course not. Teri will stay here."

"Oh, and has she said she will?"

"She loves me. I know she does."

Mary Kate wiped his face with the towel, then ran it over his hair. Her voice became serious when she said, "Teresa is wearing a wedding ring, or have you been too blind to notice?"

"Her husband died two years ago." He took the towel and began to wipe the back of his neck.

Mary Kate placed another piece of turf on the fire, then looked deeply into her son's eyes. "Twelve years is a long time. The young girl you told me about is a mature woman now, and a businesswoman at that. She's sure to have ideas of her own about how she wants to live her life and where she wants to live it. And she's an American woman. They don't like to be told what to do, I hear. So you'd best not get your hopes up that she'll fit into whatever plan you see as best."

Kevin smiled broadly, leaned down and kissed his mother's cheek. "Haven't you heard? Where there's a will, there's a way. And I plan to find one. I'm not going to lose her a second time."

Mary Kate silently noted the set of her son's lips, aware it meant his stubborn streak had surfaced once more. Quietly she said, "I hope so—for both your sakes."

CHAPTER FIVE

WHEN TERI CAME out of the bathroom, she went to the kitchen, but saw only Mary Kate. "Where's Kevin?"

"He's in his room changing," the older woman said with a smile as she stirred a pan on the gas stove. "Would you like to give me a hand here?"

"Certainly."

"Put a little of this rosemary and crushed garlic on that roast there." She nodded toward the rack of lamb in the roasting pan.

"Like so?" Teri asked.

"Perfect." Turning the flame under the pan a little lower, she said, "When Kevin came back from America twelve years ago, he told me he had met you there."

Teri's hand paused over the roast, then she continued to rub the garlic in the meat. "I gathered that when you knew I was from New York."

While pouring melted butter into the saucepan, Mary Kate asked, "Has he told you about Moira Fitzgerald?"

"A little."

"Kevin was sorely hurt when she married Denis, but I've always believed his pride was damaged more than his heart." She chuckled softly. "He's so like his father. Padraig never forgave or forgot when his pride had been hurt." She added wine vinegar to the sauce, then set concerned eyes on the younger woman's. "You're not going to hurt Kevin, too, are you?"

As Teri wiped her fingers on a towel, she looked at Mary Kate and saw the worry in her eyes. "I would never intentionally hurt Kevin," she told her sincerely.

Mary Kate nodded, and seeing that her helper had finished, she said, "We'll need to chop two tablespoons of that fresh mint." As she focused her attention on the sauce again, she continued to speak of her son. "The boy was unhappy enough when he first came home. Things weren't right between him and Moira. When she broke off their engagement, he went to pieces. Somehow he felt she had shamed him." She shook her head. "I never want to see Kevin like that again. At the time I asked him why he didn't write to let you know what the situation was, but there was no talking to him."

Teri stopped chopping the mint for a second, then began again. "I wish he had. Both our lives could have been different."

"Maybe," Mary Kate agreed. "He was in no mood to listen to me or to his father at the time. Padraig liked his whiskey some, but Kevin had never drunk the way he started to then. At first I was thankful he went into the army. I thought it would put some order in his life. But I was worried sick when he volunteered for Lebanon." She looked over at Teri. "It was as though he didn't care what happened to him. And when he left the army, he threw himself into his work in Dublin, as though some demon were chasing him."

Removing the saucepan from the stove, she said, "Kevin seems happy now, but I know he still feels a great deal of anger toward Moira and Denis. I also know it will take a very special woman to help him shake off that anger."

"After all these years, though," Teri said, trying to understand, "why is he still so angry?"

"It goes way back to when Padraig worked for Denis's father. He didn't have his own boat then. Mr. Fitzgerald owned a fleet of boats in Bantry Bay at the time. The Fitzgeralds lived in Bantry in those days, and both Kevin and Denis had eyes for Moira." Mary Kate's brow furrowed. "Denis was never a happy child, and Moira didn't make things any better for him or for Kevin. She played one against the other, but she finally had the sense to choose Kevin. When he came home from America, though, he was different somehow, more of a grown man."

She took hold of the roasting pan. "It's time to put this in the oven." As she carried the pan, she said, "Moira must have noticed it, too, and soon after she decided to marry Denis. And the rest you already know. Just remember—"

"Remember what?" Kevin asked, coming up to the kitchen door.

Both turned their heads, and Mary Kate told him, "Never you mind. It was women's talk. Why don't you busy yourself by setting the table?"

During dinner, Mary Kate regaled Teri with stories of Kevin's boyhood in Glengarriff, and afterward they sat around the fireplace. Teri became oblivious to the sound of the howling wind; she was too engrossed in listening to Kevin playfully taunt his mother about her belief in the "little people." He delighted Teri with stories about mischievous leprechauns constantly on the alert to protect pots of gold stored under rainbows, little men who chased milkmaids and robbed wine cellars, and merrows—Irish mermaids who led many a hard-drinking bachelor on a merry dance, always to return to the sea.

When he began to talk of banshees, though, Teri noted that Mary Kate's face lost its smile. But she, too, was quiet when he spoke of the awesome female lamentor who cried and wailed and rapped on windowpanes to warn of death. When the wind blew something against the door, Mary Kate jumped and told her son to stop frightening Teri.

"Kevin's so like his father," she said, "and he's got as good a temper. He even looks like Padraig did when I first saw him on a boat, sailing into Bantry. He was standing straight and tall at the prow, and I said to myself, 'There's the man I'm going to marry.'"

"And she did," Kevin said, grinning. "My poor father never had a chance."

"Not that I chased him, you understand," she informed Teri. "It was all done very properly in those days. The rules were clear and uncomplicated. The banns were read and Padraig courted me—under strict observance, mind you. There were no patty-fingers until we were wed." Mary Kate picked up her cup of tea and smiled. "There were parties and walks—" she looked over at Teri "—and I had my fortune from my mother and my grandmother... a hundred and fifty pounds! That was a lot of money in those days. And Padraig gave me a bouquet of yellow gorse. It's a common weed that grows on the moor, but they were the loveliest flowers I ever saw."

Over two more cups of tea, Mary Kate continued to tell Teri of life with Padraig in Glengarriff, and it became obvious to her that while Kevin's parents had shared a life devoid of luxury, theirs, indeed, had been a life filled with love.

IN THE MORNING, after Mary Kate had fortified them with a hearty breakfast and packed them a lunch, Kevin and Teri set out for the nearby bog in the family's horse-drawn jaunting car. The car itself was more like a wagon with two parallel seats, larger than the jaunting cars she had seen on the road so far. Kevin had removed the wooden back seat, and as Teri rode next to him she glanced down at his Wellingtons and the calf-high boots Mary Kate had loaned her.

Smiling, she said, "I can't wait to get back to New York and tell Colleen I went turf cutting in a jaunting car."

Kevin flicked the brown mare's reins to hurry her along. "One-seventh of Ireland is covered with bog-land, mainly in the west and the midlands. Rural families use turfs in lieu of electricity, oil or coal."

"Your mother has gas and electricity," Teri commented.

"Yes, but she likes the old ways. I'm surprised she didn't come with us. She, my father and I always made a holiday out of turf cutting. Mary Kate would pack a picnic basket, and the three of us would spend the entire day out here."

Teri glanced around at the flat, vivid green sunlit fields with patches of indigo and violet wildflowers. A trio of speckled grouse shot up from the edge of the dirt road just ahead, and she raised her hand to shade her eyes as she watched them fly off.

A little later, Kevin guided the horse to the side of the road and pulled the jaunting car to a halt. "Hope you're feeling energetic this morning," he said, then jumped down and helped Teri off the wagon.

"That remains to be seen," she told him, and took the wooden-handled tool he gave her. The metal cutting end was long and flat and had a sharp edge. A slane, Kevin called it. He lifted the wheelbarrow from the back of the car, laid a turf fork in it and Teri followed him over the bog. The rolling carpet of mosses and heaths was springy under her step.

When he stopped, she looked down at the massive hole in the bog that was perhaps four feet deep and a half mile long and wide. The rectangular area had been so neatly dug she decided it could have been excavated by an archaeologist. Reddish water covered the bottom.

Using the slane, Kevin removed a layer of turf and spread it on the lower area to provide a dry surface for working. Then he made a number of vertical cuts in sweeping, graceful movements.

After half a dozen pieces of turf had been cut, he said, "If you feel like it, you could use the turf fork and move the cut pieces back a ways. Line them up like that pile over there."

He pointed to his left, and Teri gaped at the huge dome-shaped stack.

Kevin laughed. "Don't worry, we're not going to cut that much today. I did that about six months ago. It's been seasoning, drying out. We'll cart some of it home to Mary Kate."

Teri followed Kevin's instructions, feeling very much like a pioneer woman building a sod house on a Kansas prairie, and two hours later, she felt aches in muscles she didn't know she had. When Kevin suggested they have lunch, she was only too happy to oblige.

While Teri got Mary Kate's basket and a blanket she'd given them, Kevin started a small fire, using several pieces of dried turf as fuel, and made tea in a kettle.

As they ate the thick cheese sandwiches on home-made brown bread, Teri decided she was getting used to the strong tea. Maybe it was the hard work, but it actually tasted good to her. The sun was high in the clear sky, and she inhaled the aromas of the bogland, the turf fire, the tea and the brown bread. She looked over at Kevin, who had removed his shirt earlier. She now knew how, despite his white-collar job, he had maintained his lean but powerful body. Turf cutting, she realized, was a backbreaking job, and she imagined that he was also the one who kept the cottage and the barn so beautifully whitewashed.

Kevin spooned some blackberry jam onto a soda biscuit and handed it to Teri. "These bogs actually move, particularly the ones in the center of the country. After heavy rains, bogs lying on steep slopes slide like avalanches of molten lava, sometimes going onto farmlands and into woodlands. Only last year the road from Ballycastle to Belmullet in County Mayo was blocked by a bog that moved down a hill for a mile and a half." He scanned the area with alert eyes. "And it's in bogs like this throughout Ireland that antiquities are found."

"Like the ones that were hijacked?" she asked.

He nodded and rested back on his elbow. "The bogs have been growing and burying things in them ever since prehistoric settlements were first constructed. Even the remains of Viking strongholds have been discovered. There's one bog, near Cullen in County Tipperary, in which so many gold objects have been found buried that it's become known as the Golden Bog of Cullen. Irish gold," he said as though to himself, then told Teri, "Just this year they've found unmined gold in the Connemara region of County Galway. It could be worth as much as half a billion dollars, they say."

His jaw muscles tightened. "But that's new gold with no history yet, not like the gold and silver artifacts that were found in the boglands near Denis Fitzgerald's turf plant." Shaking his head, he said quietly, "I don't trust the man."

Remembering what Mary Kate had told her about Kevin's animosity toward Denis Fitzgerald, Teri wondered how much of Kevin's lack of trust had to do with the fact that Denis was Moira's husband. "But they are being found. That's good, isn't it?" she asked.

"Not when so many are being destroyed by the huge machines Denis's workers use. Their cutting arms are 180 feet long. They scoop up the turf, and chew and shape it into foot-long briquettes. Many antiquities that happen to get dug up are crushed and chopped up."

He reached over the edge of the blanket and picked a small pink flower. Showing it to Teri, he said, "It's a bog orchid." His eyes drifted over the land. "The bog is so beautiful on top, and underneath it hides clues to our past and to our cultural identity. Sometimes whole bodies are found, the skin and hair preserved by the humic acids in the bogs, and we can actually see the faces of our ancestors." He looked over at Teri and smiled. "There I go again . . . talking my head off."

Quickly he pushed himself up and brushed his hands together. "If you'll take care of things here, I'll load some of the dried turf onto the car and we'll head back."

But he stood quietly for a moment, looking down at her attentive eyes and watching as the pleasant breeze ruffled her sunlit hair. When she smiled up at him, he felt a surge of excitement rush through his body. He knelt beside her and wiped a smidgen of turf from her cheek with his fingers.

"You are so beautiful," he whispered, and kissed her lips gently. Their sweet, warm softness sent another shock wave of desperate longing surging through his veins. For long moments he tottered on the edge of urging her down on the blanket and giving in to the primeval need that racked his loins. Only the threat of rejection saved him, and he drew back from her quickly and jumped up again.

His chest almost ached from the deep breaths he had to take. "It won't take me long to load the turf," he muttered, quickly grabbing the wheelbarrow and heading toward the pile of dry turf.

Teri had been equally affected by Kevin's fleeting kiss. As she watched him move away, she sat there startled and more uncertain than ever that they could only be friends.

IT WAS EARLY EVENING when they bade goodbye to a sad Mary Kate and began the seventeen-mile drive to Kenmare. Even though Teri had known Kevin's mother for only a short time, she realized she was actually going to miss her. And, she had to admit, it was going to be even more difficult to leave Kevin. No, she told herself, she wouldn't think about that now; she would deal with it when she had to.

In Kenmare, Kevin checked them into separate rooms at the Park Hotel, a large Victorian-style country house on a beautiful eleven-acre park overlooking Kenmare Bay. After sipping Irish coffee in the quiet lounge, they walked hand in hand through the moonlit garden of stately palms, tall tropical ferns and flowering plants.

As they sauntered down a moonlit pathway toward the bay, a string quartet on the terrace serenaded them with lovely Irish melodies. Singing quietly, Kevin looked over at Teri and offered a slightly altered version of the song presently being played. " 'She was lovely and fair as the rose of the summer. Yet 'twas not her beauty alone that won me. Oh, no, 'twas the truth in her eyes ever dawning, that made me love' Teri, 'the rose of Tralee.' "

She smiled and laughed softly. "You're a man of many talents. A government executive, a turf cutter and a singer."

"The singing I got from Mary Kate."

"Thank you for taking me to meet your mother. She's a lovely woman."

"That she is and always has been. She doesn't let on, but I know she misses my father very much."

"Padraig," Teri said, and asked, "Irish for Patrick?"

"Yes. I'm sorry you never got to meet my father. You would have liked him." Kevin placed an arm around Teri's shoulder. "And he would have loved you. My father had an eye for beautiful women. Ah, he had a temper, though, but he was honest and hardworking. He hammered into me the belief that a man needed to have a keen sense of duty and that he had to protect his honor above all, or he wouldn't be any good to himself or to anybody else. I've never forgotten that."

Again Teri remembered the conversation she had had with Mary Kate. Kevin's mother suspected his pride had been hurt more than his heart when Moira had married Denis, but now Teri had to wonder if Kevin believed his honor had been assailed, as well. Try as she did, though, she couldn't help but be troubled by the thought that perhaps he had never quite gotten over Moira.

On impulse, Teri asked, "Why haven't you ever married?" She felt his hand tighten around her shoulder.

"The right woman came along only once, and I foolishly let her get away."

"Moira?" she asked, despising herself for fishing so obviously.

Kevin led Teri off the path to a boulder beside a clump of palms. Leaning back against it, he slipped his hands under her sweater and placed them around her waist. Absorbed in looking at her moonlight-bathed face, he said softly, "No, not Moira. Teresa Rosario."

Teri's breath caught, but just as it evened she felt Kevin's hands begin to move softly up and down her sides. It was cool in the garden, but she knew that her shivers were not due to the night air. She had been experiencing so many similar sensations since seeing Kevin again that she recognized the cause instantly—him. But his touch did feel wonderful, and, she had to admit, *he* was wonderful.

In many ways she knew more about the man holding her so lovingly than she did about the younger Kevin O'Shea. She admired the work he was doing now and his deep commitment to his country. She also admired the loyalty and love he showed his mother.

Teri closed her eyes, and her thoughts flashed her a mental picture of his kneeling before her on the bogs in the afternoon. She had wanted to press her palms against his chest and test his body with her fingertips, but she hadn't. She'd been too afraid it wouldn't have stopped there. But now she could almost feel his lips on hers again.

Almost? They were! Her eyes flicked open for a second, then she closed them again and rested her hands on his shoulders as his kiss became more insistent. The subtle sensations she had felt moments before now grew to a thrilling heat that spiraled wildly in her abdomen and jolted her equilibrium, causing her to thrust her arms around his neck and hold to him for support.

When Teri whimpered, Kevin broke off the kiss and rested her head on his shoulder. He could feel her heart pounding against his as he held her close. "I've never stopped loving you," he whispered. "If you don't believe anything else in your life, believe that. It's always been you, and it always will be."

As he spoke, his breath wafted on her ear, and the heat of his body molded to hers created an inner fire that flamed where his eager maleness pressed boldly against her soft flesh. She could feel herself reaching the point of no return, the point at which she would be able to deny him nothing. But she had to be sensible, she warned herself; she just had to! With an emotional strength she wasn't certain she possessed, she tried to break free of his embrace, but the moment she attempted to move, stronger arms held her firmly against him.

"Kevin," she pleaded, "we have to be reasonable."

"Then let's be reasonable," he countered. "I love you, and you love me." Without giving her a chance to speak, he asked, "You do, don't you?"

A light-headedness overtaking her, she kissed the side of his neck and admitted hesitantly, "Yes... I do."

"Then what's more reasonable than our being together, tonight, right now?"

Teri sighed, feeling her determination weaken. "And tomorrow, next week, next month? What then? What chance do we have for a future together? Your life is here in Ireland. Mine is back home in the States."

For several moments, the only sound that broke the silence of the night was the cool breeze rustling the palm fronds above them. Then Kevin kissed her forehead and said, "Let's not think about the future right now. We lived and loved for the present once before. Why can't we do it again?"

She turned her face toward the twilight sea spread out beneath velvety hills. "I . . . I don't know."

"Please, luv," he breathed against her ear, "if you have any feelings for me, stay with me tonight. I need you. God, how I need you! I've thought about you so much, even fantasized about holding you like this, and now that I can actually feel you in my arms—" He sighed deeply. "I want us to make love. Please...please say you want that, too."

As she felt his warm lips nuzzle the side of her throat, her inner struggle abated, and she realized that reason had lost again. But when she slowly lifted her head and saw the burning desire in Kevin's eyes, she was happy that her love for him had won. "Yes," she said in a thread of voice, "it is what I want."

In his room, Kevin doused all the lights save for the little table lamp in the sitting area by the window. His body fairly shook with the urgency of his need for Teri, but he promised himself that he wouldn't satisfy his own desperate hunger until he had pleased her first.

When he turned, after closing the drapes, he saw her waiting motionless by the four-poster. The last time they had made love he had asked her to come to him; this time he would go to her. He did, and gently began to undress her, kissing her shoulders, her arms and her throat as he dropped garment after garment to the carpet. When she stood before him in all her natural beauty, he saw that she was trembling. Quickly he drew back the quilted spread and the top sheet, swooped her up in his arms and laid her gently on the bed.

As he removed his own clothing, his eyes remained fixed on the exquisite form lying so near, waiting for him. He could feel his breath pressing hard against his chest and a steady ache heating his loins. For one terrifying instant he wondered if he was dreaming the moment as he had so many times in the past. A near panic overtook him and he blurted out her name. "Teri!"

She raised herself onto her arm and looked over at him. "Yes?"

He went to her, sat on the bed and took her in his arms. "I had to make sure you were really here with me."

Drawing her head back a little, she saw the strained expression on his face and she ran her fingers over his cheek. "I'm here, Kevin . . . with you."

He reached for her left hand and kissed her palm. Then he gently removed the two rings from her finger and set them on the bedside table. Teri made no protest, and in her heart she knew she would never wear them again.

Kevin slipped down beside her on the bed and covered their legs with the sheet and spread. After she lay back and rested her head on the pillow, he slowly traced the soft curves from her hip to her shoulder, then trailed his fingertips across her breasts and up over her throat.

In a whisper, he asked, "What can I do to please you, luv?"

Teri placed her palms against his warm chest and closed her eyes. "Just being here with you is wonderful," she told him just as softly.

He kissed her eyes, her cheeks, then brushed her lips with his as he fondled the swell of her breasts and teased their burgeoning tips. When her sigh filled his ears, he lowered his mouth to one breast, then the other, suckling slowly and gently and nibbling their sweet peaks. The ache in his groin became unbearable, and he guided her hand until her palm encased his throbbing flesh.

"Oh, God, luv," he moaned, and buried his face in the soft valley of her bosom as he tried desperately to control his mounting desire to enter her immediately.

Teri basked in the warmth of the lovely sensations she was experiencing: the moist heat of his breath on her bosom, the feel of his hand on her thigh, the fullness of his desire for her. But when his fingers drifted inward and tangled in the silky hairs of her most sensitive place, she began to feel a stronger and deeper sensation that caused her to shudder. As his gentle fingers entered and probed her warm moistness, she felt his kisses descend over her abdomen and into her inner thigh. She flattened her palms against the cool sheet, and when his fingers gave way to his searching tongue, she arched her body to better meet his intimate kiss.

Her pulse raced as a searing heat began to burn deep within, making her feel as though she were floating higher and higher. To steady herself, she cupped the back of his head and arched even more to meet his warm, demanding lips. A trembling began in her legs that she couldn't control. Nor could she keep from rocking her head from side to side as her breaths came out in quick, uneven gasps. She tensed and heard her own silence-splitting sigh as her closed eyes viewed a kaleidoscopic whirling of all the colors of the rainbow.

When reality returned, she found herself in Kevin's arms; he was kissing her forehead and stroking her back in long, easy motions. She lifted a hand and placed her palm on the side of his face. Ever so slowly her fingertips traced his full, symmetrical lips, and she realized that history had indeed repeated itself. She was right back where she had been twelve years ago: desperately in love with Kevin.

His heart thudded against her breasts, and the heat of his pulsating need pressed hard against her abdomen. Slowly she ran her hand up and down his firm thigh, delighting in the feel of his silken hair under her fingertips. Yes, she told herself, she loved Kevin with all her heart, and she knew she was going to suffer when they parted once again. Then she remembered his words: *Let's not think about the future right now.*

No, she agreed silently, she wouldn't. The only reality she would recognize was that of the man holding her so lovingly, so patiently. When she eased herself onto her back, Kevin moved with her and braced himself on his elbows as he gazed down at her lovely smiling face.

Softly she said, "Now I want to please you."

His quiet chuckle echoed in the stillness of the room, and he smiled back at her. "What do you think you're doing, luv?"

"Kevin," she whispered, "I want to feel you inside me. I want you to be a part of me, have me be a part of you. Now," she said, and guided him to her waiting silky moistness.

He raised himself slightly and felt her open to him. Savoring each and every wonderful sensation, he lowered himself slowly, luxuriating in the exquisite feel of her ardent welcome as she absorbed and encased him deep within her.

"Aaaa." He sighed and gazed down at her. Seeing that her lids were lowered, he said, "Open your eyes, luv. Let me see them."

She did as he asked, and in his eyes she saw a sparkling light born of contentment mingled with passion. She felt him twitch inside her and then drive deeper until he filled her completely. Placing her palms on his chest, she dug her fingers into his firm muscles, then slid her hands over his shoulders and drew him to her.

"You feel so wonderful," he murmured, and wrapped his arms about her before claiming her lips with his own.

With each tantalizing thrust, Teri found her own excitement mounting again. She dug her nails into Kevin's back, and when his movements became more rapid, she wrapped her legs around him and arched to meet the pressure of his powerful body. His loving kiss became more urgent; their sighs mingled and his mouth ravaged hers when he lost all control. No longer did they seem *like* one; they *were* one as he drove into her again and again with the force of a wild man. He tensed and drew his head backward, then felt every muscle in his body turn to molten steel and heard Teri cry his name.

Long moments later, as they lay quietly, taking in deep breaths of cool air, he realized his weight was pressing against her, and he rolled onto his side, bringing her with him. Kevin reached for the covers and pulled them up to ward off the chill that had settled in the room.

Wrapping her arms around his waist, Teri kissed his shoulder and closed her eyes, immersing herself in the warm comfort of his body. She nuzzled against the side of his neck and felt herself drift slowly toward sleep.

"Are you happy?" he asked quietly.

"Umm, yes," she whispered against his throat.

"If you were to stay in Ireland, it could always be like this."

Her eyelids flicked open.

"We could have an exciting life," he told her in quiet tones, picturing the two of them together. "I often have to travel in my job. I'll be going to Tokyo and Hong Kong soon, and I'd want you to come with me. I'd want you to be with me wherever I went."

Teri rolled onto her back, slipping loose from Kevin's arms. He raised himself up, and resting on his forearm, he looked down at her and asked, "You want to be with me, don't you?" He was unable to conceal the tone of doubt in his voice. "I need you."

She felt cold suddenly and pulled the covers up a little. The word "need" echoed in her ears and she asked herself if Kevin didn't realize that she had needs, too. Even more disturbing was his automatic assumption that she would want to live in Ireland.

Alarmed by her silence, he tilted her face toward his. "Will you stay?"

Her eyes took in his pleading expression, and she said, "I can't stay in Ireland, Kevin... whether I want to or not. Just as you have responsibilities here, I have them at home. Colleen and I have a business to run, and she depends on me. You have Mary Kate to watch out for here, and my parents are getting on and will need my help eventually."

Kevin rested his head on his pillow and stared up at the ceiling. "We could work those problems out when the time came."

Moving to him, she placed her cheek on his chest and drew her arm across his waist. "I don't see them as problems. They're choices I've made in life...commitments, just like yours."

As he began stroking her nape, he said, "We missed an opportunity years ago. Let's not turn our backs on it again."

She raised her head and looked at him. "'We,' Kevin? If you had let me know you hadn't married Moira, I would have come running to you then, no questions asked, no apologies requested. I wouldn't have spent eight years with Angelo."

After studying her face, he asked, "Weren't you happy with him?"

Slowly Teri raised herself to a sitting position, brought her knees up and clasped them to her, oblivious now to the chilly air that caped her shoulders. "I suppose I was, but I went into the marriage without great expectations or fanciful dreams. I wasn't very assertive then, and Angelo was. I let him make all the decisions for both us. At the time I was happy that he took care of everything. When he died so young, though, I paid for that mistake. Suddenly and without warning I had to take charge of my life, of everything."

She glanced down at Kevin. "Nothing had prepared me to sort through insurance policies and bank statements. I had foolishly let Angelo take care of all those things. It was a nightmare, but a learning experience." She stared blankly into the semidarkness. "I was forced to take control of my own life, and I'm not ready to turn it over to anyone else."

"You've never once said you missed him," Kevin commented in a strange tone.

Quietly she said, "I did at first." Abruptly she faced Kevin. "Why are we talking about all this? It's making me miserable."

Reaching up, he pulled her down and folded his arms around her. "Maybe it needs to be said, but we won't discuss it anymore...not now." He smoothed back the strands of hair that lay across her forehead. "Only one more word about the past. You're right. I'm the one to blame for the wasted years we had to spend apart. But I've paid for that. I've learned that inside me I have all these feelings just waiting to come out, but without you, those feelings are trapped, luv, and I'm not a whole man."

Teri turned onto her side, facing away from him. She didn't want to listen to what he was telling her. Nor did she want to risk giving in completely to the powerful attraction she felt for Kevin O'Shea. Not again.

CHAPTER SIX

THE MORNING SUN was looming over the eastern mountains, warming the cool air, when Teri and Kevin left Kenmare to drive the eighty-eight-mile scenic Ring of Kerry route to Killarney. Following the Kenmare estuary, they rode through rugged mountains and unspoiled forests, and passed breathtaking sea views and riverscapes. Kevin pointed out the medieval castles of Dunkerron, Cappanacuss and Derryquin, but Teri, although she was interested, spent the majority of the time perusing Kevin's features. Now and then he would touch her hand or brush his fingertips over her thigh.

At Cahirciveen, a small farming and fishing village that was located at the foot of Bentee Mountain and overlooked Valentia Harbor, they stopped for lunch. In the rustic pub they chose, Teri felt as though she had stepped back in time. Most patrons spoke only Irish; even Kevin ordered for them in his native language— shepherd's pie, fresh-baked brown bread and strong stout.

They had both tried to put the previous night's conversation out of their thoughts, and so far Teri had done a good job of it, but there was something about seeing Kevin in the very Irish pub that made her fully appreciate the strength of his ties to Ireland. The realization that she was an outsider, a foreigner, only accentuated the cold fact that she would soon have to return home.

That same realization brought with it the painful decision to put as much distance between her and Kevin as she could—and quickly.

As they drove inland toward Killarney, she told him she had decided against further shopping, since she had already ordered more merchandise than she had planned to. She also asked about the train schedule to Dublin.

"First you want a car and now you want a train," he said, smiling. "Is my driving that lousy, or is it my company?"

Would that it were, she reflected. Aloud, she said, "How am I supposed to get back to Dublin... hitchhike?"

"You'd have no trouble at all. The Irish are very friendly people."

"Seriously, Kevin—"

"Seriously," he repeated, "I'd like you to come with me to the Fitzgerald estate."

"What?"

"My business with Denis won't take long. We could drive back to Dublin together."

"I can't just show up uninvited," she protested.

"The Irish are the most hospitable people in the world. If Moira happens to be there, she'd be pleased to show off her home. It's a refurbished castle with a view of the River Shannon."

The place sounded intriguing, Teri had to admit. And the more she heard about Moira, the more curious she became.

"We'll drive there after you've finished your business in Killarney," Kevin said. "We can be there in little more than an hour. We'll spend the night in

Limerick, and I'll have you back in Dublin by noon to-morrow.''

He was doing it again, she warned herself. Kevin was finding a reason to keep them together. Why did he have to be so appealing? She glanced over at his finely sculptured profile and ordered herself to think of the present, only the present.

Just then they reached the outskirts of Killarney, and, taking Teri's silence for consent, Kevin turned north and headed for County Limerick.

"I hope they haven't shipped Patrick off some-where," he said. "I'd like you to meet him."

"I guess his father is expecting you," she com-mented, wondering if this was what she really wanted to do.

"He is. I spoke to him on the phone last week to make sure he'd be home."

"Do you think you'll be able to convince him to back the financial center in Dublin?" Teri asked, really wondering if Moira would be there, too—and what she would look like.

"I doubt it."

She regarded him quizzically. "Then why make the trip?"

"I really want to try to find out just where the secu-rity fell apart when the artifacts were being transported from his plant to Dublin."

"You don't think he would have done anything amiss, do you?"

Kevin's brow furrowed. "Right now I'm not sure what to think."

As they approached the Fitzgerald estate, Teri straightened a little in her seat. When Kevin had said they lived in a refurbished Irish castle, she had visualized a foreboding stone structure similar to the ones she had seen thus far in her travels through Ireland. But ahead of them, far down the long driveway, sat a gleaming three-story blue-gray edifice that was almost cheerful. The afternoon sun was strong and steady, the acres of lawn and gardens green and bright. The battlements of the castle stood out sharply against the sheer blue sky.

"There's Patrick!" Kevin said excitedly.

She glanced to her left and saw a blond-haired boy meandering across the lawn, his head lowered, his hands shoved into his pants pockets.

Slowing the car, Kevin remarked, "He's a little shy, but a wonderful boy once you get to know him."

Teri smiled at Kevin's enthusiasm, and she acknowledged that she had learned one more thing about him: he liked children.

Kevin beeped the horn and stopped the car, hopping out when Patrick came running toward it. Teri watched as man and boy met halfway, each yelling the other's name. She felt a warm glow in her heart as Kevin grabbed Patrick under his arms and swung him around several times. Then, his hand on the boy's shoulder, Kevin led him to the car.

As they came closer, Teri saw that Patrick was an adorable-looking child, with straw-blond hair cut straight across the middle of his forehead, faint freckles dotting his pale cheeks and the bridge of his nose, and large eyes of cornflower blue.

"Patrick," Kevin said, when they reached the car where Teri was sitting, "I'd like you to meet Mrs. Teresa Manzoni. Teri, this is Patrick."

Extending her hand through the open window, Teri smiled. "I'm so pleased to meet you, Patrick."

The boy looked briefly at Teri's hand; then his eyes, which were disturbingly sad looking, shifted to her face for a second before he lowered them and backed away.

"Patrick," Kevin said gently, "is that what they teach you at school?"

His eyes still downcast, Patrick shook his head.

"Well, then?" Kevin urged.

Still not looking at Teri, Patrick said, "I'm pleased to meet you, Mrs. Manzoni."

To put him at ease, Teri said, "When I was young, I was shy, too," but as he looked up at her, she saw something in his eyes that made her believe he was actually frightened of her.

"Come on, Patrick," Kevin told him. "Get in and we'll drive you back to the house."

Once the boy was in the back seat of the car, Teri turned to him. "I imagine it must be a lot of fun to live in a real castle."

His eyes lowered again. "I suppose."

Glancing in the rearview mirror, Kevin said, "Mrs. Manzoni is from America, Patrick."

The boy lifted his eyes and glanced at Teri before he asked Kevin, "How long will you stay?"

"Not long, I'm afraid. I need to talk with your father. He's at home, isn't he?"

Patrick merely nodded and stared down at his nervous fingers, and Teri, who hadn't taken her eyes off him, was struck by how tense he appeared.

As Kevin pulled onto the circular driveway in front of the imposing structure, Teri saw a tall, black-haired man standing outside the castle's double wooden entry doors under a Gothic arch. He wore a bulky wheat-colored sweater, gray jodhpurs and riding boots. If he had been smiling, she thought, he would have been attractive.

Patrick's eyes darted to his father, then he asked Kevin, "You won't leave without saying goodbye, will you?"

"Of course I won't." After switching off the ignition, he got out of the car and opened the door for Teri.

"Patrick!" the dark-haired man said sharply, "go upstairs...now."

Teri's head swung back toward the car, and again she saw that troubled expression on the boy's face. When she glanced over at Kevin, she noticed a muscle was twitching at his jaw.

"Yes, sir," Patrick said, promptly hopping out of the car and hurrying up the three steps to the doorway.

With little enthusiasm, Kevin made the introductions, and Denis Fitzgerald led them inside, across a spacious entry hall and into a huge salon. Teri was instantly entranced. From the ceiling of the elegant green, gold and white salon hung a magnificent chandelier that sparkled and was reflected in an equally magnificent mirror across from a huge stone fireplace. Coming from outside the tall window next to her was the gentle sound of gurgling water. A fountain, she supposed.

"How are things in Dublin?" Denis asked, resting an arm on the stone mantel of the fireplace. "I've heard that the millennium exhibition is a great success."

"It would have been a greater success if we could have displayed the antiquities found near your plant last month."

Dark eyes challenged cool blue ones. "Yes, it's a shame about the hijackings."

"You know," Kevin said purposefully, "I'm certain the museum would pay to retrieve them."

Denis smiled—sort of. "If they haven't already been melted down by whoever has them."

Before Kevin could reply, Denis moved closer to Teri and asked, "Are you in Ireland as a tourist, Mrs. Manzoni?"

"No, I'm here on business, but I have been enjoying your beautiful country."

"Business?" he said, reaching for her hand.

An uncomfortable feeling rippled through her as he held her unoffered hand in his, and the sensation was heightened when she caught a whiff of overly sweet shaving lotion. In the next instant, when he held her eyes with his, she thought them rather strange looking. They were dark, almost black, but it wasn't the color so much as the strained, glassy look of them that she thought odd.

Rude or not, she withdrew her hand and, to answer his inquiry, said, "Yes, I operate an Irish import shop in New York."

"Irish imports," he repeated, and chuckled wryly. "Smoked salmon and shamrock-painted teacups?"

Kevin moved next to Teri. "Really, Denis, you should get around your own country a little more. Irish craftspeople have a great deal to offer. If you didn't spend so much time in London and Paris, you'd know that."

Denis set his hands on the back of a Chippendale chair. "What do you suggest I do? Tour the island, stop at rustic bed-and-breakfast inns and dine on Irish stew and stout?"

"You could do worse."

Whenever Kevin had spoken about Denis Fitzgerald, Teri had gathered that no love was lost between them, but now the air was so thick with tension it was almost suffocating. She saw that Kevin's face had reddened, but the other man's retained an aloofness that she was sure belied his feelings.

As Denis moved to a richly carved high-backed chair and sat down, he asked Kevin, "Is that why you wanted to talk to me? To try to interest me in Ireland's cottage crafts?"

Dryly Kevin told him, "You know why I'm here."

Denis's expression turned condescending. "Oh, yes, I remember now. You're still trying to drum up backers for the Custom House."

"Exactly, and you're too good a businessman to pass up the generous tax incentives the government is offering. Your money would be invested here as safely as it is in London."

"Ireland has no track record as a financial center."

"How the hell are we going to build one if we're not given the chance?"

From where Teri stood she could see that Kevin's eyes had turned dark, as they did whenever he was about to lose his temper. She was relieved when she saw him physically calm down and lower his voice as he continued.

"Belgian Kredietbank has already applied for a license to operate out of the center, and U.S. Citicorp may do so, too. A group of Chicago financial traders plan to open an exchange, as well."

"You've been busy," Denis commented.

"Yes, and I'm traveling to Tokyo and Hong Kong to invite their major financial organizations."

Denis glared at him. "Then why come here begging for my support?"

After flipping back the sides of his suit jacket, Kevin put his hands on his hips. "I'm not begging, but it would make my job a lot easier if I could show prospective backers a list of Irishmen who have faith in their own financial institutions."

Denis rose and strode to a marble-topped table, where he picked up a pipe from its holder. Without looking at Kevin, he said sarcastically, "Faith. I'm a businessman, not a priest. If I do have any faith, it's in the English pound." His eyes swept over to Kevin. "Unlike you, I don't have time for flag waving."

"But you do have time for—"

"Kevin!"

Teri turned toward the entrance to the salon. Walking directly toward Kevin was one of the most beautiful women she had ever seen. She was tall and slender, and her long, thick red hair cascaded in natural waves around her classically lovely face. She wore a white silk blouse that was ruffled at the collar, and a simple navy skirt, yet the overall effect was elegant and entrancing. Teri was happy she had decided to wear the chic yellow suit she had bought at Bloomingdale's.

"Moira," Kevin said in a soft tone.

She kissed him on the cheek and turned toward Teri, who could tell the other woman was assessing her from her brown pumps to her dark hair. A brief moment passed, then Moira's gorgeous lips parted in a pleasant smile that exposed beautiful white teeth. "Welcome," she said in a musical tone.

After introductions, Teri remarked, "Your home—" she smiled apologetically "—your castle is overwhelming."

Moira's gentle laugh echoed in the high-ceilinged room. "Exactly the right word. Yearly maintenance is forty thousand pounds, and that's before you start fooling with the roof and things like that." Her gaze drifted around the room. "But it is rather nice, isn't it? Would you like a quick tour? That way the men can go to it—" she aimed a piercing glance at her husband "—as they always do."

"Go ahead, Teri," Kevin said. "Denis and I still have some business to discuss."

No sooner had the women reached the doorway than Teri heard Kevin start in on Denis again, telling him he had the manners of a goat. That was not, she told herself, the way she would have gone about trying to enlist the man's support for the project in Dublin. She had learned something else about Kevin: he wore his temper just under his skin.

As the two women crossed the gray stone floor their high heels made clicking sounds. Teri took time to study the display of fierce-looking seven-foot hunting spears that hung on a wall in the foyer before they started up one of the curved staircases that had obviously been added.

"Have you known Kevin long?" Moira asked.

"Yes and no," Teri replied, noting the interest in her hostess's green eyes and putting her guard up. "We met briefly many years ago, and quite accidentally in Dublin this week."

"I see. I've known Kevin all my life. We grew up together."

"How nice." *And what was the reason for that comment?* Teri wondered.

"In fact, we were engaged once." Moira smiled softly, then added, "The problem was that we were engaged for too long."

Moira led an unresponsive Teri down a long hallway and into rooms that had either a plush coziness or an airy elegance. As she did, she pointed out favorite objets d'art, paintings and curios she had brought back from the Continent. "Collecting," she admitted, "is a habit of mine."

"You and your husband must travel a great deal," Teri remarked as they walked through a lovely morning room.

"Yes—but rarely together," Moira said, her voice losing its well-modulated quality.

From that comment, Teri could only infer that the Fitzgerald marriage was not in the best shape, and she suspected Denis was to blame. The insensitive way he had ordered Patrick upstairs was unforgivable in her opinion. She remained silent.

"Do you ever travel to the Continent, Teri?" Moira asked.

"No, but someday I hope to."

"You'll adore it." Moira went to a table by the window and picked up a carved crystal bowl. "I found this Baccarat piece in Paris last month." Her eyes drifted over the furnishings. "This is my favorite room in the entire castle. I love to just sit in here and read, and Denis and I have aperitifs and after-dinner drinks in here when we happen to be home at the same time."

Teri noted that Moira wasn't at all hesitant in implying that the ties between her and her husband were not strong ones. She also wondered when Moira was going to mention Patrick, but then she recalled Kevin's comment that the woman seldom had time for her son. That saddened Teri, and she became even more impressed with Kevin's obvious affection for the boy. It certainly seemed to be returned.

An hour later, the tour completed, the two women reentered the salon. Denis was leaning against the grand piano and Kevin was standing close by, his eyes fixed on the man. Neither appeared to take note of the women's return, but Teri was happy to hear Kevin's voice sounding more reasonable. In fact, it was almost too reasonable, considering the topic of discussion.

"The Dublin police are wondering how the hijackers knew when the crates were being shipped," he said.

After Denis sipped his drink, he responded, "Just as I was advised, I told no one about the transport schedules. Even the men who crated them didn't know. The boxes remained in the plant and were guarded by the Limerick police until they were picked up."

Quietly Moira took a seat near the archway at the entrance to the salon; Teri did, too.

"Who was in charge of the crating?" Kevin asked.

"Gary Dillon, and he's to be trusted. He's been my plant manager for almost fifteen years."

Kevin eased his fingers over his jaw. "Well, someone told the hijackers, and as a result three men are dead and one is in a coma. If he ever comes out of it, he may be able to give the police some description of the thieves."

Without warning, Denis's stolid face contorted, and his voice rose in pitch. "And you'd like him to describe me, wouldn't you...lay the thefts and the murders at my doorstep?"

Kevin raised a hand, palm forward. "I didn't say that. I'm just trying to figure out what went wrong and where."

"*You* knew when they were being shipped!" Denis said accusingly, pointing at Kevin. "And you wouldn't have any trouble with customs getting them out of the country, not if you had them in one of the minister's diplomatic pouches. Have the Dublin police thought of that?"

Kevin crossed his arms and shook his head slowly. "You're being ridiculous."

"And do they know just how badly you want money for that damn financial center of yours?" Denis asked excitedly.

"It's not *my* project, you idiot."

"Please," Moira interrupted from across the room, starting toward them. "We have a guest. The two of you are being boorish."

Standing, Teri watched as Moira went to Kevin and took him by the arm.

Looking over at her husband, Moira said, "Really, I wish you'd conduct business at your office and not here at home."

Denis smiled snidely. "You really wish I'd never again set foot in this place, don't you? That way you could entertain your ex-lovers whenever the mood struck you."

"Mother," Patrick said, coming into the salon.

Denis wheeled around. "I thought I told you to stay upstairs!"

"For God's sake," Moira said, "will you leave the boy alone!" Turning to her son, she asked calmly, "What is it, Patrick?"

"May I go outside and play?"

"Of course."

Before Denis could object, Kevin said, "Wait up, Patrick." He looked at Moira. "I promised him we'd spend some time together before I left."

Smiling, Moira said, "Wonderful. Why don't you spend the night and stay for the hunt tomorrow?"

"I'm afraid we can't. I told Teri I'd have her back in Dublin early in the morning."

"Dinner, then—" her voice took on a beseeching tone "—please?"

"Oh, by all means," Denis chimed in, "stay for dinner. Perhaps I'll change my mind about helping you build your financial center."

Kevin studied him for a moment, not taking his words seriously, then he nodded at Moira, took hold of Teri's arm, and with Patrick, they left the castle.

Teri and Kevin spent a good hour and a half with Patrick, and although the boy showed no signs of warming up to her, she couldn't help but notice how he blossomed with Kevin. And she noticed a change in him, too. Inside, talking with Denis, he'd been in a rage. Now, as he and Patrick jockeyed for a ball with hurling sticks, Kevin exuded a gentleness that was truly heartwarming.

When the three of them headed back toward the castle, Patrick asked Kevin, "Can you spend your vacation here again this summer?"

Ruffling the boy's blond hair, he told him, "No, not this year. I have to go to Tokyo, then to Hong Kong."

"Could I go with you? I hate it here when I'm alone with Father."

"Is your mother going away again?" Kevin asked.

Patrick nodded. "She's going to Rome and then to Venice."

Teri wondered why he wasn't going with Moira, but she knew better than to ask.

His hand still on Patrick's shoulder, Kevin said, "Tell you what we'll do. As soon as I get back from my trip, you can spend some time with me in Dublin."

"Could I?"

"I'll talk to your mother about it. I think she'll say it's all right."

Moira was coming down one of the curved stairways as they were crossing the foyer. "Patrick, go upstairs and wash. Nanny has your dinner ready."

"Yes, Mother." He turned to Kevin and whispered, "You won't forget to ask her, will you?"

"Not a chance," he said, and watched him scoot up the stairs.

"He is a dear, don't you think, Kevin?" Moira said, leading them into a sitting room off the entry hall. Turning to Teri, she asked, "Would you like to freshen up before dinner?"

"I would, yes."

Moira pulled a bell cord and moments later a young, uniformed maid entered.

"Sheila, would you take Mrs. Manzoni upstairs to the Rose Room, please."

"I think I'll wash up, too," Kevin said.

Touching his arm, Moira told him, "I'd like to speak with you first."

Teri glanced over at him, then followed Sheila out of the room.

Once they were alone, Moira asked, "Why do you always make Denis so furious?"

With little emotion, he answered, "It's a natural talent I have."

Moira curved her arm around Kevin's, and he followed her to the tall, Gothic window overlooking the gardens. "It certainly doesn't take much to unglue him lately, but when will you ever learn? You should realize by now that when you ask him to do anything, he'll do just the opposite out of spite. You know he's insanely jealous of you."

"Of all your ex-lovers, according to what he said before."

Her eyes sparkled, and her red lips curved into a lovely smile. "You don't believe that for a second." Her smile evaporated, and her tone became serious. "It's always been you, only you."

"Moira—" he began, but she interrupted.

"I could leave him. Just say you want me to. Getting a divorce wouldn't be easy, but possibly I could get an annulment."

Kevin shook his head and pulled his arm from her grasp. "We've been through this before. Why do you insist on believing there's anything left between us? It's finished, Moira. It's been finished for a long time."

"Eight years, to be exact," she told him.

He studied her with eyes that were icy and unresponsive before he turned away. "That was a mistake, a damn big one, but I'm not going to go on paying for it to my dying day. When you told me Denis had hit you—"

She placed her palms on his back, then slipped her fingers up over his shoulders. "You comforted me, and I appreciated it more than you know. But I made you happy that night, didn't I? I could make you happy again."

"I am happy," he told her, "happier than I've ever been."

She moved her hands inside his suit jacket and ran her fingers over his chest. "You're just trying to make yourself believe that. You know you'll never get me out of your system completely."

"I already have."

Disregarding his words, she rested her cheek on his back. "Divorce or annulment, I'd come out of this marriage a rich woman. We could be together... travel, do anything you want to do."

Kevin pushed her hands away and turned to face her. "You haven't given a minute's thought to Patrick, have you? What would you do with him while we were *traveling*?"

"He'd be in school, where he should be."

"Damn it, Moira, the boy's a human being, not a curio you picked up because it caught your eye. He has feelings, and you're his mother!"

"And you're—" she stopped, then pasted on a smile "—you're acting as though I don't love him."

He took hold of her shoulders firmly and asked, "Do you? Do you really?"

"Of course I do."

"You and that pig of a husband of yours have a hell of a way of showing it."

She placed her fingers on Kevin's cheek. "He is a pig, isn't he?" she agreed. "I can't stand for him even to touch me."

Kevin edged away, letting her hand drop. "Why the hell did you marry him, then?"

Her green eyes drifted around the lavishly appointed room. "There were some benefits."

"Then you'll just have to continue earning them."

Moira's expression turned hard. "It's this Teri, isn't it?"

"Let's leave her out of it."

"Are you sleeping with her?"

"That's none of your business."

"Maybe it is."

"What the hell is that supposed to mean?"

Moving directly in front of him, she guided her hands up and around his neck. "No matter who you're sleeping with, you'll always belong to me, and I have good reason for saying that."

"What are you talking about?"

"About this."

In the next instant Moira's lips were on Kevin's, but he pulled away sharply, went to the window and looked back at her. "You're right about Teri. I do love her."

Moira turned momentarily, her expression pained. "Oh," she murmured, then her green eyes sent him a troubled but longing look.

At that moment Teri reentered the room and couldn't help but notice the way Moira was gazing at Kevin. Cheerfully Teri remarked, "You do have a lovely home, Moira. The Rose Room is almost as big as my entire apartment in Manhattan."

Before Moira could comment, her maid Sheila knocked on the open door. When Moira acknowledged the woman's presence with lifted eyebrows, Sheila said, "Mr. Fitzgerald is waiting in the dining room, madam."

"Thank you, Sheila," Moira said, taking hold of Kevin's arm. "I hope you're hungry."

He glanced at Teri with concerned eyes and said, "Not really."

When they reached the dining room, Teri took note of the red-flocked wallpaper, the nineteenth-century chairs and the elaborate ormolu chandelier. A formally dressed butler waited by the Irish baroque sideboard laden with venetian glass and heirloom china. One look at Denis, who was sitting at the head of the table, which could accommodate sixteen, and Teri had to wonder when he had started on his cocktails.

"Be careful, Kevin," he warned, seeing that Moira held his arm. "The woman's like a leech once she gets hold of you...a bloodsucking leech." In the next instant, much to Teri's amazement, he complimented his wife pleasantly. "You look lovely, dear. Is that a new dress?"

"Yes, I bought it in Paris."

Teri had to admit that Moira did look fabulous in the silver-beaded champagne silk dress. If, as Kevin had told her, Ireland was having a difficult time economically, it certainly didn't show in the Fitzgerald household.

After they joined Denis at the table, dinner was served: artichoke hearts, venison with morels and watercress salad, followed by French cheeses and an intricate but light dessert. All the while, Denis was utterly charming, and attentive to Moira. Teri began to wonder about his mood swings.

After dinner they had French brandy in the salon, and Moira played Chopin softly at the grand piano while Denis stood beside it, listening. Out of the blue, he asked his wife, "Have you talked our guests into staying the night?"

She glanced up at him. "I haven't tried to."

"Pity." Looking over at Teri, he held up his brandy snifter. "It might have proved interesting."

"Denis," Kevin said in a warning tone, "don't make an ass of yourself."

"Strange advice coming from you," he said, his alcohol-glazed eyes widening. "Or are you worrying about my stealing your American friend from you as I did Moira? Well don't! I'm damn tired of your leftovers."

Kevin jumped up.

Teri lurched forward in the chair she was sitting on, afraid of what would happen next. She couldn't blame Kevin for becoming angry; Denis Fitzgerald was crude and obviously enjoyed taunting him, but she didn't want the men to come to blows.

Moira moved quickly and took Teri's arm. "Would you like to see the garden?" Without waiting for a reply, she led her through the French doors out onto the terrace and down into the beautifully landscaped grounds.

Although it was nine-thirty in the evening, the sun had not yet set, and there was a pleasant breeze. As the two women walked, Teri tried to shake off her bad feelings about the Fitzgerald household. Denis's behavior toward everyone was exceedingly ill-mannered, and he had all the earmarks of a deeply disturbed man. She wondered how Moira put up with him and what was going on between the two men they had left behind.

When Teri and her hostess passed a miniature waterfall and began walking under a series of wrought-iron arches entwined with climbing red roses, Moira said, "I must apologize for Denis's behavior. He's not been well lately."

"Nothing serious, I hope," Teri offered, wondering just how well he'd be when Kevin got through with him.

Moira tapped her temple with her forefinger. "It's all up here. It runs in the family." She chuckled, but with little humor. "His brother's built an underground shelter stocked with perishables, no less. He claims that the wee folk are out to get him."

"I am sorry," Teri offered sincerely.

The pathway curved at a large stone urn on a high pedestal, which overflowed with white ivy geraniums, and Teri remarked on the surrounding violet rhododendrons and scarlet-flowering trees, but her hostess had other things on her mind.

"I admire your independence," Moira said.

Thinking that an odd comment, Teri replied, "From the way you travel, I would gather you're pretty independent yourself."

"Not really." She stopped and glanced back at the castle. "I can go just so far from this place and for just so long. Denis has me chained here with invisible bonds."

Patrick, Teri guessed but said nothing.

"When exactly did you first meet Kevin?" Moira asked.

Teri knew the date by heart, but replied only, "Many years ago when he was in New York on business."

"Oh. I imagine you saw each other every time he was there."

Stopping, Teri said, "I didn't realize he had ever returned to the States."

"Oh, yes," she said, a glimmer playing in her expressive green eyes. "Not long after he left the army and went to work in Dublin, he made several trips to New York. I'm surprised you didn't know."

Stunned by that bit of information, Teri had to come to the conclusion that Kevin's actions—or nonactions—spoke louder than his words. Why had he never tried to contact her? Of course she had married by then, but she was deeply hurt that he hadn't at least tried to see her.

"Are you in love with him?" Moira asked casually.

Looking directly at her, Teri decided Moira wasn't as beautiful as she had at first thought. Her features were symmetrically perfect, but an inner discontent blighted them, for the moment, anyway. Lifting her chin a little, Teri answered, "Yes, I guess I am."

"Kevin has that effect on women. I've never stopped loving him, and I believe he's never really stopped loving me."

Annoyed by Moira's probings into personal matters, Teri said rather curtly, "I'm surprised you didn't marry him when you could have."

As they continued down the garden path, Moira remarked, "I wasn't ready to dedicate my life to helping him in his career, and that's exactly what you would have to do if you're even entertaining the idea of marrying him. Kevin's first love is his country. I wasn't prepared to take second place in his life." Her voice softened somewhat. "I threatened to marry Denis, thinking Kevin would change his priorities."

"But he didn't," Teri said.

Moira shook her head. "And now I'm saddled with a man who's half-crazy." Looking at Teri, her voice and expression darkened when she said, "Sometimes he behaves so irrationally he frightens me. I'm also afraid for Patrick."

"But surely he wouldn't hurt his own son."

Moira reached up and plucked a scarlet blossom from the tree overhead; then she gave Teri a passionless sideways glance. "He knows Patrick isn't his son."

CHAPTER SEVEN

AGAIN TERI CAME to a halt, but this time she looked at Moira with incredulous eyes as a fearful tremor jolted her heart. Quietly she asked, "If Denis isn't Patrick's father, who is?"

"Kevin," Moira said with a note of triumph in her voice.

Feeling the blood drain from her face, Teri sat down slowly on the stone bench along the side of the pathway and stared down at the gravel. *Kevin, a father. Moira, the mother of his child.*

Just when she thought she had learned so much about the mature Kevin O'Shea, she now had to come to terms with the realization that there was a side to him she knew nothing of.

When her thoughts ceased reeling, she began to understand that the affection between Kevin and Patrick was more than a man's concern for a child who desperately needed love and attention. No wonder he had spent his vacation with the boy and expressed such concern for his well-being. What she couldn't comprehend was why Kevin hadn't told her himself.

As she tried to recuperate from the shock of Moira's admission, Teri looked up and asked, "Does Patrick know?"

"Of course not. Nor does Kevin."

"What?" she exclaimed in disbelief. "You mean in all these years you haven't bothered to tell him he's a father, that Patrick is his son?"

"I hadn't wanted to...until recently. I can take Denis's verbal abuse, and a few times he's actually hit me, but I don't want him hurting Patrick."

"If you weren't going to tell Kevin, why on earth did you tell your husband?"

"Two years after Patrick's birth, Denis wanted another child. When I couldn't conceive, he insisted we both be checked for medical causes. Denis learned that it was physically impossible for him to have any children, that he could never have had any. I had to tell him."

"So that's why he hates Kevin so."

"That's only part of the reason. Denis was jealous of him even when we were growing up. The Fitzgeralds used to live on an estate in Bantry, near Glengarriff. Kevin was always so much better at everything than Denis was. He always bested him, and even though Denis had so much more financially and socially, it seemed to eat at him. I think he was half-crazy even then."

Teri pushed herself up from the stone bench. "Why are you telling me all this? I'm little more than a stranger to you."

"Because I'm planning to leave Denis, and I want Kevin, Patrick and myself to have a chance to be a real family, as we should be. I don't want you to ruin that chance, for Patrick's sake more than Kevin's or mine."

The throbbing at Teri's temples was becoming more painful by the moment, but she was determined not to give Moira the satisfaction of knowing just how bad she felt, how terribly disillusioned she was. After a deep breath she asked, "You are going to tell Kevin, aren't you?"

Starting back toward the castle, Moira said, "When the time is right I will, but if you say anything to him before I'm ready, I'll deny it, and you'll look like a desperate, jealous woman. Besides, you really don't know if I'm telling you the truth, do you?"

Still feeling upset and confused, Teri merely shook her head, but she couldn't believe the woman would lie about something like that. *Oh, Kevin,* she murmured silently.

When they reached the terrace, a red-faced Kevin came rushing out. "Come on," he told Teri, taking hold of her arm, "we're leaving before I kill him."

"But my purse," she protested.

"Where is it?"

"On the table near the piano."

"Wait here. The man in there is a raving maniac."

As soon as Kevin was inside, Moira said, "You can see how important it is that I get Patrick away from Denis, don't you?"

Teri fixed her eyes on the woman, and deep inside she had to agree that it was necessary. "I think you should tell Kevin. He has a right to know. If you were truly concerned about your son's safety, you would tell Kevin now."

Moira checked the open French doors, then said, "I don't think Patrick's in any danger at the present, and as I said, I'm the one who will choose the time and place to tell Kevin the truth."

"I've got it," Kevin said as he came back out and gave Teri her purse. To Moira he said, "Do you have any objections if Patrick visits me in Dublin when I get back from my business trip?"

Her reply was instant and sweetly spoken. "Of course not. We both know how he adores you. Anytime it's convenient, Kevin, and for as long as you like."

"You don't think his father will object?"

"I know his father won't—" her eyes met Teri's briefly "—believe me. If you'll let me know when you want to take him, I'll plan to be here to see that nothing stops you from doing so."

"Good. Tell Patrick that and say goodbye for both of us."

"I'll tell him right now." She offered Teri her hand. "Will we be seeing you again?"

Not accepting the other woman's hand, Teri said, "No, I'll be in Dublin for a few days. Then I'm returning home."

Kevin looked at them, sensing that something was going on, something he knew nothing about. Taking hold of Teri's arm again, he said his final goodbye to Moira, and he and Teri headed for his car.

During the short drive to Limerick, an inland port city on the River Shannon, Teri sat silently, close to tears as she mulled over her conversation with Moira. She only half heard Kevin as he ranted on about Denis's state of mind and said the man should be committed. She was too preoccupied with yet another barrier that had been set firmly in place between her and Kevin, one she couldn't even tell him about—Patrick.

After checking them into separate rooms at their hotel, as Teri requested, Kevin suggested they go into the Copper Room for tea and coffee.

"I'd really like something stronger," Teri said grimly.

Kevin spoke with the desk clerk, then led Teri to the piano bar, where he ordered two Irish mists.

"You've hardly said a word since we left the Fitzgeralds," he commented, studying her expression, which he thought rather impassive.

"It's been a long day," she offered as an explanation.

"And not a very pleasant one for you."

Nervously toying with the single strand of pearls at her throat, she said, "I wasn't prepared for the fireworks."

After their waiter served the Irish mists in glistening pony glasses, Kevin said, "To be honest, I wasn't quite prepared for the way he acted. I never would have taken you there if I'd thought he would carry on as he did. There's definitely something wrong with him." Noting the strained look on Teri's face, he added, "And I really hadn't expected Moira to be there. She rarely is when Denis is at home for any length of time. Staying for dinner was a mistake. But let's forget the Fitzgeralds. We've better things to talk about."

So easy to say, she thought, but how could she forget what Moira had told her? Teri's determination not to let Kevin complicate her life had begun to waver in spite of the problems she foresaw. *Problems,* she repeated silently. She had thought they would have minor problems ahead of them, but now Teri knew enormous problems lay ahead. And Teri certainly did not want to become involved in them. As sympathetic as she was to Patrick's plight, that issue would have to be settled between Kevin and the Fitzgeralds.

"*Sláinte,*" Kevin said, raising his glass, but Teri was so preoccupied she didn't hear him. "Teri?" he said curiously.

She looked up from the small glass she was absent-mindedly turning on her napkin. "Yes?" She saw his glass poised in midair.

"To your health," he said again.

To my sanity, she added mentally, then said, "To yours," and took a hearty sip. She pursed her lips slightly. "Sweet, isn't it?"

Kevin glanced at her glass and saw that two-thirds of the liqueur was gone. Grinning, he warned, "And potent."

"That's just what I need right now."

"Did Denis's behavior bother you that much?"

Meeting his questioning eyes, she commented, "Yours wasn't that much better. I had the feeling you were trying to pick a fight with the man. It was as though you were carrying a grudge."

After a sip and a moment's honest reflection, he admitted, "I've never liked Denis."

Teri finished her liqueur, and with uncharacteristic bravado, she asked, "Because Moira married him?"

The frankness of her question took Kevin by surprise, and he polished off his drink and signaled their waiter for two more. "That didn't exactly place him on my Christmas list, but my not liking the man has nothing to do with the fact that Moira married him. It's the way he treats his own son. Denis is making the boy withdrawn and unsure of himself."

Since the bar was nearly empty, their refills came quickly. Teri sipped this time, then looked over at the young woman playing a melancholy Irish melody that Teri couldn't identify. Against her better judgment, she said, "You certainly seem to be concerned about Patrick."

"Wouldn't you be if you had known the boy all his life? You saw how he's treated in his own home . . . as though he didn't belong there."

Teri asked, "Aren't there relatives to see to his well-being?"

"None who have paid as much attention to him as I have."

Kevin's reply was firm and stated with a finality that made Teri wonder if it was instinct that made him feel protective of Patrick. The thought was at once wonderful and distressing: wonderful because it indicated the strength of the bond that could exist between father and son; distressing because Moira could at any time tell Kevin the truth and create a stronger bond between him and her. If and when Moira did tell him, Teri knew he would take full responsibility for Patrick. And where would that leave Teresa Rosario Manzoni? She knew exactly where. His sense of duty had caused him to leave her once before, hadn't it?

"I can't explain it," Kevin continued, "but I do worry about Patrick. Maybe it's because he's so bright and could look forward to such a happy and productive life if only he were given support and direction. Right now he's afraid of just about everyone he meets."

Teri easily detected the sincerity in Kevin's words. "Yes," she said quietly, "I noticed that."

Kevin grunted ruefully. "Denis is not the greatest role model a son could have."

But you are, she thought, and sipped her liqueur.

Brightening, Kevin said, "Enough about problems. This is supposed to be the vacation part of your trip." He took hold of her hand, stood and pulled her up beside him. "I want to hold you in my arms—" he glanced around at the few couples seated in the cozy room "—but here we're going to have to dance for me to do it."

Teri let him lead her to the small dance floor by the piano, and when he placed his arms around her and drew her to him, she expelled a sigh that carried some of her tension with it. The music was soft and slow and a little too sad, she thought as she swayed in Kevin's arms. Why couldn't she just pretend she was on holiday and didn't have a care in the world? Why couldn't she take Colleen's advice and spread her wings and soar without worrying about crashing to earth again? Why hadn't she gone ahead and taken the train to Dublin earlier?

When she felt Kevin's warm cheek rest against her forehead, she knew why. She was destined to love him. But now destiny had again played an awful trick on her, making it impossible for them ever to be together permanently.

The music seemed to go on and on, and she continued to relax in Kevin's embrace, but suddenly she was becoming quite warm, as though someone had just turned the heat up in the lounge. She touched her cheek; her face was warm, and she could feel a tingle of heat on the curves of her ears. Softly she asked, "Is it getting hot in here to you?"

He pulled back a little and smiled at her. "It's the Irish mist. I warned you it was potent. Are you feeling a little sleepy, too?"

"Kind of drowsy, but not sleepy."

"Then I think it's time we called it a night."

The way he said it was sobering, and she agreed. "I think you're right."

"I know I am," he told her. He guided her back to their table, and after she retrieved her purse, he took her to their adjoining rooms on the second floor.

When he unlocked her door and opened it slightly, Teri looked up at him. "This part of the evening has been pleasant. Good night, Kevin."

"It has been nice," he said quietly, glancing inside her room. "Are you going to ask me in?"

Teri's thoughts came in a jumble. Yes, she did want to, but, no, she couldn't—not after what Moira had told her. Knowing she had to take control of the situation before it took control of her, she said, "I'm exhausted, and I imagine you are, too. Let's both get a good night's sleep."

Scrutinizing her expression, he saw that she wasn't able to keep her eyes fixed on his, and he wondered why. Again he cursed himself for taking her with him to see Denis Fitzgerald. But he couldn't erase it now. Nodding, he said, "Sleep well, Teri," then he went to his room.

GRAY CLOUDS HOVERED over the land in the morning when Kevin and Teri checked out and began the drive to Dublin.

"I want to stop at Denis's turf plant," he said. "It's on the way, so we won't be losing any time. I'd like to talk to Gary Dillon, the man who was in charge of crating the hijacked artifacts."

"Haven't the police already questioned him?" she asked.

"I'm guessing they have, but sometimes a man will tell someone else things he's hesitant to tell the police."

When they arrived at the outskirts of the bogland on which Denis Fitzgerald's plant was located, Teri saw only a vast, flat plain of brown grasses with streaks of rust and occasional white tufts that Kevin said were called bog cotton. As they continued along the dirt road, the bog stretched endlessly on all sides.

They passed a long line of railroad cars laden with turf, and Kevin explained, "The trains carry the turf to power stations. Twenty-one percent of our electric power comes from it. But, like Mary Kate, a lot of people still use it the old way. It burns better than wood and about half as well as coal." He pointed to the left. "There's one of those monster machines I told you about."

Teri looked out the window. In the distance the cutting machine resembled a giant farm tractor, and indeed it did have a cutting arm attached, which appeared to be many times the length of the tractor. She watched as the arm moved slowly over the bog and saw that it left unbelievably neat rows of turf bars behind it.

"There's the plant," Kevin said, following the road that curved to the right.

Teri saw that the mammoth, dingy gray building was three stories high at one end and shot up another story in the main section. Several trailers were lined up next to a loading dock. Kevin pulled onto the blacktop, circled the building and parked in front of the administrative office.

"Best that you wait here," he suggested. "I'll find out where Dillon is."

Soon he was back, though.

"Our friend Dillon no longer works here," he reported as he got back into the car. "Seems he recently came into some money and bought property near Thurles. How much of a hurry are we in?"

Just as Kevin had, Teri put two and two together. Hijacked gold and silver, a man suddenly coming into money, quitting his job and buying property. It might just have been a coincidence, but she didn't want Kevin trying to find out. She reminded him, "You promised me I'd be in Dublin by noon." She glanced at her watch. "It's one-thirty now."

"I guess that means we are in a hurry." After fastening his seat belt, they were off once again.

IN DUBLIN, Kevin made a quick stop at the Department of Foreign Affairs, where his secretary chatted with Teri over tea while he spoke with his boss. Then they went directly to Seamus's office.

The man was effusive as he welcomed Teri back and scanned the order forms she had filled out at the craft center in Cork. Fiona joined them, looking as elegant as ever, Teri thought.

"I just saw the minister," Kevin told Seamus. "As we all are, he's troubled by the recent hijackings. He said the police believe the people involved may be part of a smuggling operation centered here in Dublin."

"What would they be smuggling?" Seamus asked.

"Mostly valuables stolen from museums and private collectors."

"Do they have any idea who these people are?" Fiona asked.

"We didn't have time to talk very long," Kevin told her. "The minister had to leave for a meeting at the Bank of Ireland."

"Oh," she said, then she smiled at Seamus. "I'll process Teresa's order."

After handing her the papers, Seamus told Teri, "Your merchandise from Enterprise Tower arrived. Would you like to see it before we ship it?"

"I really would," she said excitedly.

"Fiona," Seamus said, "if Mr. Ryan returns my call, tell him to hold. I'll be right back."

"No, no, stay here, Seamus. I'll take them." As the three of them started toward the office door, Fiona glanced back at the chair next to Seamus's desk. "Teresa," she said, "you forgot your briefcase."

"It'll be fine right here," Seamus promised.

"Better to be careful in case you have to leave the room. Teresa carries her valuables in it." Fiona picked up the briefcase and handed it to Teri.

The mailing room employees had already left for the day, so after showing Teri which boxes were hers, Fiona excused herself and returned to her office, leaving Teri and Kevin alone in the quiet room to look over the merchandise.

A half hour later, as they left the building and walked to his car, Kevin asked, "How long are you planning to stay in Dublin before you leave for home?"

Teri knew Colleen didn't expect her back for another week, but she also realized that each day with Kevin would make it more difficult to say goodbye. Not looking at him, she said, "I've changed my mind about staying here. I've decided to go on to Galway tomorrow."

He opened the car door for her and closed it a little harder than necessary. When he sat down next to her, he looked at her with steely eyes and said, "Well, before you run off again, we still have some unfinished business to settle."

During the short drive to his town house, Kevin remained silent, and Teri was busy formulating the reasons she was going to give him for her change of plans. Once there, though, she became concerned. Kevin's eyes had darkened just as they had when he and Denis had argued. She refused his offer of a drink, but after he belted one down, he stretched out an arm and pointed a finger at her from the other side of the room.

"You've been acting very distant ever since we left the Fitzgeralds. Is there something you want to tell me?"

Lowering her eyes, Teri thought, *How can I? I don't even know if what Moira said is true.*

Teri's silence always got to Kevin; he didn't know how to handle it. After a frustrated breath, he calmed himself and said, "You can't just reenter my life and walk away like this."

Quietly she reminded him, "That's exactly what you did to me twelve years ago."

"Is that what this is all about? Are you trying to make me pay for the mistake I made?"

"Of course not. I only want you to know you don't have the corner on being hurt." She recalled what Moira had told her about his having returned to the States. Looking up at him, Teri's expression turned stony. "Why didn't you try to contact me when you returned to New York?"

"Who told you I did?"

"Moira...."

"Did she also tell you that on my first trip back I found out you had married?"

Surprised by that, Teri shook her head, and after several painful moments, she said, "I would have liked to see you, anyway."

When he finished pouring himself another drink, Kevin turned; his eyes lacked their usual sparkle. "And how do you think I would have felt meeting your husband, the man who slept next to you every night?"

"Kevin, a woman can love a man and still—"

"And still what? Marry someone else...the way Moira did, the way you did?"

She shook her head. "You're doing it again. *You* left *me*, damn it. And I'm not proud of the fact that I loved you even while I was married to Angelo. In fact, until seeing you again, I hadn't realized just how much I did." She forced her next words out. "And it's very possible that Moira still loves you, too."

"Is that what she told you?"

"Yes, but she didn't have to. A woman can tell."

"Oh?" he remarked, sitting down in the chair opposite her and crossing his legs. After an awkward silence, he said, "You don't know Moira the way I do. She's selfish, greedy and manipulative."

"That doesn't mean she doesn't love you."

"I don't think she knows the meaning of the word." He studied Teri, and the pain he saw in her eyes made him ask, "Just what else did she tell you?" When Teri didn't respond, he guessed. "Did she also tell you she came here to Dublin just after I found out you had been married? Did she say that Denis had hit her, that I felt sorry for her and made love to her? Not that it was my idea, mind you."

So, Teri thought, feeling more dismal by the second, *Patrick could be your son.*

Kevin's voice rose slightly. "Did she?"

Softly Teri said, "No, she didn't tell me that, but I do know she's afraid of her husband and worried that he might hurt Patrick."

"That's crazy. Why would Denis hurt his own son?"

Because Patrick is your son! she wanted to scream. Biting the inside of her lower lip to keep from speaking, she vowed again that she was not going to be the one to tell Kevin.

"Well, why would he?" Kevin asked again.

"The man seems unstable enough to do anything. You said so yourself."

Kevin rose quickly and rammed a fist into his palm; Teri's head jerked up. "If that bastard so much as touches that boy... No wonder she wants to leave Denis."

"And if she does?" Teri asked.

As he moved toward the sofa, he said, "If she's smart enough to, maybe she can make some kind of decent home life for Patrick."

Quietly she remarked, "He seems very fond of you, Kevin."

Looking down at her, he realized what Teri was insinuating. "And I'm very fond of him, but if you're thinking there's any chance that Moira and I could—"

"Could give Patrick the support and direction you told me he needed." Her words came fast and with conviction—as much as it hurt her to say them.

Kevin sat down next to her and took her hand in his. "You're forgetting one important thing," he said quietly. "I'm not in love with Moira. I'm in love with you. Besides, Patrick thinks of me as an uncle, and he knows I'm always here for him if he needs me. So no more of this talk about me and Moira."

Teri wanted to believe him in the worst way, but Moira's hope that she, Kevin and their son could be a family wouldn't leave her. In her confused emotional state, Teri saw herself as the "other woman," and the feeling stung unmercifully. Then Kevin put his arm around her and cradled her against him.

As he held her firmly to him, she placed her hand over his and moved her fingers over his knuckles. Softly she said, "Moira may not be perfect, but I think you sometimes become disappointed in people who aren't perfect. And you have a crazy way of taking it personally." She sat up straight and looked into his attentive eyes. "And that scares the hell out of me. I'm not perfect, either."

He tried to hold her, but she got up quickly. "Perhaps, like Moira, there are things I want from life that love alone can't give. I'm proud of the fact that Colleen and I, through hard work, were able to create a successful business. And I love New York and the friends I've made over the years. I'm in charge of my life for the first time, and I refuse to go back to letting someone else run it the way Angelo did."

"And you think I would try to?"

Her lips formed a semblance of a smile, but there was little heart in it. "Be honest with me and yourself," she said slowly. "Would you even discuss the possibility of your relocating to the States? Would you leave Mary Kate and Patrick behind, see them perhaps once a year? Would you be content to read about Ireland's problems in the *New York Times*?" When he looked away and didn't respond, Teri said softly, "I thought not. Yet you have no problem in assuming I'd be more than happy to pull up my roots and live here."

A heaviness centered in Kevin's chest, and confusion masked his expression as he mulled over her words. Clasping his hands together so tightly that his knuckles whitened, he said, "I guess I did take it for granted that you were more than casually interested in Ireland. After all, you've built your job around things Irish.''

Teri lowered her eyes, knowing that she had involved herself with "things Irish" to keep some part of him alive in her heart. Quietly she said, "My job is not my life, Kevin, but yours *is* your life...your duty, as you put it." Looking directly at him again, she added, "I don't want to compete with that or have to settle for just a part of you when it's convenient for you."

"Compete?" he asked in disbelief, then rose from the sofa. "I would have thought that loyalty to my country would seem admirable, but you make it sound like I'm being disloyal to you."

Teri was in no mood to ponder Kevin's words. Instead, as she reached for her purse, she said, "We all have to make choices, don't we?"

She headed for the door, but he moved more quickly and took hold of her shoulders. "Stay here tonight...please."

Avoiding his eyes, she said, "I think it would be better for both of us if I checked into a hotel."

Gently he took her purse and set it down on the chair by the door. "If you're going to leave, let's at least be together every moment we can." He drew her closer and wrapped his arms around her. "What's the point of your making me crazy, of my walking the floor tonight, knowing you're only minutes away in some hotel?"

Caught in Kevin's embrace, Teri realized just how emotionally exhausted she really was. And—God help her—how vulnerable she was where Kevin was concerned.

"Please," he whispered close to her ear, and she felt all her sensible resolve begin to evaporate like the morning mist when the sun rose.

On the verge of tears, and unable to help herself, she slipped her arms around his waist and pressed against him. His body heat warmed her hands, and she closed her tired eyes as she rested her head on his shoulder. "It wouldn't make much sense, would it?" she murmured against his neck.

He stroked her back as he held her. Then in a low tortured voice he asked, "What's going to become of us, luv? I don't think I want to live without you. I don't know if I can. With you, everything seems so right. Without you, everything would be so wrong."

As Teri listened to Kevin's plea, she knew he had won again. But she didn't care. Nor could she think about anything at the moment except that Kevin's arms were about her. And he needed her, wanted her—just as she wanted him. Cursing her weakness, she said softly, "I guess we did agree that we would think only of the present... our present."

Although it was early evening, the sunlight was streaming through the sheer drapery panels in Kevin's bedroom.

Hungrily they caressed, kissed and touched each other as though to memorize for all time the exquisite experience. For brief periods they drifted into a light sleep, Kevin holding Teri, she clinging desperately to him. But for both of them sleep was uneasy, and the first to wake would renew intimacies that would send the two of them spiraling breathlessly over the edge again and again. Time, their enemy, was passing all too quickly.

MIDMORNING ON SATURDAY, when Teri awoke, she touched the side of her face and realized that Kevin's stubble had left its mark. She saw that he was lying on his stomach, his hands under his face, and felt guilty at the discovery that she had pulled all the covers over to her side of the bed during the night.

It was cool in the room, so she carefully pulled the sheet and blanket up to his waist. Slowly she began a trail of kisses upward over his smooth back, then across his broad shoulder and on his angled arm, not stopping until she placed a lingering and loving kiss on his cheek.

"Umm," he moaned. "Good morning." He rolled onto his back, pulling her with him.

"Kevin," she said in a warning tone, "I think we should slow down . . . just a little."

He opened his eyes and gazed up at her. "Didn't I tell you? I did slow down."

"When?" she inquired, amusement flashing in her dark eyes.

"About four o'clock this morning."

"Oh," she said, and moved a fingertip over his chin. "When you finally passed out."

He caught her finger between his lips and ran the tip of his tongue over it. After kissing it, he corrected her. "When I decided you needed to rest."

"Rest," she repeated playfully. "I used to know the meaning of the word."

As his hand lingered over her smooth bottom, he said, "You're rested now, aren't you?"

She set her forearms on his chest and told him quietly, "Rested enough to get ready for my trip to Galway." She started to get up, but his arms captured her and held her firmly.

"Why can't you wait until Monday?"

She knew she could, but she had promised herself she would leave today—the sooner the better. She knew that prolonging their separation would only make her more miserable than she already was. "Be reasonable," she told him in as firm a voice as she could manage. "Remember, I'm in Ireland on business."

"And a vacation." He rolled her onto her back, thrust a heavy leg over her and began to run his fingers through strands of her dark, silky hair. "I'm not asking you to stay the weekend. I'm telling you."

"Kevin!"

"All right—" he smiled his apology "—I'm asking."

"Seriously, Kevin—"

"I am being serious. You won't get much done in Galway on the weekend, and part of this trip is your vacation." He leaned down, brushed her lips with his, then whispered in her ear, "How better to spend it than with a friend?"

As Kevin nibbled her earlobe and smoothed his warm hand over her thigh, Teri moaned, feeling wonderfully defeated again. Wrapping her arms around him, she murmured, "Why fight it? I'm yours for the weekend."

At least, he thought, and smiled.

They both heard the chime of the front door downstairs, and Kevin's head reared up. "Who the hell could that be?"

When the chimes sounded again, she suggested, "There's one way to find out."

He got up and reached for his robe, which lay over the back of a chair. Grinning, he told her, "Stay right where you are. I'll get rid of whoever it is."

She watched him leave and close the door behind him, and couldn't help but wonder who was downstairs. She had to smile at her own curiosity, and reminded herself that Kevin had a social life she knew nothing about. For that matter, so did she. Deciding to shower, she went into the bathroom, looked for shampoo and saw it on a rack in the shower stall.

Her mind wandered as the water pelted her, and she thought how proud she would be to introduce Kevin to her friends in New York. As what? she wondered, working the creamy lather into her hair. A visiting statesman? A husband?

She smiled at her foolish musings and tilted her face up to let the water cascade over it, telling herself there was no harm in indulging her imagination while she was on holiday.

A half hour later, Teri went downstairs, feeling refreshed and crisp in her beige slacks and the white silk top Colleen had given her as a send-off gift. "Kevin," she called when she entered the living room.

"In here," he called back, and she went to the kitchen.

There sat Patrick in jeans and a blue-and-green striped T-shirt, a half-eaten ginger cookie in his little fingers.

CHAPTER EIGHT

"WE HAVE A VISITOR," Kevin said, his expression indicating a mixture of pleasure and disappointment.

Patrick stared up at Teri, but said nothing.

Teri smiled at him. "Hello again." Still he said nothing, and she looked back at Kevin.

"Moira dropped him off and asked if I'd be able to take care of him for the weekend. Denis is in Belfast, and she had to rush off to London."

"How wonderful," Teri commented for Patrick's benefit. *And how convenient for Moira and inconvenient for us,* she added silently, remembering that Kevin had said the woman was a manipulator.

"Kevin," Patrick asked, "can you and I go to the zoo like we did the last time I was here?"

"Finish your milk, and we'll talk about it a little later, okay?" With that he hustled Teri out of the kitchen and over to the far side of the living room.

Whispering, he asked, "What was I suppose to say, no? Patrick was standing right there with her."

In just as quiet a voice, she answered, "You don't have to explain. Of course you did what was best for Patrick. I would expect you to. And you're helping Moira out, also."

"I'd like to help her out...out of the country for good. She pulled this emergency trip on purpose. Don't you see that?"

"The thought did cross my mind."

"She knows there are only two bedrooms upstairs." He placed a hand on her arm and rubbed it lightly. "Do you mind if Patrick bunks with me tonight? He may not understand why you and I are sleeping together."

"These days seven-year-olds probably would understand why, but I agree with you," Teri said with a wry smile.

"We can smooch on the sofa after I put him to bed," Kevin said, tapping the tip of her nose, "and we have tomorrow night."

"When is Moira picking him up?"

"Tomorrow, around noon."

Teri thought about that, then said, "Maybe I should go on to Galway now. I'm sure Patrick would rather be with just you."

"Don't even think it," he said firmly. "The three of us are going on an outing."

AT THE DUBLIN ZOO, located in the 1760-acre Phoenix Park at the city's northwest end, Patrick led Teri and Kevin on a merry chase as he ran from one exhibit to another, mimicking monkeys, lions and disinterested giraffes.

They watched part of a hurling match, then went on to the race course, where a motor car competition was in progress. Despite her walking shoes, Teri had begun to slow down a bit, and she shook her head when Kevin suggested they take the pathway to the residences of the president of Ireland and the American ambassador, which were both situated in the park. Taking his cue from her, he started them back to the outdoor restaurant near the zoo, where they dined on Ireland's version of the hamburger. It was tastier and more tender than the American fast-food version, Teri thought, but the catsup was a touch sweeter than she was used to. Coca-Cola, she decided, must be the same the world over.

Every now and then she would try to strike up a conversation with Patrick, but his responses continued to be polite, his attitude wary.

With double-dip strawberry ice-cream cones in hand, they set out again and explored the lovely Zoological Gardens. By then Teri felt like a basket case, but she trudged along, bolstered by the easy, affectionate interaction between Kevin and Patrick. Watching them, she could see—and wondered how Kevin hadn't—the resemblance between the boy and the man: the blond hair, the blue eyes, even their confident gait as they walked along the beautifully landscaped pathways. And she recalled that Kevin's father's name had been Padraig—Irish for Patrick.

By six-thirty, Teri was begging for a reprieve, and they left Phoenix Park. Kevin suggested that they stop to have dinner before returning home and he noted the smile of appreciation that settled on her face. He parked near a pub on Wicklow Street, and while the grown-ups had chicken and fish platters, Patrick had a submarine sandwich and more cola.

Teri was more than surprised when he suddenly looked up at her and asked, "Have you ever seen an Indian, Mrs. Manzoni?"

"As a matter of fact, I have. My parents live in Florida now, and the last time I visited them, we went to a Seminole Indian village and saw an Indian wrestling an alligator."

Patrick's eyes widened. "A big one?"

"It looked pretty big to me." Wanting to believe that he was beginning to feel more comfortable with her, she suggested, "You can call me 'Teri,' if you like."

He glanced over at Kevin, who smiled and nodded. The boy's voice was a little more animated when he asked, "Have you been to Disneyland?"

"No, but I have been to Disney World in Florida."

He pondered that while he took another bite of his huge sandwich, then asked, "Do you know Corey Millen?"

Teri looked at Kevin, who explained, "The young American hockey player who did so well in the winter Olympics in Canada."

"I'm afraid not," she apologized to Patrick, "but if you'd like, when I get home I'll mail you some sports magazines. They have lots of pictures and stories in them." She looked over at Kevin again, thinking she'd see an expression of appreciation on his face for her offer. Instead she saw that his smile had disappeared.

Back at his town house, Kevin suggested that they all kick off their shoes. Even the energetic youngster was happy to comply. A short while later, Teri rested in one corner of the sofa, her tired, aching feet curled under her as she smiled down at Kevin, who was lying on his back on the carpet, his hands propped behind his head. Patrick, too, was on his back, his head resting on Kevin's waist. Teri listened, amused, as Kevin helped Patrick with his Irish.

"Good," Kevin complimented the boy. "Now tell Teri."

Patrick looked over at her and actually smiled. *"Go n-éiré an bóthar leat*, Teri."

She knew from listening to them that Patrick was telling her to have a safe trip home, but if home was where the heart was, she thought, perhaps she was already there. She loved Kevin with all her heart, and in the brief time she'd known Patrick, he had become important to her, particularly now that he seemed more relaxed with her. And the probability of his being Kevin's son made her particularly concerned for his well-being.

"Thank you, Patrick," she said. She was speaking to him, but she was looking at Kevin, wanting to thank him, too—for coming back into her life, for making her feel truly loved and for letting her love again.

Patrick didn't see Teri turn her head a little and run a finger under her eyelid, but Kevin did, and he gently moved the boy's head and pushed himself up from the floor. "Okay, it's bedtime for you," he said.

"Aw, do I have to?" Patrick looked over at Teri with pleading eyes, but she could only offer a shrug of sympathy.

"Go on, now," Kevin said, pulling him up. "I put your overnight bag in my room. I'll be up in a little while to tuck you in."

With downcast eyes and a hint of a pout, Patrick mumbled, "Okay," then turned and started toward the stairway.

Kevin grabbed him by the seat of his jeans. "Whoa! Say good-night to Teri first."

Smiling again, Patrick said, "Good night, Teri. I had fun today."

"Good night, Patrick," she returned, and followed him with her eyes as he scrambled up the stairs.

Kevin sat on the sofa and moved Teri's feet so that they rested on his lap. Slowly he began to massage them with strong but gentle hands. "He likes you—and he doesn't make friends easily."

"How could anyone not love him? As you said, he's quite a boy. He's like you in many ways." The instant she said that she wished she hadn't.

Glancing over at her as he continued his massage, Kevin asked, "How do you mean?"

Teri smiled away her concern. "He's intelligent and very handsome."

"Ah, so the lady thinks I'm handsome."

"Yes, I do."

Kevin moved her legs onto the sofa, leaned closer to her and kissed her softly on the lips. When he drew back, his eyes met and held hers. "You keep looking at me like that and I'll make love to you right here, Patrick or no Patrick."

"You wouldn't dare."

"I wouldn't?" He slipped a hand under her top.

"No, you wouldn't," she said, pulling it back out. "You're too much of a gentleman."

"So much for civilized society," he complained, sitting up and resting an elbow on the back of the sofa. Taking one of her hands in his, he began stroking her fingers. "You know what I'm thinking?"

"Nothing would surprise me," she said playfully. "What are you thinking?"

"That I just might go upstairs and have a man-to-man talk with Patrick."

"And tell him about the birds and the bees?"

"Uh-huh, and that I've got this uncontrollable urge to make love to you."

She freed her hand from Kevin's, pulled her legs out from behind him and slipped her feet into her walking shoes. "Patrick's arrival was a blessing in disguise. We could both use a good night's sleep. I don't know about you, but I'm going to start getting ready for bed in about five minutes."

As she rose from the sofa, Kevin reached out and took her hand again. "Today was nice, Teri, in ways that I've never experienced. Don't laugh, but I kept hoping people would think we were a family."

Teri's heart began that agitated thumping again. It happened every time Kevin looked at her a certain way or said something sweet, as he just had. Gazing down at him, she placed her other hand over his. "Funny you should say that. I was hoping the same thing."

He stood and placed his hands around her waist. "We could start a real family of our own. How about a girl like you and a boy like me?"

Children, she repeated silently, and the very thought awakened a long-suppressed desire that she had just about given up on.

"You do want children, don't you?"

She nodded, even as she reminded herself that Kevin was suggesting the impossible.

"I do, too," he said. "See, that's something else we know about each other now."

"Kevin, I—" she attempted a soft smile, but a somberness lingered in her expression "—I enjoyed today, also, but right now I'm going to enjoy my pillow more. I'll see you in the morning. Good night."

"Good night," he said, holding her hand until she forced it from his.

SUNDAY MORNING WAS SPENT enjoying a leisurely breakfast that a rested Teri prepared while Kevin and Patrick discussed the latest hurling and football scores. True to her word, Moira arrived to pick up her son a little past noon.

When the front door chimes sounded Patrick went to the window, and without a great deal of enthusiasm, he told them it was his mother. Teri started for the stairway.

"Please," Kevin said, "don't go."

Hesitant to remain, she nevertheless did, following his movement to the door and watching as an elegantly dressed Moira kissed him on the cheek. Her muted green linen suit set off her lovely red hair to perfection.

"Thank you for taking care of Patrick," she said, walking like a model into the living room. "London is as dull as ever, but the trip had to be made. Where's Patrick?" She turned and saw him, then the woman standing by the staircase. "Teri," she said with surprise, "I thought you had returned home."

I bet you did, Teri said to herself, forcing a pleasant smile. "Not yet, obviously."

"Patrick," Moira said, "take your overnight bag out to the car. I'll be right there."

"Yes, Mother." He picked up the bag, went to Teri and held out his hand. "Will you really write to me?"

Holding his hand, she assured him. "I promise. And I haven't forgotten about sending you the sports magazines. I'll do that first thing when I get home." Not caring whether Moira would like it or not, she stooped down and kissed Patrick on the cheek. "You promised to write, too," she reminded him.

"I will," he said, adding quietly, "I'll miss you, Teri."

As Patrick hurried out the door, Moira turned to Kevin. "Really, you ought not let the boy address adults so familiarly. It's not good breeding."

"I'm afraid it's my fault," Teri explained. "I asked Patrick to."

"Oh," she commented, lifting her finely arched eyebrows. "Well, in that case, I suppose there's no harm done." She eyed Teri's casual slacks and denim top, then asked, "Which hotel are you staying at? The Shelbourne, I hope...in the new wing?"

Kevin walked over to Teri and put his arm around her. "Teri's my guest," he said pointedly, giving her shoulder a squeeze.

"Really," Moira remarked. She aimed her green eyes at Teri and smiled. "I'm certain you were circumspect. Patrick is extremely sensitive."

"He spent the night with Kevin in his bedroom," Teri informed her.

Kevin took hold of Moira's arm and urged her toward the front door. "Your son is waiting for you in the car."

"When will you be visiting us again?" she asked, her voice taking on a sudden warmth. "Soon, I hope."

"I'll see you when I come to get Patrick after I return from the Orient."

At the door she said, "Yes, we'll need to discuss that. I'll phone you later in the week." She glanced at Teri, then told Kevin, "Better yet, I plan to be here in Dublin for a few days next week to do some shopping for Patrick. He's growing so fast. We could do that together, and also some early shopping for his birthday." Kevin started to say something, but she didn't give him the chance. "Don't decide now. We'll make our plans when I phone you." Facing Teri again, she smiled and said, "Enjoy your trip home."

Teri nodded, then went to the far side of the living room and looked out the window. She could see Patrick sitting in the Mercedes parked in front of the town house. Moira's invitation to Kevin to go shopping together for the boy's birthday presents resounded in Teri's ears, and she wondered if Kevin, once he found out the truth, would eventually give in to Moira for their son's good. Even if he didn't, Teri now realized that if she were to marry Kevin, he would probably allow Moira to have such a huge part in their lives that it would be unbearable. No, she warned herself again, even fantasizing about a life with Kevin was ludicrous.

When she heard the front door shut, she turned and saw unbridled anger on Kevin's face.

"Do you still see a possibility of my ever getting together with that woman?" he asked.

"I'm certain of one thing. Moira does."

Kevin chuckled wryly. "That wouldn't be her first crazy idea."

Crazy or not, Teri reminded herself, the woman did have a solid claim on Kevin—Patrick. Quickly she said, "I've decided to go on to Galway today."

"Today? It's Sunday. You won't get any business done there on a Sunday." His voice turned sharp. "Why the sudden change in plans?"

As she ran a finger along the edge of the desk she was standing next to, she said, "I've decided to rent a car and drive there and—" she looked over at him "—act like a tourist. Remember, I'm here on vacation, too."

The deadly serious look on his face instantly wiped the tenuous smile from hers. "I'd better get packed," she told him, promptly rushing across the room and up the stairs.

Her throat tight and her pulse pounding at her temples, she hurriedly set her suitcases on the bed and began packing. Moments later she noticed Kevin's form filling the bedroom doorway. For long moments he stood there watching her every move.

In a low voice he said, "I can't go with you this time. I have a job to see to." He smiled caustically. "But I imagine you thought of that already."

As she placed her lingerie in one of the suitcases, she said, "We both have jobs to take care of."

A dismal silence followed, and he continued to watch her. After a while he remarked, "You're a very neat packer. Wish I could say the same for myself."

Folding a nightgown, she said, "I would think that with all your traveling, you'd have it down pat."

He didn't respond to that; instead he said, "In fact, everything you do, you do with style and grace."

Teri's hands poised in midair and she glanced over at him. He looked so miserable, she thought—the way she felt. Tearing her eyes away, she quickly placed the nightgown in the suitcase, closed it and began to pack her makeup case.

"When are you returning to Dublin?" he asked.

"Wednesday," she told him, "or maybe Thursday."

"Then what?"

"I'll give the last of the order forms to Seamus, and it's back to New York." Snapping shut the makeup case, she said, "Well, that should be it." She met his eyes again, and her voice took on a false cheerfulness. "Galway, here I come."

Kevin said nothing. He was too busy trying to cope with his feelings. He raised a hand in a gesture of frustration, then slammed his fist against the door. Turning quickly, he charged down the hallway.

Teri watched him leave, feeling a dull ache in the pit of her stomach. She didn't want it to end like this, but end it had to. Of that she was certain. Leaving was the only course of action that made any sense.

Her movements sluggish, she went to the closet, took down her garment bag and walked downstairs. Kevin was staring out the living-room window at the little garden at the rear of the town house. Draping the garment bag over the back of the sofa, she said, "These past days have been wonderful. You've given me so many beautiful memories to take with me."

He turned, his facial muscles taut, his steely eyes boring into hers. "I'm happy to have made your visit to Ireland interesting, or dare I hope that the better word is 'exciting'?" For a moment he glanced away, then he faced her again. "Seems the tables are turned this time, and I'm the one who was *convenient* for you." He saw the blood drain from her face, and he raised a hand in a mock gesture of apology. "There I go, being cruel and callous again."

"Please, Kevin," she murmured, trying to steady her voice, "let's be kind to each other now."

"Kind...I see. You want me to make your leaving easy for you, is that it?"

Speaking past the lump in her throat, Teri whispered, "I'd like it to be easy for both of us."

He nodded slowly, never taking his eyes from her. "All right, I'll even carry your luggage downstairs for you while you phone for a taxi." He took long, heavy steps past her, but at the bottom of the stairway he stopped and looked back at her. After chuckling wryly, he said, "I don't understand why I feel so lousy. Leaving each other should be easy for us. We've had enough practice." Then he took the stairs two steps at a time.

FOR TERI, driving on the left side of the street again was bad enough, but having to wipe the tears from her eyes made it even worse. As she turned west onto Conyngham Road, she automatically steered the car she'd rented to the right side of the street, but swerved quickly to the left when another car came at her head-on. The near accident was sobering, and she had just about gotten herself together, when she began driving past Phoenix Park.

Again the tears started as memories surfaced of the day she, Kevin and Patrick had spent there. "Stop thinking about it!" she ordered herself, and she purposefully visualized Colleen and Betsy—and just about everyone else she knew in New York.

Once out of Dublin and in the countryside, she tried to concentrate on the deep green hedges and sloping pastureland. But then her eyes drifted to the empty seat next to her, and again she thought of Kevin. She remembered his saying, "Two shorten a trip." How right he was, she decided.

Pressing her foot on the gas pedal, she decided to make the hundred thirty-six-mile drive to Galway in record time.

It was almost 6:00 p.m. when a road sign indicated she was approaching the city. The air rushing in the open car window took on a salty tang, and soon she found herself driving through a maze of narrow streets. She suspected that not much had changed in Galway for many years. And she was surprised to note an obvious Spanish influence in the city's architecture. As she drove slowly past a beautifully landscaped square, she saw a sign that indicated the area had been dedicated to John F. Kennedy. Stopping to ask for directions to the Galway Ryan Hotel, she heard passersby speaking in Irish, and once more she thought of Kevin.

After checking in at the ultramodern hotel, she purchased a handful of postcards, bypassed dinner and spent the remainder of the evening writing cards and letters, trying to forget the Irishman she had left back in Dublin.

The following morning, she located Stephen Faller, Ltd., where she admired Waterford, Galway and Cavan crystal and settled on the Galway, as she thought she would. At Padraig O. Maille's she came across finely handwoven tweed capes, shawls and skirts. But Teri's heart wasn't in her work; she had left that back in Dublin, too.

In early afternoon she decided to bolster her spirits by playing tourist, and drove south, following the road around Galway Bay. The ever present salty odor from the ocean filled the automobile as she drove. Strange, she thought, how an aroma could rekindle memories from long ago and far away. On the other hand, she mused, maybe it wasn't so strange. No doubt the Atlantic smelled the same on the west coast of Ireland and the east coast of the States. She and her husband had spent many a summer day at Jones Beach on Long Island; Angelo had loved the water, the sand and picnics.

As thoughts of him crept into her consciousness, she glanced around at the landscape. It was now totally different, a rocky limestone area devoid of trees or hedges, a stony place that filled her with a sense of great stillness. She passed a sign that read Burren. When she pronounced it, she thought how appropriate it was that it sounded almost like the word "barren."

Soon she found herself driving along a desolate winding road high atop a cliff, with a magnificent view of the Atlantic Ocean to her right and a desert to her left. After pulling off the narrow roadway, she walked toward the edge of the cliff. Overhead, seabirds soared and screeched, and the tangy smell of the water became even stronger, bringing back memories of the nighttime walk she and Kevin had taken along the shore at Crosshaven.

She remembered his question: *"As for the barriers you mentioned, are they real, or are you erecting them because you think you need to?"* "Need to?" she questioned aloud, then discounted his accusation, telling herself she had not been responsible for the barriers Moira and Patrick created.

A strong wind from behind jostled her, and she moved away from the edge of the high cliff, crossed her arms and grasped them tightly with her fingers.

Angelo, Kevin, she said to herself, wondering why true love and happiness didn't seem to be in the cards for her. She brushed back the hair the wind had whipped over her eyes, thinking that with Angelo, she had come closest to having a family to call her own. If only she'd had children, she thought sadly.

Her regret brought back the tormenting idea that Kevin, Moira and Patrick were indeed a family. Patrick needed Kevin. For that matter, so did Moira, Teri told herself, deciding that for all the woman's material possessions, she was miserable. But what did Kevin need?

"Me, he claims," she murmured, adding silently that she needed him. She stared down at the wildly churning water and shook her head slowly. No, she had been right in leaving when she had. Once Kevin had found out that he was a father, his sense of duty would surely have taken over and destroyed any relationship between them.

Slowly she walked back to the car and drove off again, this time inland.

Passing through a wooded valley, she came to a small village. Ennistymon, the sign read. She glanced at the steplike falls of the River Cullenagh, then scanned the narrow gray-and-white row houses along the bank, trying to play the role of carefree tourist. With the slender windows and slanted roofs, the scene was like one out of an Utrillo painting. Utrillo, she mused, recalling the prints that hung in the bedrooms at Kevin's town house.

She forced that recollection from her mind, turned left to circle back to Galway, and in minutes found herself riding through neatly plowed land dotted with farmhouses. She passed the ruins of an ancient castle and smiled at the incongruity of the thoroughly modern golf course adjacent to it.

Soon the land became flat. Bunched up clouds were mirrored in deep blue lakes and floated over picturesque whitewashed cottages—cottages that reminded her of Mary Kate . . . and Kevin.

When she saw a Celtic stone cross at the side of the road, her fingertips went to the little gold cross at her neck, but of course it wasn't there.

A dark cloud drifted overhead, and suddenly she was driving in a summer shower, but not for long. When the sun shone again, she saw the most beautiful rainbow imaginable. Kevin had been right, she decided; it did look like a lovely ribbon of pastel colors arching over the emerald fields brilliant with yellow flowers.

"Kevin," she murmured, wondering if there would ever be anything that wouldn't remind her of him. She doubted it.

IN THE MORNING, Teri tried to busy herself at The Treasure Chest, an Irish crafts shop on Eglington Street, but neither the Royal Tara fine bone china or the gossamer-weight laces could lift her depressed mood. Only one thing might, she decided: leaving Ireland as quickly as possible.

She drove back to Dublin with haste, and when she arrived at Seamus's office, she gave him the order forms she had filled out in Galway, thanked him again and told him she'd be leaving in the morning.

"So soon?" he asked. "Margaret and I had hoped you'd spend a few relaxing days at the house before you left."

Teri shook her head. "That's kind of you both, but it's best that I return home. I've so many things to do."

"I understand," he said, "and I do hope you've enjoyed your stay in Ireland and that you'll visit us again soon."

Smiling, Teri told him, "Perhaps Mrs. Parnell will make a trip next year."

"Where will you be staying until you leave? The Royal Dublin?" Seamus asked.

She nodded, touched at his obvious concern for her, then said her goodbyes to Seamus and Fiona.

After checking into the hotel, Teri phoned Aer Lingus and made reservations on a morning flight to New York. For a while she sat in her hotel room, but the quiet became suffocating. Grabbing her purse, she decided to go downstairs to the Oyster Bar for a quick snack. Not that she was hungry, but she felt the need to hear voices and pretend she was having a good time.

She was just about to close the door behind her, when she was startled to see Kevin coming down the hotel corridor, his stride hurried, his features grim.

"Welcome back," he said dryly, then hustled her inside her room.

In one quick motion, she shrugged her arm free and asked, "What are you doing here?"

"Trying to get you to stay put long enough so that we can talk."

"There's nothing for us to talk about," she insisted.

"Yes, there is. Seamus told me you're leaving tomorrow morning. Why? I thought you weren't due back in New York until Monday."

"My business here is finished," she said with an effort.

"Not quite."

Teri saw the fire in his eyes; turning away, she asked sorrowfully, "What is it you want from me, Kevin?"

He moved behind her and placed his hands on her shoulders. "I want you to tell me how to stop feeling, how to stop thinking about you . . . tonight, tomorrow, next month."

Her response came in a strangled tone. "I . . . I can't."

Kevin heard the distress in her voice, turned her around and saw the gleam of moisture in her eyes and the desperate expression on her face that pleaded for understanding. He sighed long and hard, then took her in his arms and rested her head against his shoulder.

Teri shuddered as pent-up emotion drained her of willpower, and when she felt an overwhelming weakness in her knees, she let her body go limp against his. Without thought she kissed the side of his neck and felt his Adam's apple jerk upward, then descend.

After taking a deep breath, Kevin stared across the room and said in a low, hollow voice, "It's possible I would be granted a preference visa because of my profession, but if we were married here first it would simplify everything."

She pushed herself back from him. "What are you talking about?"

With emotionless eyes, he said, "Or I could just get a visitor's visa, and we could be married in New York."

She knew by his cool and determined expression that he was seriously contemplating leaving Ireland. Taking measured steps, she moved away from him, twirled around and clasped her hands firmly. What a simple solution, she thought. Marry here or in the States and she and Kevin would never have to be separated again. They could remain far from the problem that haunted her: his finding out that Patrick was his son. But of course Kevin would never be happy living in New York, far from the work he had committed himself to, far from Mary Kate and from Patrick. Sure, he could pretend, but for how long?

Besides, another worry consumed her: what would Kevin's reaction be when he found out that she had known the truth about Patrick and hadn't told him? One phone call from Moira and the cat would be out of the bag. Then what? He'd leave her again, that's what. Experience had taught her something. No, she wasn't going to let him put her through that again.

She faced him once more, and her voice was clear and crisp when she said, "You realize that this talk about your relocating to the States is nonsense, don't you?"

"Does our being apart for another twelve years make more sense?"

"Either one of us can cross the Atlantic in a matter of hours now."

"And you'd be willing to settle for that... an occasional night of breathless lovemaking?"

"Don't make it sound crude," she said quietly. "You mean more to me than that and you know it." She glanced at her watch, then went to the phone and picked up the receiver.

"What are you doing?"

"I'm going to see if I can change my reservation for a flight home tonight."

"Now who's talking nonsense?" He grabbed the receiver from her hand and slammed it down. "What else is it that you want me to do, Teri? I'm willing to turn my back on my country, throw duty and honor out the window to be with you."

Bitterly she said, "For how long? For another week in New York, just like the one we had twelve years ago?"

Kevin's expression froze, then his eyes narrowed. "You can't forget that, can you?"

"Apparently you have."

Raking his hair with tense fingers, he said, "All right, I admit it. I shouldn't have left you then, but it was something I thought I had to do."

"To marry Moira, wasn't it?" she asked dolefully.

Fighting hard to remain calm, he commanded his voice to stay steady. "Yes, at the time I thought I had to, but I also felt very passionately about needing to do my part here in Ireland—to try to make things better. Was that a crime?"

"You said you loved me then, Kevin."

"I did and I still do. You know that."

An image of Patrick flashed through her mind before she said, "Until someone or something else looms that you feel you have a duty to," she said quietly.

Taking hold of her firmly, he said, "Please, just tell me what it is that you want me to do!"

"I want to be considered important to you. I want to be right up there on your list of priorities."

His arms flew out in frustration. "Who do you think is more important to me than you are?"

Patrick, she screamed silently. Then, seeing the obvious confusion in his eyes, she groaned and said, "Kevin, I can't take much more of—"

The knocking on the hotel room door cut her off, and Kevin went to answer. Soon the decision about when Teri would leave was academic.

Two police officers had come to arrest her for attempted smuggling.

CHAPTER NINE

WHEN THE OFFICERS learned who Kevin was, they told him he was wanted for questioning, too, but they would say nothing else. At headquarters, Teri and Kevin were led to different rooms for interrogation.

The experience was hardly routine for her. Nor had she ever been as frightened. She felt as though she were dreaming. How could this be happening to her? Instructed to follow a uniformed man, Teri did, and as they passed a room with a large glass window, she glanced in and saw Seamus being questioned. From the pallor of his usually red-cheeked face, she could tell he was terrified, too. What was he doing here? Where had they taken Kevin? Why were they doing this to them? Smuggling? Smuggling what?

"Right in here, please," the uniformed man said, opening a door that led into a small room.

Hesitantly Teri entered, and saw a pudgy, middle-aged man sitting at a little table. His suit jacket was draped over the back of his chair and the cuffs of his white shirt had been rolled up a few turns.

The sound of the door being closed startled her, and then the man at the table stood and asked blandly, "May I have your passport, please?"

Teri swallowed hard and placed her purse on the table. Her fingers trembled as she found her passport and handed it to him.

"Please—" he gestured with his hand "—have a seat."

She did so, then glanced around the narrow, stark room and back at the man, whose metal-rimmed glasses caught the light emanating from the metal lamp hanging overhead.

Sitting on the edge of the table, he opened her passport. "You're an American citizen, Mrs. Manzoni," he said matter-of-factly.

"Yes, and I demand to know why you've brought us here."

"In due time." He flipped through several blank pages and remarked, "You don't travel very much, do you?"

"No. This is my first trip abroad."

"Yes...according to *this* passport." He looked down at her with cool gray eyes. "I believe you're in the import business."

"I own a shop in New York City."

After studying her face for a while, he said, "I'm Officer Crowley." He set her passport on the table, but when Teri reached for it, he picked it up again. "We'll be keeping this for the time being."

"Why? And what in heaven's name is this all about?"

"How long have you been doing business with Seamus McFadden?"

"For almost two years. Why?"

"And this is the first trip you've made to Ireland?"

"You just saw that in my passport."

"Why this trip?"

"I had a special arrangement with Mr. McFadden."

"'A special arrangement,'" he repeated, obviously interested now. "And just what was that?"

"Officer Crowley," Teri said with false bravado, "I'm not going to answer any more of your questions until you tell me exactly why I've been brought here."

"Smuggling is a nasty business, Mrs. Manzoni."

"Smuggling. That's all I've been told. Smuggling what?"

He reached down and set a black suitcase on the table. Teri watched intently as he opened the suitcase and drew out a protective cloth.

Her eyes widened as she stared at elaborately fashioned gold torques and rounded collar ornaments. Next to them was a round, ornate silver piece, its handle intricately engraved. She had seen enough Celtic designs to recognize that the engraving was of that period. Possibly a mirror once, she thought. Alongside that piece was a carved ivory animal similar to ones she'd seen pictures of. Scattered about were sundry coins, necklaces and gold chalices studded with rubies and emeralds.

Teri lifted her eyes to meet Officer Crowley's. "What do these items have to do with me?"

"They're part of the collection of artifacts that were hijacked recently. They were found by customs...in the merchandise Seamus McFadden attempted to ship to you in New York."

Teri was struck silent as the pieces of the nightmare began to fit in place. This man actually thought she was a *smuggler*! She didn't know whether to laugh or cry. Deciding against either, she asked incredulously, "Are you serious? Do you actually think I know how these got mixed in with my merchandise?"

Seemingly unaffected by her surprise, he continued his questioning. "How well do you know Mr. O'Shea?"

"That's another thing you haven't told me. Why was Kevin brought here?"

"Have you know him for some time?"

"Yes, for a very long time."

"Perhaps that was why you came to Ireland," he suggested.

"It was not! I'm here on business."

His eyes drifted down to the artifacts, and he picked up a gold chalice. "What kind of business?"

"Officer Crowley, let's not play games. You know what kind of business I'm in, and I'm certain Mr. McFadden has already told you of our arrangement. As for my relationship with Kevin O'Shea, that's no concern of yours. Just why you think that either I or the assistant to the minister of foreign affairs would have anything to do with—" she waved a nervous hand over the suitcase "—with this is beyond me. As for smuggling...that's ridiculous."

He sat down, removed his glasses and looked at her for long moments, as though analyzing her frank remarks. Then he said, "I'm afraid it's not just a matter of smuggling, Mrs. Manzoni. Three men are dead and another is in a coma. We're also talking about hijacking and murder."

Teri jumped up from her chair and glared at him, his words ringing in her ears. Grabbing the edge of the table for support, she asked, "And you think Kevin or I could be implicated in something like that?"

"Mr. O'Shea is on the board of the National Museum. He would have known exactly when the artifacts were to have been transported from County Tipperary to Dublin. Are you telling me you just happened to make a business trip here at this time, and that these items just happened to turn up with your merchandise?''

Slowly she sat down again, beginning to feel like a trapped animal. Taking a deep breath, she went on. "I told you, I don't *know* how they got there. How could Kevin or I possibly have put them there?''

"Were you and Mr. O'Shea in McFadden's mailing room for a time last Friday—'' his next word was shaded with import "—alone?''

She honestly had to think back to remember. "Well…yes, but only while I spot-checked some of the merchandise Mr. McFadden ordered for me. Did he tell you we were?''

"No. I also questioned his assistant, Fiona Riain. She mentioned you had a large briefcase with you in the mailing room.''

Teri gaped momentarily as she looked the man directly in the eyes. "You're implying that I had these things in my briefcase and tried to hide them in the boxes being shipped to me, aren't you?''

"At this point we are investigating all possibilities.'' What settled on his face might have passed for a smile under other circumstances. "But you will agree that my hypothesis is quite plausible.''

"Not considering the people involved! Kevin would no more treat Ireland's historical finds the way you've suggested than he would rob a church. He's devoted his life to working *for* his country, not against it.''

A sigh of exasperation followed. "Mrs. Manzoni, here in Dublin we're very aware of Mr. O'Shea's dedication to his job, and because of his position in the government, neither you nor he will be held at this time.'' He placed Teri's passport in the inside pocket of the jacket dangling on his chair. "Meanwhile you are not to leave Dublin until our investigation is completed."

Watching her passport disappear, Teri said firmly, "I'll see what the United States embassy thinks about that."

"It might be wise to consult them, for your own protection, but you do understand that my telling you not to leave the city is not a request."

She stood and raised herself to her full five-foot-six-inch height. "I want to speak with Kevin."

"You're both free to leave just as soon as his statement is taken."

"And Seamus McFadden?"

"He's being held for the time being. If, as you say, neither you nor Mr. O'Shea had any part in the attempted smuggling, someone else obviously did."

"Obviously. May I go now?"

He nodded, and she turned to leave. "Mrs. Manzoni," he called, and she looked at him over her shoulder. "I do hope you're enjoying your visit to Ireland."

"Is that an example of the Irish humor I've heard so much about, Officer Crowley?"

He smiled. "No, no . . . Irish hospitality."

She lifted her brows and left the room.

After closing the door behind her, Teri tried to steady her knees. She scanned the large and noisy main room that bustled with policemen and busy clerks, hoping to see Kevin, but he was nowhere in sight. Starting toward a water fountain, she passed the room where she had seen Seamus; it was empty now. At the fountain she took a drink, then wet her fingertips and dabbed her forehead.

"Teri!"

She turned, relieved to see Kevin coming toward her.

"Let's get out of here," he said grimly. Taking hold of her arm, he led her to the front entrance of the police station.

Outside, Teri told him, "They took my passport."

"I thought they would after they explained what had happened."

"Kevin, they actually think—"

"I know what they think, and I can't say that I blame them."

"What?"

As they headed toward the taxi stand at the corner, he said, "Look at it from their point of view. The artifacts were found in the boxes being shipped to you. Someone succeeded in making it look as though you were interested in more than Irish craftsmanship."

"What am I going to do, Kevin?"

"Right now we'll get my car and your luggage from the hotel. You're going to stay with me until we can get this business straightened out."

At this point, Teri was grateful for his offer.

Inside the taxi, Kevin gave the driver the name of the hotel, then took hold of Teri's hand. "Was it rough in there? Are you all right?"

"Of course I'm all right," she said sharply. "You don't think this is the first time I've been hauled off to jail and accused of smuggling and murder, do you?"

They both felt the taxi swerve to the right, then jerk back, and Teri saw the driver's eyes widen in the rearview mirror.

Under her breath she said, "I can't leave without my passport."

Fighting a smile, Kevin agreed. "I know."

At the town house, Kevin poured them each an ample portion of Bushmill's Black Label, an Irish whiskey. "This should help," he said, handing her the glass. "It seems to get stronger each year, and they've been making it for four centuries."

Teri sipped and winced. "Dear God! How can you drink this stuff?"

"It grows on you," he told her, and took a healthy swallow. "Helps clear the brain for hard thinking."

"For you, perhaps." She set her glass down on the coffee table, sat on the sofa and pondered her situation. She could very possibly be dragged through a criminal prosecution in a foreign country for heinous crimes she had nothing to do with. Smuggling and murder! Quickly she reached for her glass again and hoped Bushmill's firewater would clear up something.

After sipping again, she shuddered and asked, "Shouldn't we get a lawyer?"

"The minister will be back in Dublin late this afternoon." Kevin checked his watch. "I'll talk to him. Our department has some of the sharpest legal minds available."

"Are they current on murder charges?"

The grin he gave her was reminiscent of the one she'd seen on Officer Crowley's face. "My, but you do go right for the bleak picture, don't you?"

Removing her suit jacket, she said, "That way things can only get better."

Kevin sat down beside her on the sofa, placed an arm around her and kissed her cheek. "They can't get any worse. Isn't that a consolation?"

"No. If you're so big on looking at things from other people's points of view, look at things from mine. You're at home here in Ireland, and you have powerful friends. I'm the alien—without a passport, I might add."

"If I have friends in high places, so do you. We're a team now."

He set down his glass, and when he started to move closer, Teri put her hands up. "Kevin, aren't you the least bit concerned? *We* are in trouble—big trouble."

"Not real big trouble. The Irish police may not be Scotland Yard, but they're pretty good at their job. They had to question us and compare our stories." He cocked his head. "You did tell them exactly what happened, didn't you? I did."

"As much as I know about what happened."

Kevin crossed his arms and leaned back against the sofa. "It's Seamus I'm worried about. I've known the man for years. He's just not capable of being involved in such a thing."

"I'm inclined to agree, but it's just instinct. We could both be wrong, though. The police must have some reason for holding him."

"Well, the antiquities were found in boxes he was shipping out of the country. But the whole thing doesn't make much sense. You or Colleen would have discovered the artifacts once the boxes reached New York."

"I would have phoned Fiona as I did the last time there was a mix-up in our order," Teri explained.

"Even if the items were gold and silver?"

"I probably would have guessed they were supposed to be shipped to a museum." She thought a moment. "Or that they were replicas like the ones I saw at the Enterprise Tower."

He reached for his glass and took another sip of whiskey. As though thinking out loud, he said, "There's always the possibility that the artifacts never would have reached your shop. If your boxes passed through customs here and in New York, it's possible that someone would have been waiting to intercept them before delivery. It wouldn't have been difficult to remove the valuables, then deliver your merchandise without your being the wiser."

He looked at his watch and pushed himself up from the sofa. "I'm going to try to meet with the minister. Will you be all right if I leave you alone for a while?"

Teri nodded. "I'd better call Colleen. She's expecting me home this weekend."

He leaned down and placed his palms on the back of the sofa. "But you won't be. See, things are looking up already." The kiss he gave her was short but sweetly given. He started to move away, but had second thoughts. Again he leaned down. "That was nice," he whispered, and kissed her once more. This time his lips lingered a little longer.

When Kevin did leave, Teri dialed her boutique in Manhattan. Colleen was delighted to hear from her, but before Teri could explain why she had called, Colleen burst forth with her own news.

"Charlie got a job today, a great one in his own field...with the Hansen Freiberg Agency. He'll start as an assistant to the man in charge of producing their television commercials, but you know Charlie once he gets going. I'm so thrilled for him, and he's so happy. *We're* so happy!"

Teri began to have second thoughts about telling Colleen why she had to stay on in Dublin. "How are Betsy and the little one in your tummy?"

"Betsy's gained five pounds and the little guy's gained fifty, I think."

Teri smiled. "Twins, I told you."

"Oh, I almost forgot! Mr. Keller said we could have the shop next door, and he's going to have it painted. I'll order the sign extension tomorrow."

"You have been busy."

"Busy? This place has been jammed! I thought Saint Patrick's Day was in March." After a slight pause, Colleen asked, "Are you in a good mood?"

"So far. Why?"

"I hired a woman to help out temporarily. Her name's Loretta, and she's fabulous. I told her we were expanding and that the job could turn into a permanent one, but I want you to meet her first, of course."

"Things are looking up," Teri said, remembering Kevin had said the same thing to her before he had left. "Well, you certainly seem to have everything under control there. Sure you want me to come back?" The second she asked that in jest, Teri knew what she was thinking in her heart.

"You'd better come back! I'm great at getting some things accomplished, but we both know you're the business brains behind our little gold mine here. Oh, Teri, all our hard work is finally paying off. I only hope we're not going in too deep expanding right now. Do you think we're doing the right thing?"

Teri spent the next ten minutes reassuring Colleen that together they had everything under control, citing cost figures and projected profits as proof. When she finally got her partner back to a high level of enthusiasm, she decided not to dampen her good spirits by telling her about the mess she was in. Not until she had to, anyway.

"Well, since everything is going so smoothly," Teri said, "would you mind if I stayed in Ireland a few more days...a week, maybe?"

"Of course not. I thought you were crazy for going for such a short time."

"Good," Teri said, relieved. "I'll let you know exactly when I'll be home. We'd better hang up now, or the phone bill will take care of our profits this year."

"Not so fast, friend," Colleen said. "Is there any special reason you decided to stay? As in a fabulously handsome Irishman who has the body of a Greek god and the heart of a passionate Italian?"

That certainly described Kevin, Teri thought. Smiling into the receiver, she said, "I didn't know you were clairvoyant."

"You did meet someone!"

"Since I've been here I've met lots of people. You were right. The Irish are a friendly lot."

"That's not what I mean and you know it. There's someone special, isn't there? And you can't bear to leave him."

"Colleen—"

"I knew it. Didn't I tell you you were too nice and too attractive just to watch life go by? Didn't I?"

"Yes, you—"

"Go for it, Teri. Be happy. But for God's sake, come back!"

"I fully intend to. Now say goodbye and kiss Betsy and Charlie for me."

"I will, and remember...spread those wings and soar a little. Bye, now."

The sudden silence weighed heavily on Teri. While talking with Colleen, she had almost been able to blot out the events of the past few hours. Now they came rushing back. Replacing the receiver, she looked around the living room. It was so quiet, and she felt so alone.

But then her inner ear played a trick on her, and she could almost hear Kevin and Patrick laughing as they had on Saturday night while lying on the floor. She had to admit that in spite of Kevin's temper, which could flare at the slightest provocation, and his exaggerated sense of duty, she was hopelessly in love with him. He was always sensitive, yet he was the most masculine man she had ever known. And she loved the way he enjoyed touching her, even if it was just a brush on the shoulder on the way to the kitchen, or how he held her hand when they were roaming through Phoenix Park with Patrick.

Sweet little Patrick. What was going to become of him? she wondered anxiously. *I'll miss you,* he had told her, and Teri found she already missed him.

Kevin, Patrick, Moira. Kevin, Patrick, Teri. Which would it be? Which should it be? Despite Moira's aloof attitude toward the boy, Teri knew the woman had to love her son. And what woman in her right mind would give up her son if she didn't have to? Certainly Moira wouldn't. Patrick was her ace in the hole. With only one word to Kevin from Moira, Teri would lose him forever. Yes, Patrick was worth that much.

Standing, she glanced at the pendulum clock on the wall and decided she had time to shower and change before Kevin returned. As she slowly climbed the stairs, she wondered just how much the minister of foreign affairs could do for them. After all, it wasn't as though they'd been given a speeding ticket.

She unpacked again—it seemed as though she'd been packing and unpacking for an eternity—and wondered how long the Irish government would hold her passport. Quickly she undressed and sought the relaxation of a hot shower.

Afterward, she put on a floral shirtdress that she had bought before leaving Manhattan. It was cheerful, and Kevin hadn't seen her in it. Actually, the fabric had been too light. Ireland was cooler than she'd thought it would be in July.

She took special care with her hair and makeup, inserted small pearl earrings into her pierced ears, then went downstairs. It was almost eight o'clock and still there was no sign of Kevin. With the shower on, though, she wouldn't have heard the phone if he had called. Just then the front door opened.

"Sorry I was gone so long," Kevin apologized. "I had a talk with Fiona on the phone. She's understandably upset, but she said Seamus might be released tomorrow. I also called Margaret to see how she was taking his arrest. The butler told me her doctor gave her a sedative."

"What did your boss say?" Teri asked, seeing that Kevin looked especially tired as he walked over to an easy chair and slumped into it.

"That we weren't to worry, but he doesn't want to put any pressure on anyone just yet—not unless things become more difficult for us. He suggested we let the police do their job." Kevin's face brightened. "He also told me to take some time off, but to keep him informed." His low laugh was short and halfhearted. "I know he doesn't think I'm involved, but it would be an embarrassment for him to have a suspected smuggler on staff."

Kevin's eyes drifted over her. "You look beautiful," he said, "but, then, you always do."

"The eye of the beholder," she suggested.

"Uh-uh." He extended his arms to her, and she went to him gladly and sat on his lap. "Put your arms around me, luv. I need you to hold me." His voice was strained.

Teri now realized how worried Kevin was, how worried he had probably been all day. No doubt he had put up a front for her benefit. She slipped her right arm around his shoulder, and with her left hand she smoothed back the stray locks of blond hair that had gone askew.

Softly she asked, "You are concerned, aren't you?"

"Only because this whole matter is upsetting you."

"I'm not upset anymore...honest." Hoping to cheer him, she added, "I spoke with Colleen, and she had loads of good news. She's doing fine. Her husband got a great job in advertising, and our landlord is renting us the shop next to ours. We're going to expand the boutique."

"How many children does Colleen have?"

"A daughter who's five and a baby who's due in October."

As he stroked her hip, he said, "You're anxious to get back, aren't you?"

Leaning her forehead against his, she told him honestly, "I am and I'm not. I don't want to leave you, Kevin, but I'm also excited about enlarging the boutique. And Colleen's going to need me to be there pretty soon."

"I need you."

She smiled. "You're not pregnant."

He tilted back his head. "Is that what it would take to keep you here? Should I let you have your way with me?"

"I've already had my way with you."

"How was it?"

"Wonderful."

"How about a replay, then?" he asked, and kissed the hollow at her throat.

She pulled loose from his embrace and rose. "After we eat. We haven't had a thing since breakfast. You go shower while I fix us something. It'll make you feel better."

"I'd rather take you out for dinner." Still sitting, he took hold of both her hands. "You look so lovely I want to be seen with you."

"It will be more relaxing to eat here. Come on, go shower," she ordered, pulling him up from the chair.

"Are you going to be this bossy after we're married?"

The present, Teri told herself quickly, *think only of the present.* "If I do marry again," she informed him, "I intend to have my say in matters."

"Good," he said, reaching for her. "I like that."

She grabbed his arm and aimed him toward the stairway. "Now go, or I'll wind up fixing breakfast."

Concerned, Teri watched him as he crossed the room and started up the stairs, his steps slower than usual. On the way to the kitchen, she wondered if there was something he hadn't told her, something that was preying on his mind.

After checking the fridge and cupboards, she set a package of frozen flounder fillets in warm water to defrost partially, then took out some fresh broccoli. Once she had peeled potatoes for home fries, she placed the fillets in aluminum foil and seasoned them, adding butter and rings of green peppers and onions before closing the foil over them.

As she laid out cutlery on the oval mahogany table in the dining room, Teri smiled, thinking how easy it would be for her to slip into domestic life with Kevin. With Patrick, too, she mused. *Be realistic,* she promptly ordered herself. A seven-year-old boy would need a lot of attention. And Kevin had talked about a baby girl. *Instant family,* she thought, wondering how she would handle all the changes in her life that would have to be made. With Kevin at her side, though, she would manage somehow. Wouldn't she? With that question left unanswered, she returned to the kitchen.

During dinner both she and Kevin avoided talking about the day's events, and conversation settled on Teri's parents in Florida and Mary Kate's life in Glengarriff. Afterward, when they sat together on the sofa listening to soothing music, Kevin asked about Teri's life in Manhattan: the things she enjoyed doing, with whom she did them. And he learned more about Colleen and her family.

When they finally retired for the night, Teri lay peacefully in Kevin's arms. They had been silent for a long while when she said, "You're worried about Seamus, aren't you?" She felt Kevin breathe deeply and she smoothed her hand over his velvety skin.

"Yes. I'm afraid the police think they have an open-and-shut case against him."

"But don't they realize that any one of his employees could have placed the artifacts with my order? Or couldn't they have been put in my boxes after they left his building?"

"They're checking out those possibilities. Still, it's his firm, and he's responsible until they know differently."

"How long do you think it will be before they come up with something?"

"I don't know. It depends on the extent of the operation. They can't be sure if this was a one-time thing, or if it's been going on for some time. Whoever is behind it would have to have people at both the shipping and receiving ends."

"And the police think it's Seamus, you and me."

Placing his hands over hers, he said, "No one is going to accuse us of anything."

"I'll believe that when they give me back my passport." After mulling over Kevin's news, she asked, "Do you think I should let the American embassy know the police took my passport?"

"They already know. The minister contacted the ambassador, and on my recommendation he told him he was confident you weren't involved in the matter and that no charges would be brought against you."

"Charges," Teri repeated morosely, and sat up. There was desperation in her voice when she stated flatly, "We've got to do something. We can't just wait and see what happens."

"I don't intend to. I've an idea."

"What are we going to do?" Teri asked quickly.

Kevin pushed himself up and leaned on his elbows. "Not 'we'—me. Tomorrow I'm going to Thurles to talk to Gary Dillon."

Adamantly she said, "I'm going with you."

"No, you're not. The police would be after both of us once they found out we left Dublin."

"I don't care. If you go, I go. There's no way I could just sit here idly, wondering if you're all right."

"Look, I don't know what I'll run—"

"It's not a matter for discussion," she interrupted. "Remember, you said we were a team. Or was that just talk?"

Kevin shook his head. "You don't take no for an answer, do you?"

"Uh-uh," she whispered.

Running his fingers through her silky hair, he said, softly, "Neither do I."

CHAPTER TEN

KEVIN AND TERI started out for County Tipperary and reached the outskirts of Thurles in early afternoon. They stopped at a pub, where Kevin checked to see if anyone knew of Gary Dillon. No one did, but the owner directed Kevin to the local sugar-beet factory that employed many of the town's residents, suggesting that someone there might have heard of him.

But they hadn't, so Kevin drove into the heart of Thurles and inquired at several shops. Still no luck. Since they were less than fifty miles from Denis's turf plant, Kevin decided to return there and speak with the man who had told him Dillon had bought property.

At the plant, the same gray-haired man said, "No, I don't have an address, but I'm sure Gary said Thurles." He called over to another workman, who was checking an invoice with one of the truck drivers. "Justin, wasn't it Thurles where Gary bought property?"

The man looked over, eyed Kevin, then said, "No, he changed his mind. He bought a place in Silvermines, a village about ten kilometers south of Nenagh. He lives somewhere in the vicinity of the Dunalley Castle ruins."

Kevin thanked the men, then he and Teri were off once more, this time northward, toward the Silvermines Mountains. It was after 8:00 p.m., but it was still light when they reached the small village at the foot of the mountains. People there were tight-lipped. Kevin wasn't sure if they really had never heard of Dillon or they simply didn't want to tell him where he lived, so he followed the road to Dunalley Castle, which was two kilometers west of the village. They checked the mailboxes at several dirt roads leading to cottages off in the distance, and just as they were about to give up, Teri told Kevin to stop.

"Look," she said, pointing to her left.

"Dillon," Kevin read on the mailbox, and pulled onto the dirt road. It curved twice and they passed some sheep grazing, then they saw a thatched cottage with brownish stains running down the sides of the white-washed exterior. Blue-gray smoke streamed upward from the stone chimney. Off to the side was a barn, its doors open.

"If it's our man," Kevin said, "it looks as though he's home."

He drove closer to the cottage and parked. Just as he switched off the ignition, Teri saw a man about Kevin's age come around from the back of the house. He was tall and muscular, and wore only jeans and boots. A dark stubble covered his jaw and upper lip. He had on gloves and was carrying a roll of rope in one hand. When he saw the car he stopped, and a startled look shaped his features.

"You wait here," Kevin told Teri as he got out of the car. Heading toward the cottage, he inquired, "Gary Dillon?"

His dark eyes alert, the man asked, "Who wants to know?"

They were close enough so that Teri could hear them. The man's belt was slung low on his hips, and she could see his abdomen tighten nervously.

"I'm Kevin O'Shea, a friend of Denis Fitzgerald's."

The man said nothing.

"You are Gary Dillon, aren't you?"

"And if I am?"

"Denis told me you were in charge of crating the artifacts found near his plant."

"I used to work there."

"You managed the plant, didn't you?"

Dillon nodded.

"I was wondering how many men knew when the crates were to be transported to Dublin—other than you, of course."

"I *didn't* know that, and neither did anyone else. Only Mr. Fitzgerald knew. It was all kept very hush-hush."

"The hijackers found out somehow."

"Yeah, I heard about that. A shame, isn't it. What's the world comin' to?"

Kevin decided he wasn't going to get very much out of Gary Dillon, but he sure was going to try. "The crates were kept under lock and key at the plant, weren't they?"

"They were, and only Mr. Fitzgerald had the key."

"Was he there when the truck from the museum picked them up?"

"Don't know. I left a few days before it arrived."

"I thought you said you didn't know when the crates were to be picked up."

Teri saw Dillon tense, and she gasped when he lifted his hand with the rope in it slightly. But then he lowered it and said, "The crates were in the plant when I left, and I heard about the hijackin' a few days later."

"Here?" Kevin asked.

"No, I had business in Dublin at the time." Dillon glanced over at Teri and said, "It's gettin' dark, and

I've still got a lot of work to do around here. There's nothin' else I can tell you about the crates or either of the hijackings."

Kevin nodded and began to turn, but then he looked back. "Tell me, Gary, where did you suddenly get the money to buy this place?"

"That's none of your damn business. Now get the hell off of my property!"

"Take care," Kevin said. "Maybe we'll be talking again . . . soon." Then he got back into the car, turned it around and they drove off slowly down the bumpy dirt road.

"Well?" Teri asked.

"The man knows more than he's saying, but I don't think he's smart enough to have planned the thefts. Seems that security was pretty tight while the pieces were in Denis's custody, though. Still, I can't help but believe he had something to do with the hijackings."

"But why would Denis have been involved? Surely he doesn't need the money."

"No, he doesn't, but I think he'd get a kick out of passing historical Irish treasures around to select friends in London."

"That doesn't add up," she said. "He couldn't very well pass them around if they were with my merchandise in New York."

"The ones found in your boxes were only a small part of the two shipments hijacked. Denis could have had some of the other pieces flown out in a private plane, or he could have smuggled them to England in his yacht." He shook his head. "But he would really have to be crazy to take a risk like that."

It was a possibility, Teri had to admit, but she felt Kevin was working awfully hard to implicate Moira's husband. Then she thought of Patrick and said, "If Denis was involved, it would bring a lot of grief to his entire family, including Moira and Patrick. It's Patrick I'm really concerned about."

Kevin pulled onto the main road and headed toward Limerick, where he planned for them to spend the night. "If the man's guilty, he's the one bringing the grief on his family."

"It doesn't bother you that Patrick would suffer, too?"

He glanced over at her. "Of course it bothers me." He reached over, took her hand and kissed it. "I appreciate your being so protective of him."

Why shouldn't I be? she thought. *He's your son.*

As the road ribboned up and down through dark, low-lying hills, Teri remarked, "It's deserted out here, isn't it?"

Kevin checked his rearview mirror. "Not really," he said, smiling. "There's a truck keeping us company. It's been with us for a while now."

Glancing over her shoulder, Teri saw the truck bearing down on them. "I think he wants to pass us."

"Bad place to pass," Kevin said, quickly looking in the rearview mirror again. "There's an S-curve coming up."

She looked ahead, but in the next instant something struck the back of Kevin's car—it felt like a giant demolition ball—with an earsplitting thud, jolting the two of them in their seats. Teri screamed and Kevin yelled "Stupid bastard!" as he pushed the gas pedal to the floor. In seconds the truck banged into them again, throwing Teri against the door.

The car skidded and Kevin wrestled with the wheel, his eyes glued on the sharp curve directly ahead of them.

"Kevin!" Teri hollered, grabbing hold of the padded dashboard as the car scraped against the wooden safety rail and lurched back onto the road.

Panic caught her in an icy grip when the truck smacked into them again. All she could see in the darkness were the blurred tops of the trees in the ravine on the other side of the safety rail.

Acting instinctively, Kevin struggled against his seat belt, reached to the back seat and grabbed a heavy knit sweater he'd placed there in case Teri got cold. "Put this over your head!" he ordered, then checked the rearview mirror. "He's pulling back. No, here he comes again. Cover your head!"

Before she could, the truck rammed into them and sent the car crashing through the safety rail and down into the ravine. "Hold on!" Kevin yelled. He needn't have. Teri's hands had a crushing hold on the dashboard. She was so terrified her scream caught in her throat, gagging her. The car bounced and lurched from side to side as it scraped against rocks and careered off of low-growing branches. Teri felt as though she were on a runaway roller coaster, going down, down, down—

The left front wheel hit something, throwing both of them sideways in their seats. The car tipped to the right, and Teri thought they were going to flip over. But then the car hit some thick branches and was set on all four wheels again. Still they sped downward, and when she saw a huge tree trunk in the beam of the headlights, she screamed again.

Kevin's face was grim as he wrenched the wheel hard to the left and veered away from the tree just in time. "Cover your head, damn it!" he yelled.

She did, and in the next instant her ears were filled with the sickening sounds of metal and rock colliding as the car bumped and bucked in its downward plunge.

Suddenly she felt Kevin's arms protectively cradling her head. The car was level for seconds, then it tilted up in front. It jerked and rocked a few times, then stopped; the sudden silence was deafening.

Half-conscious, Teri tried to raise her head. She felt weak, emotionally drained, and her shoulder hurt. Her eyelids fluttered as she tried to organize her jumbled thoughts. The car. A truck. Kevin!

She sat bolt upright. He was slumped sideways, his arms now over her legs. She saw that he had broken away from his seat belt. No doubt he had jerked free of it to cover her when he had realized they were going to crash into the hill that had suddenly loomed up in front of the car.

"Kevin!" she cried in a weak voice as she pulled his body up until he fell back against his seat.

"Oooooow," he moaned, and shook his head. "What the hell happened?"

"Darling, you saved our lives. That's what happened. That truck rammed us into the ravine."

Pressing the heels of his palms against his closed eyes, he mumbled, "Yes...the truck." He opened his eyes and jerked his head toward her. "Are you all right?"

"Yes, yes." Then she saw the cut on the right side of his head. "You're bleeding."

He raised a hand to his head. Looking at his fingers, he saw that there wasn't a great deal of blood. "It's nothing. I'm fine."

"Thank God."

Kevin scanned the terrain, then forced open the door on his side. After getting out, he said, "There's a dirt road behind us. I guess we sailed right over it." He looked at the car, which sat at a thirty-degree angle at the bottom of the hill, then walked around the vehicle to give a cursory check.

Getting in again, he said, "If this thing decides it wants to move, maybe we can get to a busier road." He switched on the ignition, and the engine groaned and sputtered. "Come on," he pleaded, "don't leave us out here." He turned the key again and hit the gas pedal; this time the engine cooperated—kind of. Slowly he backed the car onto the moonlit road.

Again he asked, "Are you sure you're all right?"

"I am, but we've got to see about that cut on your forehead."

"We will, as soon as we reach civilization."

Which way? he wondered, and decided one direction was as good as the other. The road was rough, but after the ride they had just taken, it felt as though they were driving on blacktop. The car chugged along, then died, but Kevin got it started again.

Fifteen minutes later, the dirt road ended, and he turned onto a macadam road. After driving for a while, they came to an inn, but all the lights were out. Kevin pulled into the parking area and saw only one automobile there.

Teri remained in the car while he went to the front door and knocked. He paced as he waited, then knocked again. She saw a light appear in a second-story window. When a man opened it, Kevin said something to him in Irish. Within a minute he was at the front door. The two men talked briefly, and Kevin returned to the car.

"The inn is closed, but when I explained what happened, he said we could spend the night."

The building wasn't at all luxurious, but it was extremely neat and clean. Their room was on the second floor, and as soon as the innkeeper left them, she examined Kevin's head, then took him down the hall to the bathroom, where she washed the cut. Back in their room, she found the box of bandages she carried in her suitcase and put two over the wound.

They were both exhausted, so it wasn't much later that they piled into the high four-poster. Only when Kevin had undressed did Teri see the bruise on his right shoulder. Cradling him in her arms, his head resting on her breast, she stroked his hair until he drifted off to sleep.

But it was a while before Teri slept. Going around asking questions was one thing; having someone try to kill them was another. She hadn't wanted Kevin to get mixed up in this business any more than he was already, and now her worst fears were coming to pass. They should have stayed in Dublin, she decided, wondering just what her chances were of getting Kevin to drive back there in the morning. Her last thought before closing her eyes was, *not too good.*

A GRAY MIST hovered outside the window as the innkeeper served them a hearty country breakfast the following morning. Kevin had phoned a garage in nearby Nenagh to have his car towed there, so after eating, they rode with the mechanic, and in the city he rented a car. This time, although they drove in daylight, Kevin kept a watchful eye on the rearview mirror the whole time.

"Is your shoulder hurting?" Teri asked.

"Not really. In fact, I feel pretty rested. How about you?"

"I'm fine," she lied. Then she saw a sign saying Silvermines was off to the right. "Kevin, we are *not* going back to see Gary Dillon," she said firmly. He shook his head, and the muscles that had suddenly tensed in her relaxed. "Good," she said. After they were well past the sign, she asked, "Do you think he was driving that truck last night?"

"I'd bet a winning sweepstakes ticket on it, but we couldn't prove it. I wouldn't even be able to identify the truck." He glanced her way and grinned. "I was too busy to notice."

Failing to see the humor in his remark, she asked, "If it was Dillon, why would he want to try to kill us?"

"Maybe we're getting too close to finding something out."

"Like what?"

"Beats the hell out of me . . . unless I unnerved him when I asked where he got the money to buy his property. That's something the police can check into when we get back to Dublin."

"That's where we're going, isn't it?" Teri had had enough of sleuthing if last night's experience was a sample of what they would come up against.

"Limerick," he told her. "I want you in a place where there are lots of lights and lots of people while I run an errand."

"You're going to see Denis, aren't you?"

"Exactly."

Hopefully she said, "He may not even be at home."

"I'll find out where he is."

Teri didn't like the sound of that or the tone of Kevin's voice. "Why don't we just let the police handle things? I don't want you getting any more hurt than you already are. It's just not worth it."

He put a hand on hers. "It is to me. We've already had two hijackings. If it's not stopped soon, the same thing can happen all over Ireland. Remember, the bogs are continually releasing treasures they've held for centuries, and that's a lot of Irish history that should be passed on to future generations."

"I remember," she said with a sigh, realizing that once Kevin got an idea in his head, little could be done to change his mind. At that moment, she would have welcomed a patrol car pulling them over and ordering them back to Dublin.

Just outside the city, Kevin checked them into the Limerick Ryan, a hotel situated on an eight-acre park near the Shannon airport.

In their room, he told her, "I don't want you leaving the hotel until I get back. Have lunch in the restaurant downstairs, or have it sent up here. And if I'm not back by four o'clock, I want you to take a taxi to the airport and get a flight back to Dublin."

"But Kevin—"

"No buts about it this time. If what I suspect is true, I'm not sure what Denis will do, and I don't want you anywhere nearby. Now promise me that if I'm not here by four, you'll get back to Dublin. Promise?"

"All right," she said quietly.

"Do you have Irish currency?"

"Some, but I've also got my credit cards."

"That'll be okay. Remember...four o'clock."

She nodded.

Cupping her troubled face with his hands, he kissed her. "I love you, and I always will." Then he left, leaving a frightfully worried Teri behind.

WHEN KEVIN ARRIVED at the Fitzgerald estate, he was shown directly to Denis's study on the second floor.

"Back so soon, Kevin, and without your American friend? Are you losing your touch?" Fitzgerald's stony dark eyes narrowed. "What's the attraction that keeps bringing you back to us?"

"The only thing that keeps me coming back is concern for Patrick."

"An unnatural concern, wouldn't you say?"

"Look, Denis, I don't have time right now to give you my opinion of what I think of you as a father."

"Then why are you here?"

"I've talked with Gary Dillon."

"Oh," he said with an indifferent air, and walked behind his desk. "Just what business do you have with Dillon?"

"I thought it interesting that he suddenly had enough money to quit his job and buy property in Silvermines."

Denis's face screwed into a condescending grin. "Ah, yes. Kevin O'Shea, the flag-waver with the great concern for the working class. No doubt Dillon had a relative who died and left him the property, or perhaps his luck at the races improved."

"Apparently his luck improved after you put him in charge of crating the antiquities."

"That again. Don't you have anything better to do than play detective?" Denis sat down in the brown leather-backed chair, his cold stare never leaving Kevin. "Who is it you're trying to impress? The minister?" He leaned forward and put his hands on the desk. "Or are you trying to get your friend Seamus off the hook?"

Slowly Kevin moved over to the desk. "I don't happen to think Seamus had anything to do with the hijackings or the attempted smuggling."

"Apparently the police differ with you, and the media suggest otherwise, as well."

Kevin leaned over and placed his hands on the desk, too. "The police won't after they talk to Dillon."

"And what can that sod buster say that would interest them? He quit the plant before the artifacts were picked up."

Kevin decided to play out his suspicions. "Only because he had to be somewhere else . . . waiting between Kildare and Newbridge for the truck carrying the crates he'd packed."

"Dillon?" Denis leaned back in his chair, his eyes curiously remote. "He told you that?"

"You and I both know he doesn't have the brains to plan two successful hijackings, particularly the elaborate assault on the armored car. And since he no longer worked for you, someone would have had to tell him when the shipments were scheduled and what route the drivers would take to Dublin. You told him, Denis. You masterminded both operations. Why?"

Dark eyes glaring, Denis jumped up. "So that's what you're still trying to do . . . implicate me!" He started to laugh wildly, a sound so crazed it startled Kevin. "Moira put you up to this, didn't she?" He strode around the desk and headed for the study door, but then whirled and pointed a finger at Kevin. "You have no proof, have you? If you did you wouldn't be here talking about it. You would have gone directly to the police."

"Dillon has agreed to testify against you to keep himself out of prison," Kevin lied, watching carefully for Denis's reaction.

Waving his finger at Kevin, Denis lowered his voice and said huskily, "It's Moira. She put you up to this. You're both trying to get rid of me. You think you'll get Patrick, and all my money, too."

Kevin had long thought that Denis was a troubled man, and the wild look on his face now fully convinced him. "This has nothing to do with Patrick or Moira. The only issue is—"

"She'll pay for this, and you will, too," Denis ranted.

"You admit it, then. You did plan the hijackings."

Denis smiled eerily. "You'd like to think that, wouldn't you? You want me put away so you can have my wife. You've always hated me because she chose me instead of you." Like a panther stalking his prey, he fixed his eyes on Kevin and walked behind him. "Even when we were boys you hated me because my family was cultured and yours were peasants."

Not trusting him, Kevin followed Denis's movements peripherally, finally turning to face him. In Denis's present state of mind he could do anything.

Denis looked Kevin up and down and shook his head. "What Moira sees in you is a mystery to me, but she'll never leave me. I promise you that. I'll kill her first, and I'll kill—"

The door to the study opened, drawing their attention. Moira entered, surprise evident on her face when she saw Kevin. Quickly she closed the door behind her and rushed to him. Her eyes were red from crying, and she had a nasty bruise on the side of her face.

"You bastard," Kevin growled, putting his arm around Moira. "What the hell kind of a man are you?"

Reverting instantly to his lord-of-the-manor tone, Denis smiled. As he walked back to his desk, he said in singsong manner, "A man who is undisputed master of his castle...and his family."

"He hurt Patrick," Moira murmured, and when Kevin started toward Denis, she grabbed his arm, imploring, "Don't, you'll only make matters worse!"

"Worse? How the hell could they get worse? Where's Patrick now?"

"In his bedroom. I finally got him to sleep."

"Is he hurt badly?"

"His arm is bruised, but I think he's more frightened than hurt."

Kevin turned to Denis, his jaw set firmly. "You and your cultured family," he said in disgust. "I'm going to see to it that you never hit your son again."

Denis glanced at Moira, then fixed glassy eyes on Kevin. Grinning dementedly, he said, "I never did hit *my* son, old friend."

His fists clenching, Kevin said, "Moira isn't a liar."

"No, she's an adulteress—" his accusing eyes swept to his wife "—aren't you, darling?"

Kevin's eyes followed him. "What's he talking about?"

Moira covered her mouth with her hands.

"Tell him, dearest," Denis urged sweetly, and sat down behind his desk.

"Tell me what?"

Denis snickered. "Why I couldn't possibly have hit my son."

Removing Moira's hands from her mouth, Kevin asked, "Did he or didn't he hit Patrick?"

Moira nodded and looked down, and Kevin's eyes shot back to Denis.

"But," the seated man said, "Patrick is *not* my son."

The smile of satisfaction on Denis's face caused Kevin's stomach to knot. A premonition took hold of him with a force that chilled him to the bone. Sensing what Moira's response would be, he fastened his gaze on her. His voice was low and quiet, but it had an edge to it that pierced the silence in the room. "Who is Patrick's father?"

Moira kept her eyes lowered, anxious not to let Kevin see the fear in them. There was a tremor in her voice when she murmured, "You are."

CHAPTER ELEVEN

KEVIN HAD ALWAYS BEEN a man who prided himself on his ability to face difficult situations. He had found the strength to leave Teri long ago when he had thought his honor demanded it. He had picked himself up by his bootstraps and reorganized his life when Moira had jilted him. And he had stuck with his commitment to do more than his share to help Ireland, even when others had given up.

But he didn't know how to face what Moira was telling him now.

It would have been much simpler if he could have convinced himself he was the wronged party. But he couldn't. Patrick, his *son*—the word jolted his heart—was the wronged party. There was blame enough to go around, but as Kevin tried desperately to work through his rage, he knew he had to own up to most of the blame.

Suddenly it was all so clear to him! For years he had felt such a strong bond with the boy that it was like an obsession. Yet he had never questioned it. Nor could he pass the burden of guilt on to Moira. He had long known she had never quite grown up; emotionally she was still a child. Patrick was a plaything to be brought out and enjoyed when the mood struck. Her husband's castle was her elaborate dollhouse. And Denis? He was to be pitied: he'd been handed a life that never had and never would give him a moment of true peace or happiness. But Kevin could find no excuse for himself.

That night eight years ago when Moira had come to him, he'd had a choice. He had taken the easier path, and Patrick had been the one to pay.

Embittered, Kevin leaned down and, with one powerful swoop, sent the items on Denis's desk crashing to the floor. The two others in the room couldn't possibly have known his anger was directed at himself.

Patrick, how do I explain it all to you? he wondered as he moved slowly to the window. *What will you think of me?*

Kevin's eyes burned, and the knot in his stomach tightened, but he knew he had to take charge—immediately. Turning abruptly, he set hard eyes on Moira. "Get some of Patrick's things together. I'm taking him with me."

"Kevin—" she began, edging toward him.

"Not one word," he warned in a voice that made her step back. "Just do as I say. Patrick's not staying in this hellhole one more night." His mouth curved in disgust. "You're sick, the two of you."

Moira's eyes flashed to Denis, then back to Kevin. Inching toward him, she said, "Take me with you, too. Patrick is ours. We can be a family now, just as we always should have been. I can be ready in just a—"

"You can go to hell," he spit out.

Denis's strained laughter filled her ears, and she bristled. "Shut up, you fool!" Then she faced Kevin again. "If I don't go, neither does Patrick."

"You'd let him stay here—" Kevin threw a contemptuous glance at Denis "—with him?"

Denis rose. "Moira, go and check on Patrick. Let Kevin and I have a man-to-man talk about...the situation."

"No, I—"

"Get out of here!" he bellowed.

After looking to Kevin for assistance—which didn't come—she left the room.

Denis leaned over his desk and asked, "So, my boyhood friend, how does it feel to have fathered a bastard?"

"Watch it, Denis," Kevin threatened. "I'm still aching to shove my fist in your face." Forcing a calmness he didn't feel into his tone, he said, "Are you going to let me take my son with me peacefully?"

"I'm not letting you take anything of mine...ever." In one quick motion he jerked open the top drawer of his desk and pulled out a revolver.

Kevin glanced at the black barrel aimed straight at him. He wouldn't put it past the man to pull the trigger and shoot him on the spot. "I don't want anything that's rightfully yours, but Patrick isn't," he challenged.

"Do you think I would let the world know I wasn't capable of fathering a child?" His bitter laughter filled the study, then stopped as abruptly as it had started. "Not while I'm alive."

"There are worse things," Kevin suggested, watching Denis carefully as he moved to the front of the desk.

"Yes...like having a wife who treats you as though you're half-mad. She does, you know. Sometimes she makes me feel that I've been a bad boy, that I've done something...so very...awful. I don't understand why she does that, Kevin," he whispered confidentially, tottering slightly. "She's just like my mother...always finding fault with me, never wanting me around."

"Denis," Kevin said in an even tone when the man raised his free hand to wipe the perspiration from his forehead, "you're not well. You need help."

"What?"

Kevin glanced at the gun. "Professional help."

"Yes, yes, but there's something I have to do, something I have to show you." He pointed the gun at the door to the adjoining room. "It's in there."

Dubious, Kevin walked over to the door as Denis urged him on. He tried to sense how close the man was behind him.

"Open it," Denis ordered.

Kevin did, knowing that it led into Denis's bedroom and sitting room.

"Go in."

As he entered, Kevin formulated a plan: when Denis became involved in showing him whatever it was he wanted him to see, he'd jump him.

But he never had the chance. One second he was listening for Denis's footsteps; the next he felt a bone-crushing pain at the back of his head. His body jerked, then he fell forward and an inky blackness engulfed him.

IN HER ROOM at the hotel, Teri paced, trying to control her mounting nervousness. For the third time in five minutes she checked her watch: it was almost 5:00 p.m. She had long since decided against following Kevin's instructions that she catch a flight to Dublin. He could return at any moment, she told herself, glancing out the window.

But the sinking feeling that had begun to gnaw at her an hour ago told her something had happened to him. If not, he would have called her before four o'clock. She hurried back to the phone on the vanity and checked with the clerk at the front desk again. There was still no word from Kevin.

A frightening sense of desperation filled her as she looked around the quiet room. Where was Kevin at this very moment? she wondered. Would she ever see him again? She shook the morose question from her mind. She had to do something. But what? Notify the police? Tell them what? Even if they checked with Denis, he could easily deny he'd ever seen Kevin. And they would certainly take her back to Dublin. How could she help him from there? Then she remembered that Fiona had told Kevin Seamus might be released today. Teri couldn't think of anyone else to ask for help, and Kevin did trust him.

Quickly she found her address book and Seamus's office number. She dialed and waited for what seemed like endless minutes, fearful everyone had already left for the day. Finally the receptionist answered and switched her to Fiona's phone.

"No, Teresa, he's not here," Fiona said in reply to Teri's terse query. "He's meeting with his barrister, but I told him I'd wait at the office until he returned. My God, isn't it awful! I mean, of all people, Seamus. It's ludicrous."

"Damn!" Teri mumbled, then immediately apologized.

"What is it?" Fiona asked. "You sound quite desperate. Are you all right?"

"Yes, but I'm worried about Kevin. I'm afraid he might be in trouble."

"Trouble? What kind of trouble?"

"Well, it's a long story, but we went to see Gary Dillon yesterday, and now Kevin thinks he knows who the hijacker is, or at least one of them."

"Who, Teresa?"

"Fiona, excuse me, but I don't want to tie up the line in case Kevin's trying to contact me. Would you have Seamus call me here as soon as he gets back to the office? It's urgent that I speak with him. And be sure to leave a message if you decide not to wait for him."

"Certainly I will. Let me have your phone number."

Teri promptly gave it to her, and told her she was at the Limerick Ryan Hotel. With that, she ended their conversation, and again began the terrible waiting.

Hours later she was still standing by the window, hoping and praying for the sight of Kevin's rental car, when the ringing of the phone jarred her from her thoughts. She ran to it, jerking the receiver off its cradle.

"Kevin!"

"Mrs. Manzoni?"

"Yes," she replied to the man's voice, disappointment in her tone.

"I'm afraid there's been an accident."

"Oh, God. Kevin?"

"Yes. Mr. O'Shea is asking for you. May I send someone to pick you up to take you to him?"

"Yes! What happened? Will he be all right?"

"That's hard to say, but the gentleman coming to get you will explain everything. How soon can you be ready to leave?"

"I'm ready right now."

"Good. Go to the entrance of the hotel. A car will be there shortly."

The line went dead. "Wait, where is—"

What did it matter where Kevin was? she thought. He was hurt, calling for her. Quickly she swooped up her purse and hurried from the room.

At the entrance to the hotel, her worry increased as she waited nervously. A few minutes later a black car drove up, and a burly man wearing a cap and gray sweater rolled the window down.

"Mrs. Manzoni?"

"Yes!"

"Get in, please." He leaned to his left and opened the door on the passenger's side.

Teri hurried around the small car, hopped in, and the man took off immediately.

"What's happened to Kevin?" she asked, turning to face the man's sharp profile.

"Sorry, but I don't have all the information. The man who was supposed to pick you up had an emergency at home. All I know is that there was some kind of a car accident."

There was an unpleasant sour odor in the car that almost gagged her. Fighting it, Teri asked, "Is he in a hospital?"

"From what I gathered, they were waiting for an ambulance when your friend asked that you be notified. That's about all I know." He glanced over at her. "Don't worry yourself. You'll see him soon enough."

In the dim light from the dashboard, Teri could see that the man's face was elongated. He had thick lips and a strong jaw; his gray eyes had little emotion in them.

An accident, she thought, forgetting the man beside her. Where was Kevin driving to or from? Had he been at the Fitzgerald estate for so long a time? Why hadn't he phoned her? But then she decided he'd probably thought she'd followed his instructions and returned to Dublin.

She looked out the car window, and in the darkness she could tell that they were driving in the countryside, but she had no idea where they were or in which direction they were heading. Turning to the man driving, she asked, "Where did the accident take place?"

"Not too far from here. We'll be there shortly."

The awful odor in the car was giving her a headache and making her feel queasy. "Do you mind if I lower the window a bit?" she asked.

"Go right ahead."

As she did, Teri began to wonder about the wisdom of having driven off in the night with a complete stranger. But Kevin needed her; that was all that mattered.

About fifteen minutes later the air rushing into the car took on a familiar aroma. She sniffed again and thought, *the bogs*. Carefully Teri inspected what she could of the land whizzing by. She would have sworn the dirt road was the same one she and Kevin had driven on twice when they'd gone to Denis's turf plant. Yes, there were the railroad cars, and in the distance she saw the small lights on top of what she assumed was the huge plant itself.

"Is this where the accident happened?" she asked, a wave of apprehension sweeping over her.

"Yes, just outside the plant, I was told."

"Denis Fitzgerald's plant?"

"That's right."

What was Kevin doing back here? she wondered. *Had Denis told him something that had made him return to the plant?* She didn't want to think about the other "accident," which she and Kevin had had leaving Dillon's place. *Dear God! Had Denis led Kevin into a trap here?*

One lone light shone over the entrance to the office, but the man drove past it, steered the car around to the back of the building and pulled up next to a short ramp leading to a door. Dark clouds floated overhead, obscuring the moon, as Teri scanned the parking area. There wasn't a car in sight, let alone any signs of an accident.

The man switched off the ignition and put the keys in his pants pocket. "This is it, Mrs. Manzoni."

"There's no one here." Her apprehension turned to stark terror. "Where's Kevin? You said you were taking me to him."

"Inside now. Be a good girl."

The bile rose high in her throat. Struggling to swallow, she said, "I'm not going in there. Take me back to the hotel."

The dark clouds passed, and Teri gasped as moonlight caught the steel tip of a knife the man was pointing at her.

"Inside," he ordered.

Her legs shaking, she got out and looked around at the vast and silent emptiness of the loading area. In the next instant the man grabbed her arm and hustled her up the ramp and inside the plant.

Teri's frightened eyes swept the dim interior. The center of the building was like an atrium; the open area soared four stories high and was topped with a skylight that filled the area with eerie blue-gray shadows. Metal stairs led to the three upper levels. Two monstrous-looking cutting machines were parked on the concrete floor, and wooden crates were piled everywhere. The stench of musty turf was almost sickening.

Spinning around, she blurted out, "Why have you brought me here? What do you want?"

The stranger closed the door in back of him and shoved the dead bolt; the thud echoed throughout the building. "That's your problem, yours and Mr. O'Shea's. You ask too many questions." Flashing his knife, he said, "Where is Mr. O'Shea?"

Teri backed away. "I . . . I don't know."

"Where did he go?"

Her eyes fixed on the knife, she said, "He didn't tell me."

"You're a liar," he growled, his face contorting into a grimace.

"I'm telling you the truth. I honestly don't know where he is right now." She backed away some more. "I thought you were taking me to him."

"You're going to make this difficult, aren't you?"

Teri turned to run, but he grabbed her. She screamed, then he pulled her up against him and held the knife at her throat.

"Is your memory getting any better?"

She could hardly breathe from the pressure of his arm on her chest. The disgusting smell of his breath mixed with that of the turf briquettes, and she began to choke. Desperate, she sank her teeth into his wrist as hard as she could. When he yelled and jerked his arm away, she turned and, with one fast, fluid motion, swung her heavy purse at him, smacking the side of his head. He stumbled backward and fell over one of the wooden crates.

Teri dropped her purse and ran for her life.

Where to, she didn't know—just away from the man hurling curses at her as he got up and pursued. She looked for a door, but in vain. Ahead of her was a metal staircase. She grabbed the railing and began to climb as fast as she could. Moments earlier she had cursed the darkness; now she was thankful for it.

At the top of the stairs on the first landing, she chanced a quick look behind her. She could see him nearing the bottom of the stairway, and she jumped backward out of his view. Her head jerked to the right, then to the left, as she searched for a place to hide. Then she heard his sinister voice rise up from the bottom of the stairs.

"That's it, Mrs. Manzoni. Run . . . try to hide. I like that. It makes it all the more exciting." He started slowly up the steps, listening carefully. "But I'll find you, and when I do—"

His raucous laughter sent an icy chill rushing down her spine. She was terrified. Her eyes shot to the stairway leading to the next landing, but she knew he would see her if she started up. As quietly as she could, she slipped between the piles of empty crates along the wall.

"Come on, Mrs. Manzoni," he taunted her. "We have things to discuss."

His gravelly voice came closer and closer. Teri was breathing rapidly, in quick, shallow gasps. She tried to take deeper breaths, and she placed her palm over her mouth so the wheezing sounds wouldn't reveal her hiding place.

"After our talk," he said as he passed within feet of her, "I'll show you the bogs. You'll like that. Deep under the turf it's warm, even in the winter. But don't worry. They'll find you in the spring . . . if the machine blades don't slash you into little pieces."

Again his ugly laughter enveloped her, and she had to fight to keep from fainting. Winning the battle against total darkness, she listened. His steps were growing faint. She looked to her right. There was enough space between the crates and the wall for her to make it to the stairs. If she could just get downstairs again, she thought, she might have a chance of getting out of the building before he realized it.

Stealthily she squeezed along the narrow passageway, pressing herself against the concrete wall. Her head was pounding, and her hands shook as they slid along the cold stone. Silently she stepped toward the last pile of crates. But as soon as she tried to move behind it, she knew the space wasn't wide enough. She'd have to go around it. That meant he might see her.

Where was he now? She listened, but heard only a deathly silence.

Wiping the perspiration from her forehead, she decided it was now or never. With a prayer on her lips, she edged from behind the crates to the main walkway. Hardly breathing, she listened again. Then she peered to her left. No one there. She leaned forward a bit more. Where was—

"Ha!" he cried.

Teri screamed and darted for the nearest stairway. She clung to the railing and forced herself up the stairs as fast as she could climb. Near the top she stumbled and fell. Tears of fright blurred her vision, but she pushed herself up, took the three remaining steps in a flash and ran down the long walkway as fast as her feet would carry her.

As she neared the opposite end of the building, she could hear the pounding of his feet. "Oh, God!" she moaned, seeing a blank wall in front of her. Then she spied another stairway.

She stretched out her arms, lunged at the railing and whipped around so hard she almost fell again. The sound of her shoes striking the steps one by one echoed in her ears as hot tears rolled down her cold cheeks.

At the top of the stairs she had to stop. She sucked in as much air as she could, glanced up and saw the skylight. No more stairways, nowhere else to run, no one to help her.

Exhausted, she staggered like a drunken woman, her feet flopping on the aged wooden planks in a syncopated death march. Why was she even trying? she wondered as she looked directly ahead at the flat concrete wall. It was over. He was on the landing with her now, singing her name with a bloodcurdling sweetness that made her stomach wrench.

At the end of the walkway she fell against the stone wall. Her hair hanging over her forehead, she rolled her body around and slouched against the cold concrete. Her breaths were deep and painful; she was trembling from her toes to her scalp. She forced her eyelids open and saw him coming slowly toward her, his knife raised, his horrible face set in a grim smile.

Oh, Kevin! she thought in despair, too terrorized and too weak to speak the words. *I'll never be able to tell you how much I really love you.*

CHAPTER TWELVE

THE HULK of a man slowed his steps, obviously enjoying the anguish of the petrified woman at the end of the landing. He could see that her face was wet from useless tears, could see the rise and fall of her breasts as she pressed her palms against the concrete behind her.

"One more time, Mrs. Manzoni. Where is Kevin O'Shea?"

Teri fought back the nauseating thickness in her throat. As the grinning man came closer, she became desperate again and let instinct take over. Her head jerked around as she sought for an escape. It was then that she saw the fire extinguisher hanging on the wall next to her.

With the speed of light, she yanked it free, pulled the red lock pin out and aimed the nozzle directly at him as he lunged at her.

A white chemical powder covered his face. He yelled, dropped the knife and covered his eyes with his hands. Then he danced crazily, thrashing about and cursing her. Teri watched in horror as he fell backward against the railing. His body seesawed, then toppled over. Her scream drowned out his as he plummeted through space. When her captor hit the concrete pavement four floors below, the sickening thud reverberated throughout the entire building.

Teri's knees gave way, and her body slipped slowly down against the rough stone wall. For minutes she sat sobbing, her legs tucked under her, her palms covering her face. Her eyes shut tightly, she tried to convince herself that at any moment she would awaken from the nightmare that was holding her firmly in its terrible grasp. But the pain that racked her chest and the throbbing that was splitting her head told her she was already awake.

She forced her hands to the railing and pulled herself up with great effort. Gripping the cold metal, she made herself look down. He was lying there in an unnatural heap.

She jerked her head away from the gruesome sight and leaned back against the wall, trying to calm herself. What she wanted most was to be away from this awful place, as fast and as far away as possible. But how? She was miles from civilization.

His car! But the keys— She had seen him put them in his pants pocket.

For a moment she thought she was going to be sick, but she conquered the sensation and took several deep breaths. No, she told herself, she didn't have time even to get sick. Kevin might be in just the same kind of danger she had been in moments ago. She had to pull herself together, do whatever was required of her until she knew he was safe.

A deep sigh gushed from her lungs, and she walked quickly to the staircase and started the long descent to the ground floor.

The silence was awesome. Muted light struck swirls of turf dust floating around the center of the building. Hesitantly, fearfully, she inched closer to the dark form lying at the far end of the building. Despite her resolve to be strong and brave, she felt like a child who was terrified of the dark.

But she had to get those car keys.

She stepped closer to him. What if he wasn't dead? she thought. What if he grabbed her ankle and pulled her down?

"Stop it!" she ordered, and the sound of her own voice forced her to halt only a few feet away from him.

For tense moments she listened for sounds of his breathing. She heard none. Nor did she see any movement. She made a fist with her right hand, digging her fingernails into her palm to stop her hand from trembling. At the same time her teeth dug into her lower lip.

Kevin is in trouble, she told herself, and moved closer to the body. *He needs you to be strong now!* She crouched and saw her hand move toward the man's left-hand pocket. *Just a bit more,* she ordered herself, shuddering.

"Ughhh," she moaned when his body heat assaulted her fingertips. Closing her eyes and turning her head, she reached into his pocket, felt the key ring and jerked her hand back as fast as she could. Then she jumped up and ran toward the exit to find her purse.

Once outside, Teri fell back against the door, wanting the cool night air to wash over her, hoping it could cleanse her tortured soul and aching body. For moments she couldn't move, her breaths coming deep and rushed, but eventually she forced herself to hurry toward the car.

The gunning of the engine, the sudden spinning of the wheels and the sound of gravel flying broke the night silence. Teri didn't have the slightest idea where she was heading; she just wanted to put as much distance between her and the turf plant as she could. She remembered that the drive from Limerick had been particularly desolate, but if she could just get back to the hotel, she thought desperately, maybe Kevin would be there.

"Teresa Rosario," she asked herself nervously as she drove through the dark night, "what's a nice Italian girl like you doing wandering around Ireland with people trying to kill you?" The question itself chilled her, and she faced the stark truth that she wasn't at all cut out for this kind of trouble. She'd never thought of herself as particularly brave; even harsh words with someone unnerved her. But now she had to be brave—for Kevin's sake.

When the beam of the headlights struck a sign that indicated Limerick was eighteen kilometers to the east, she turned and was back at the hotel in fifteen minutes.

She was calmer now, but her depressed mood returned in full force when the night clerk told her she had no messages. Whether it was the sigh she emitted or the drawn look on her face, something caused the clerk to inquire if she was all right.

"Yes," she lied, then asked, "Would it be possible to get a cup of coffee at this hour?"

"I'm sorry, but the restaurant and the grill room are closed." He looked at her again. "Tell you what. I'll get some coffee and bring it to your room."

Teri smiled weakly and asked, "Irish, if possible?"

It was.

Her fear for Kevin mounting, Teri stood by the window in her room, looking out at the driveway and drinking her coffee. When she glanced at her watch, she saw that it was almost midnight. She wondered why Seamus hadn't returned her call. She started to take another sip of coffee, but stopped and held the cup in midair. She put it down quickly when her mind flashed her a picture of the man she'd left in the turf plant.

How had he found her? she wondered. Who had told him where to find her? The only one who knew where she was staying was Kevin. Of course, she had left the message for Seamus.

Seamus!

But, Teri had to wonder, even if he was involved in hijacking and smuggling, would he actually have sent someone to kill her and Kevin? That possibility seemed beyond belief. Yet she knew that desperate men did desperate things.

And Kevin had said a number of people would have to be involved, in Ireland and abroad. Was Seamus one of them? Working with Denis? Right now she didn't know what to believe.

She reached for her coffee and downed the last drop, thinking that if Kevin had made it to the Fitzgerald estate, he could really be in desperate trouble—or worse.

Quickly she slipped into the shoes she had kicked off earlier, picked up her purse and went to the front desk. The clerk knew exactly where the Fitzgerald castle was and told Teri it was only a twenty-minute drive. After jotting down his directions, she asked where the nearest all-night petrol station was, and soon she was off again—in her borrowed car—heading west toward the River Shannon.

Believing Kevin was still at the castle, Teri grew stronger emotionally and physically as she neared it. She had loved him too long and too deeply to lose him now. *Please, God,* she prayed, *don't let it be too late.*

Attempting to bolster her morale, she told herself that Moira certainly wouldn't have let anything happen to Kevin, and with all the servants around, it would have been difficult for Denis to do anything crazy. It was also possible that Kevin wasn't even there. *He's fine,* she told herself. He hadn't phoned because he had assumed she'd returned to Dublin as he had told her to. Yes, that was it. She had to believe it was that simple....

For all of her feigned confidence, Teri parked the car well under the elm trees at the foot of the driveway, then walked the rest of the way to the entrance. Her heart sank when she saw Kevin's rental automobile parked near the door. The castle was dark, except for a light that came from a room on the first floor.

Moving quietly, she crept to the side of the stone building. Wind was whipping around the corner of the castle, but standing close to the high window, she could make out the sound of a heated argument between a man and a woman. A wide stone railing ended just under the arched window, so Teri climbed up and peered inside.

It was Moira and Denis, but she couldn't make out their words. A few moments later, Denis strode angrily toward the window. Teri drew her head back and listened.

"If you ever think of leaving me, I'll kill him! And if you so much as try to notify anyone that he's here, I'll kill Patrick, too."

"Denis," Moira pleaded, "be reasonable. You can't keep Kevin locked up forever. One of the servants will find out he's here. My God, his car is right outside. You're insane if you think you'll get away with this!"

Their voices drifted away, and Teri breathed a sigh of relief. At least Kevin was still alive. She chanced a furtive look into the room and saw Denis waving his arms at Moira. Then he stormed out, slamming the door after him. Teri watched as the red-haired woman fidgeted with the belt of her quilted robe and nervously ran her fingers through her hair.

Hoping she had an ally in the other woman, Teri leaned over and tapped on the window with her fingernail. Moira glanced around the room, startled. Teri tapped again, and that brought Moira to the window.

Partially opening it, she asked quickly, "What are you doing here?"

"Is Kevin all right?"

Moira checked behind her, then said, "There's a little door at the back of the castle. Go there and wait for me."

Teri did. When Moira opened the door and slipped outside, Teri noticed a bruise on the side of her face. Quietly she asked, "What happened to you?"

"Denis," Moira whispered. "He's really gone over the edge this time. He dismissed Patrick's nanny today, and this evening he threw the boy across the room. Now he has Kevin tied up upstairs in his bedroom. I don't know what to do. If I notify the police, Denis says he'll kill Patrick and Kevin."

Great, Teri thought. *Out of the arms of one madman and into the arms of another.* "We'll work something out," she told Moira with false bravado. "We have to. Remember, there are two of us and only one of him."

"Yes, but you don't know how mean he can get when he's like this, and he has a gun," Moira said nervously.

"The first thing we have to do is to free Kevin."

"How? Denis is probably with him now."

"We've got to think of a way for you to get Denis out of the room while I get in." Teri thought a moment, then asked, "Does Denis have another gun?"

"Yes, he has a collection, but it's under lock and key."

"Where?"

"In the trophy room downstairs."

"Can we get there without anyone seeing us?"

"The servants are in their rooms on the other side of the castle. If Denis is upstairs, we should be able to... but if he catches us—"

"Let's worry about that when the time comes," Teri suggested.

Moira told her to wait while she went back inside to see if the coast was clear. Moments later, Teri followed her up several worn stone steps and down a dimly lit corridor, on either side of which hung huge family portraits. Teri glanced at the faces in the paintings and would have sworn they were staring at her as she passed by. She was happy to leave them behind when they entered the massive trophy room.

Unlike the other rooms in the castle, this one appeared to have been left almost unchanged for centuries. The air was dank and smelled of mildew. The only modern touches she noted were the iron wall sconces, which had been converted for electricity. On two of the walls were mounted heads of animals not indigenous to the country and weapon collections. A stone fireplace dominated the third; tall, Gothic windows, the fourth. It wasn't a room that Teri liked at all.

"The guns are kept in here," Moira whispered, going to a tall, carved oak chest. "Are you any good at picking locks?"

Teri shrugged. "I don't know."

"I've seen it done on television," Moira said. "You have to stick something in it."

Teri glanced at Moira. "Let me have one of your hairpins." When Moira handed one to her, she jammed it into the huge keyhole. Nothing happened. "This isn't big enough." Teri looked around and saw a display of knives on the wall nearby. "Maybe one of those."

She chose a knife with a long, slender blade and pulled it off its mount. Carefully she inserted the tip into the keyhole and began to probe, first one way, then the other. Both women heard a click, and Teri turned the bronze handle on the door. It opened.

Inside the chest was an array of rifles, some ancient with carved wooden handles. Moira opened the other door and exposed a variety of long-barreled pistols and several modern handguns, none of which Teri knew anything about.

Moira picked one up. "Denis calls this a snub-nosed revolver." She reached into a drawer at the bottom of the chest, withdrew a white cardboard box and set it on a nearby table. Then she pushed the little cylinder in the revolver and it swung out. Teri watched as Moira began to insert bullets into the eight chambers.

When she finished loading it, Moira said, "Denis would use his gun without batting an eye. He's so filled with hate he's beyond the point of reason right now." She pressed the bullet-packed cylinder in, and the sharp clicking noise made Teri jump. "Now that Kevin knows that Patrick is his son—"

"He knows?" Teri gasped.

Moira nodded. "And he's furious with me . . . and himself, I'm afraid."

Teri had known the time would come when all concerned would have to face up to the deception about Patrick. She had never thought it would happen over tea and crumpets, but she had never envisioned the confrontation taking place when people were armed and at their wits' end. And she knew that that was exactly the wrong time for people to have guns at their disposal.

"Let's not take the gun," Teri said quickly. "I was wrong in even suggesting it. We'll work out some other way of freeing Kevin."

"On the contrary." Moira's cold green eyes focused on the revolver. "I'm surprised I didn't think of this myself." She stroked the black metal, then looked at Teri. "I can't take any more from Denis. Abusing me verbally and physically is one thing, but when he attacks my son...Kevin's son—I hate Denis with all my heart, almost as much as I love Kevin."

So, Teri thought, *you really do love him.* Placing her hand on Moira's shoulder, she said, "Please, give me the gun."

Backing away, Moira put it into the side pocket of her quilted robe, whose wide skirt obscured the gun's presence. "I know you love Kevin, too, Teri." One red brow arched. "And he loves you. Could you really stand by and see Denis kill him?"

"Don't even talk like that. No one's going to kill anyone!"

"I will...if I have to."

Turning away, Teri ran her fingers through her hair. There was a possibility that the woman would do exactly that. Facing her again, Teri said quietly, "You must have loved Denis at one time."

"Denis?" Moira asked, as though Teri were saying the impossible. "I never loved him."

"Then for heaven's sake, why did you marry him?"

Moira's green eyes met Teri's dark ones for long moments, then she quietly closed the doors of the gun chest. Slipping her hands into the pockets of her robe, she said, "When a young girl with grand ideas is born in a small village and the future holds only drudgery, boredom and childbearing, the scene is already set for disaster." A faint smile eased onto her face, but it had more than a touch of sadness. "Do you know what book I used to read time and time again when I was a young girl? *Madame Bovary*. Have you read it?"

"Yes, but you're not—"

"Not like Emma?" she asked, and went to the tall windows nearby. "Do you remember how often she would look out a window and wish for a life more exciting than the one she had? She was a selfish, greedy woman. I'm not sure if I patterned my life after hers, or if I was born that way, but, like Emma, I'm terrified of boredom."

Teri joined her at the window. "But hasn't Patrick made a difference in your life? He must be very important to you."

"He is . . . at times, just as Kevin is."

"At times," Teri repeated, not certain if Moira's confession made her happy or sad.

But she didn't have long to consider that point. Moira's tone hardened with her next words. "Now all we have to do is figure out a way to get Denis out of his room."

The two women thought up several plans, but none seemed feasible. Then, finally, they came up with one that had a chance. . . .

After quietly hiding Teri in the service closet directly across from Denis's bedroom, Moira woke Patrick and got him settled in one of the servants' rooms that was temporarily unoccupied. Then she burst into Denis's room, and told him that Patrick had disappeared, that Denis's rough treatment had made the boy run away.

As soon as the man stormed from the bedroom and charged downstairs, with Moira close behind, Teri rushed from the closet. Her heart sank when she saw Kevin tied to a chair and gagged, but she spied a glimmer of hope in his eyes the moment he spotted her. Quickly she removed the gag. He gasped for air and began to work his jaw from side to side.

"Get me out of these ropes before he comes back," he said quietly.

Working as fast as she could, Teri asked, "Are you hurt?"

When one hand was free, he raised it to the back of his head. "I feel as if a tree fell on me."

As she unwound the final loops she glanced at the cut in Kevin's scalp and the dried blood in his hair. "It looks like one did."

He tossed the rope aside and jumped up. "Moira told Denis that Patrick was missing. Is he?"

"No, he's sleeping in one of the servants' rooms. It was the only way we could think of to get Denis out of here. We should get out of here, too!"

"Not without Patrick, and not before I take care of Denis."

He started for the door, and Teri followed. "Please, Kevin. He's got a gun."

"I know that."

She grabbed his arm with both hands. "If you don't care what happens to you, think of your son. Denis could hurt him again!"

Kevin's face froze, then his voice turned hard when he said, "Now I know why you were always so concerned about Patrick. You knew he was my son. Moira told you that evening we were here, didn't she?''

Teri lowered her eyes and nodded.

''When were you going to tell me? After we set up house in New York?''

Her eyelids flicked up. ''That's not fair.''

''There's no time to thrash that out right now.'' He bolted from the room.

''Kevin!'' Teri called, running after him.

The picture that greeted her when she reached the top of the long stairway turned her blood cold. Kevin was halfway down the stairs, his body like a statue. Denis was standing at the bottom, his gun aimed directly at the man glaring down at him. Moira stood motionless several feet away from her husband.

''Almost rescued,'' Denis said, grinning. ''But not quite.'' He took one slow step up toward Kevin. ''Let me be the one to tell you that your son is missing. A prince captured by Gypsies, no doubt.'' His insane laughter bounced off the stone walls of the entry hall.

Kevin's eyes darted to the barrel of the gun and back to Denis's smiling face. ''Why in hell did you pretend to be Patrick's father all these years? I can't believe you ever cared about him for one second.''

Taking another step up, Denis said grimly, ''I hated the little bastard.'' Immediately his voice turned light-hearted. ''That's what he is, you know.'' He tilted his head slightly toward Moira, who was now at the bottom of the staircase, her hand in the pocket of her robe. ''Isn't that right, my love?''

''Yes, Denis,'' she answered quietly, as though to placate him.

His wide eyes shot back to Kevin. "And it was such a great pleasure owning something of yours, old friend."

Still watching the gun and waiting for the right moment, Kevin said, "We've never been friends. You've never had a real friend in your entire life. Men like you don't know what friendship or love is. You'll go to your grave never experiencing what it is to be liked or loved."

"Please, Kevin," Teri whispered down to him, "don't say anything else."

"Get back," he told her as he saw Denis take another step nearer.

Aiming the gun at Teri, Denis said, "No, no...stay. I want you to see your lover's blood color the beautiful carpet." He glanced down at the maroon carpet. "Ah, but it's so much like the color of blood already."

The instant Kevin moved, Denis jerked his head up and glared at him with coal-black eyes. "Anxious to get it over with, aren't you? You'd like to deprive me of even these few moments. Well, have it your way for the last time." He raised the gun and took aim at Kevin's heart, and Teri gasped.

"Denis!" Moira called.

He spun halfway around—and saw the revolver she had pointed at him. Immediately he flattened his body against the wall, keeping his gun trained on Kevin.

"My love," Denis asked, confusion in his smile, "what are you thinking?" He began to inch his way down the steps toward her.

Not budging, Moira said, "I'm thinking what a favor I'd be doing the world if I pulled this trigger."

Trying to watch both her and Kevin, Denis moved slowly down another step. "You can go with him, if you want," he said cheerfully, "and even take Patrick with you. You can get an annulment, and I'll make you a nice settlement. That's what you've always wanted—" he aimed his gun at her and shouted "—isn't it?"

The first shot fired sounded like the roar of a cannon. The harsh sound careered off the stone walls and echoed throughout the castle. Teri turned away and screamed. The second shot followed almost instantly, and Kevin charged up the stairs and grabbed Teri in his arms, turning her back to the sight that held him transfixed.

A third shot was followed by a fourth, then a fifth and a sixth.

Teri held tightly to Kevin, shaking, her head vibrating with each resounding crack of gunfire.

"For God's sake, stop it!" Kevin yelled.

An awful silence followed.

Teri felt the hammer of Kevin's heartbeat and the rise and fall of his chest against her breasts. Her eyes were filled with tears, and she raised trembling fingers to wipe them as she turned slowly and gazed down the long, curved stairway.

CHAPTER THIRTEEN

Sprawled facedown over the bottom steps of the stairway, quite still, was Denis. Moira's cold eyes were fixed on her husband; the gun was still in her hand.

Teri shuddered and turned away, but then she heard the sound of hard metal falling on the stone floor. Looking down again, she saw that Moira had dropped the gun. The woman swayed for a moment, then crumpled in a heap only feet away from her husband.

"There's a phone in Denis's room," Kevin said quickly. "Dial 999, the emergency number. Tell them we need an ambulance." He charged down the stairs, two at a time, went to Moira and lifted her in his arms. When he glanced up, he saw Teri staring down at them. "Hurry!" he yelled, starting up the staircase.

Teri did as Kevin said, and when she returned she found that Kevin had placed Moira on the canopied bed in her bedroom. The woman's eyes were open, but she didn't seem to see him or hear anything he was saying.

"She's in shock," Kevin explained, placing a cover over her.

"Patrick!" Teri murmured. She hurried from the room to find him.

The gunfire had awakened the servants, who were gaping in horror and bewilderment at the body lying on the stairs. Liam, Denis's manservant, led Teri to the servants' wing while Kevin tried to calm the others.

She found Patrick crouched on top of the bed, crying and frightened by the sounds she knew he must have heard. Teri took him in her arms and did her best to comfort him and assure him that everything would be all right, but she had to wonder about that herself. She didn't know how any of them were going to get through the next few hours—or the next few days, for that matter.

How would a seven-year-old boy be able to accept the fact that his mother had killed his father? *The man he thought was his father,* she amended. How was anyone going to explain to Patrick that the man he had called "father" all his life had no right to that name?

No, she told herself as she held the sobbing boy in her arms, she couldn't really assure him that everything would be all right. Everyone, it seemed to her, had different roles to play now, particularly Kevin. Teri had seen the concern on his face as he had carried Patrick's mother up the stairs. Would that concern become something more?

She well understood that Kevin had left her more than a decade ago because of a so-called duty to Moira, but that duty paled before the one Teri knew he would feel now. The bond that he shared with Moira—their son, Patrick—had to be stronger than any Kevin might have felt so long ago.

No, Teri wasn't at all confident that everything would be all right.

As she glanced down at the boy, who had fallen asleep in her arms, she felt a hand touch her shoulder. She looked up to see Kevin standing over them.

"The police will be here soon," he told her quietly, sitting down on the bed and putting his arm around her. "I'm so very sorry you had to get involved in all this."

Teri didn't have the heart to tell him about her earlier experience at the turf plant; he had so many problems facing him now. Softly she asked, "What are we going to do about Patrick?"

"I'm going to take him up to bed. Let's use the servants' stairway. That way we can avoid the mob out there."

Carefully Kevin lifted the sleeping Patrick from her arms and carried him out of the room. Teri followed them, and upstairs he tucked the boy in his bed.

"Kevin," Patrick mumbled, his sleepy eyes mere slits, "when did you come back?"

Brushing the boy's blond hair away from his forehead, Kevin replied, "A while ago, so—" He stopped before the word "son" passed his lips. "A little while ago. Now you get back to sleep, okay?"

"Okay. Are you going to be here when I wake up?"

"We'll both be right here."

"Promise?"

"We promise, don't we, Teri?"

"Yes," she said, smiling down at the boy.

Patrick rolled onto his side, then tilted his head toward Kevin. "What was all that noise before? It scared me."

Stroking his head, he told him, "We'll talk about it in the morning. Now it's time to sleep. I'll look in on you later." Kevin's face clouded with anxiety, then he leaned down and kissed his son's forehead.

Teri turned away. She had thought she had no tears left, but seeing how tenderly Kevin treated Patrick, she found there were indeed tears yet to be shed: for Patrick, for her and for the future she and Kevin might have had together.

After he closed the door behind them, Kevin braced his shoulder against the wall and ran his fingers through his hair. "Well, now we wait for the ambulance and the police. How are you holding up, luv?"

Teri saw the anguish in his eyes and managed a strained smile. "I'm too exhausted to fall down. About the police, though, do we tell them everything?"

"Not about Patrick...just that we were visiting, and his parents had a family squabble."

"And each of them had a gun? Do you think they'll settle for that?"

"That's their problem. We have our own."

"Yes, we do, don't we?" she said softly, and started toward the stairs.

A half hour later, Moira was taken away in an ambulance just as the police arrived. After hearing Kevin's story they were dubious, to say the least, and told him and Teri they would have to stay in Limerick for the inquest. Teri glanced over at Kevin, wondering how the Dublin police were going to feel about that. If things kept up the way they were going, she thought, pretty soon she and Kevin would be at the top of the most-wanted-by-the-authorities list in Ireland.

While Teri prepared for bed, Kevin checked on Patrick. He returned, satisfied that the boy was asleep. Then he undressed, slipped down beside Teri and held her in his arms.

"I need you more than ever now," he whispered. "I hate asking you to share all these problems with me, but I'm so damn glad you're here. I don't know what I'd do if you weren't."

Teri smiled against Kevin's neck. *He needs me,* she repeated silently, feeling a surge of love for him.

Stroking her arm with his hand, he said, "In the morning I'm going to phone Officer Crowley in Dublin and let him know what happened. I'm sure he'll be thrilled to hear from me."

"Archcriminal that you are," Teri said dryly.

"I'm also going to see if I can talk to the minister. There's no telling what kinds of stories will be circulating tomorrow when all this hits the news."

"He knows you pretty well, doesn't he?"

"Yes, but I want him to hear about it from me and let him know that I'll be here until after Denis's funeral."

Teri hadn't thought that far ahead. Moving her fingertips over his shoulder, she asked, "When are you going to tell Patrick what happened tonight?"

"Oh, God," Kevin moaned, staring up at the ceiling. "I've got to do it first thing in the morning before he finds out from anyone else." He glanced at the antique porcelain clock on the night table. "In about two hours, in fact. He'll be waking up by then. I don't dare fall asleep." Gently he placed his fingers over Teri's eyes and eased down the lids. "That doesn't mean you can't. I won't wake you when I get up. Just let me hold you for a while."

As she nestled against him, Teri tried to hold fast to the feel of Kevin's arms about her, to burn it into her memory. She was all too aware that a new life lay ahead of him, one that couldn't possibly include her.

A LITTLE AFTER DAWN, Kevin went to Patrick's room, awakened him and suggested they take a walk down by the river before breakfast. Once they reached the bank, Kevin sat down on the grass, and Patrick plopped down beside him, resting his crossed arms on Kevin's raised knee. Looking down at him, Kevin realized just how difficult the task ahead of him would be.

"Patrick," he began, "last night…" The words were hard in coming.

"I know," the boy said, an expression too worrisome for one so young on his face. "They were fighting again. I heard them when I first went to bed."

Kevin placed a hand on his son's shoulder. "Yes, they were, but then there was an accident." He decided just to come out with it. "There was a gun, and Denis—" No, he couldn't tell him the entire truth, not all at once. "And your father was accidentally shot."

His blue eyes trained on Kevin's, Patrick asked in an emotionless voice, "Is he dead?"

Kevin nodded and watched as Patrick lay down on the grass, clasped his hands behind his head and stared up at the elm tree branches overhead.

"I'm sorry," Kevin said quietly.

"I hate guns," the boy mumbled. "Father always said I'd have to learn to use one so I could go hunting." He looked up at Kevin. "Why would anyone want to shoot an animal?"

Looking out at the clear blue water of the River Shannon, Kevin told him, "Some people think of it as a sport, but I agree with you. I don't like guns, either."

"I even hate to go into the trophy room. All those heads stuck up on the wall. It's kinda scary." Patrick rolled over onto his stomach and gazed up at Kevin. "Is Mother all right?"

Kevin looked down at him and nodded. "Yes, but she's very upset about what happened. The doctor thought she should rest in the hospital for a while."

"Did she shoot him?"

Patrick's question hit Kevin like a bolt of lightning, and he had to wonder just how bad the boy's life had been for him to ask that so bluntly. Yet he wasn't going to lie; he knew Patrick would hear about the shooting sooner or later. "Yes," he said, "but it was an accident."

Suddenly Kevin knew he could not yet tell Patrick that Denis was not his father. He didn't know when he would be able to tell the boy, but the time would have to be just right.

For a while they were silent, then Patrick asked, "Do all married people fight the way Mother and Father did?"

Kevin lowered himself onto his elbows. After picking up a fallen leaf and doubling it over in his fingers, he said, "No. Sometimes they have disagreements, and sometimes they even yell at each other, but—" *But what?* Kevin thought. *But they don't hate the sight of each other the way Denis and Moira did?* "But it usually doesn't last long, and they make up," he said with a tentative smile. "With married people, that's half the fun of arguing."

"Are you going to marry Teri?"

Kevin's smile came to life and he laughed softly. "I hope so, but it looks as though I'm going to have a hard time persuading her."

"You'd never hit her, would you?"

Immediately Kevin said, "No, never. I love her very much—too much ever to hurt her in any way." *It's true, Teri,* he thought, gazing back at the castle, but he wondered if he'd ever be able to convince her of that. Facing Patrick again, he asked, "You like Teri, don't you?" When his son remained silent, Kevin felt a terrible tenseness in his chest. "Don't you?" he asked again.

Without looking at Kevin, Patrick asked, "If you marry her, can we still be friends?"

"Hey, partner," Kevin said, putting his hand on the boy's shoulder, "we're best friends, and we always will be. Don't you *ever* forget that."

"Okay," he said, smiling, "I like her." Then he asked, "When can we visit Mother?"

Kevin pushed himself up from the grass and pulled Patrick up next to him. "I think we ought to let her rest some. Right now it's breakfast time and I'm starving. How about you? Are you hungry?"

"Not very."

"Sure you are. C'mon, I'll race you back to the house."

AFTER BREAKFAST Kevin phoned Maude and Ian Healy, Moira's parents, who lived in Bantry. They arrived in Limerick in the afternoon and went directly to the hospital to see their daughter. When they reached the estate, they reported that Moira was still weak and disoriented and had no recollection of the shooting. Her doctor wasn't able to say when or if she ever would.

Denis's "odd" brother also made an appearance, declaring that the "wee folk" had caused the whole thing and that he was next on their list. Sundry other relatives showed up throughout the day, but more out of curiosity, Teri thought, than honest affection. Only a few said they would return for the funeral; the arrangements had been left to Kevin.

Late that afternoon Teri talked to Colleen on the phone for a long time, and in between trying to reassure her friend, she managed to tell her about the items mixed in with their merchandise and why she didn't know exactly when she would be able to leave Ireland.

While Kevin handled the comings and goings of Denis's relatives, Teri stayed close to Patrick. She found it highly distasteful when several of the boy's relatives commented on what a wealthy lad he was going to be, and she tried to steer him away when such conversations began. But mainly she was concerned that he showed no signs of grief for Denis or great worry for his mother. She couldn't bring herself to believe that the boy felt so distant from the man and woman who had raised him. Perhaps, she thought, the grief would come later.

Teri took an instant liking to Maude and Ian, but it soon became obvious to her that Ian was not a well man. Chronic emphysema, she was later to find out. She did have to wonder how such nice people could have raised a daughter like Moira. Maude and Ian were simple folk who appeared uncomfortable with the grandeur of the castle and the service heaped upon them. In the quiet of the evening, after Kevin took Patrick up to bed, they reminisced about their daughter's younger days and how they had watched her and Kevin grow up together. Maude was quite frank as she told Kevin how disappointed she and her husband had been when Moira had broken her engagement to him. It became quite clear to Teri that Moira's parents felt a deep affection for Kevin, and she wasn't too surprised that they didn't speak a word about their daughter's life with Denis or even mention his name.

The following day, while Kevin went into Limerick to check on Moira's condition and make the final arrangements for Denis's funeral, Teri and Patrick went off by themselves, horseback riding in the morning, then picnicking in a jaunting car in the afternoon. When Kevin returned, he told Patrick his mother still needed a few more days' rest before she could have visitors.

After church on Sunday, to keep the boy occupied the day before the funeral, Kevin and Teri took him fishing in a boat on the River Shannon. Still she waited for Patrick to express his grief, and still there was no sign of any.

When they got back to the castle, a police officer was waiting for them.

"Mr. O'Shea," he said, "I'm sorry to trouble you, but another situation has arisen."

Deciding that whatever the officer had to say it was probably nothing Patrick should hear, Teri said to him, "Let's go see if any of that chocolate cake your grandmother made is left."

"Save some for me," Kevin told them, nodding to Teri as the two of them left the room.

"How can I help you?" Kevin asked the officer.

"Did Mr. Fitzgerald ever mention a Peter Quinn to you?"

Kevin thought a moment, then shook his head. "No, the name doesn't sound familiar. Why?"

"He was found in Fitzgerald's turf plant...dead."

"Dead," Kevin repeated quietly. "Do you have any idea what he was doing there?"

The officer shook his head. "It looks as though he fell or was pushed from one of the landings. We may never know which."

"None of the workers at the plant were of any help, I'm guessing," Kevin said.

"Not a bit, but since neither Fitzgerald nor his wife are available for comment, I thought that perhaps you had heard of Quinn. He was from Belfast."

"No, I can't remember Denis or Moira ever having talked about him."

"Well, we're keeping his death quiet until we can do some further checking."

Wondering how the man named Peter Quinn fitted into the picture, Kevin walked the officer to his automobile. As soon as the man got into his car and drove away, Teri, who had come to the doorway, walked over to Kevin.

He put his arm around her and said sincerely, "Thanks for taking Patrick out of the room when you did. With Denis's funeral coming up tomorrow, I'm glad Patrick didn't hear any more about people dying."

"Dying? Who died?"

"Some man by the name of Peter Quinn. He was found in Denis's turf plant."

Teri blanched. She had known she would have to tell Kevin about the man who had chased her in the plant, but with Denis's funeral and the inquest yet to come, she hadn't wanted to add to his worries. What to do? she wondered, realizing that it was Peter Quinn's car she had parked under the trees. In all the turmoil, Kevin hadn't even asked her how she had gotten to the estate.

"What's the matter?" he asked, breaking into her deep concentration.

Teri sighed, wondering if she and Kevin would ever again have casual conversation about the weather or what to have for dinner. "Kevin," she said with little joy, "there's something I haven't told you."

Smiling, he asked, "What?"

"Well," she began, "you never asked why I didn't take the shuttle flight to Dublin when you failed to show up at the hotel."

"And I'm damn glad you didn't. You realize that you saved my life, and maybe Patrick's and Moira's, too, don't you?"

Taking Kevin's arm, she led him toward the driveway. "When you weren't back by four o'clock, I phoned Seamus's office."

Teri proceeded to tell a wide-eyed Kevin what happened. When she got to the part about Peter Quinn driving her to the turf plant, Kevin stopped, his mouth agape.

She tried to minimize the terror she had felt as she told him about Quinn's chasing her with the knife and how he had come at her, only to fall to his death. But as she mentally relived the experience, a tight, sickening sensation grabbed at her insides. That was soon forgotten, however, when she saw how red Kevin's face had become.

She jumped when he bellowed, "Why didn't you tell me this before?"

Why was he so angry with her? she wondered. She was the one who had almost been killed. Touching his arm, she said calmly, "You have enough problems to cope with right now. I didn't want to add to them."

Kevin pulled her close and wrapped his arms around her. "What the hell have I gotten you into?" he asked, holding her tightly.

"It turned out all right, though. I wasn't hurt."

He gently let go of her, and held her at arm's length. Now his neck was beet red, too. "But someone is going to be when I find out who's in back of this business."

Quietly Teri asked, "Isn't it obvious that Seamus told Quinn where I was?"

"Seamus?" Kevin shook his head. "No, I can't believe that. Quinn must have followed us to the Limerick Ryan."

"But he wanted to know where you were. If he—or someone—wanted us silenced so badly, why would he have waited until after you left to get to me?"

Kevin shrugged. "Someone else could have followed us, and Quinn might have thought it would be easy to get me once I learned he had you."

"That's possible," Teri admitted, but she felt it was just too difficult for Kevin to face what could be the truth about Seamus McFadden.

A grim determination colored Kevin's words when he said, "I'm going to find out just how possible it is as soon as we get to Dublin."

"There's something else," Teri said weakly.

Giving her an anxious stare, he asked, "What?"

"I drove Peter Quinn's car here. It's still parked just beyond those trees."

Kevin scanned the elm trees, but couldn't see the car.

"I drove it back," she told him, and asked, "Should we tell the police it's here?"

He thought hard for several moments before saying, "The funeral's tomorrow and the inquest is the day after. Then we've got to get back to Dublin to square things with Officer Crowley. But if we tell the police now about Quinn coming after you, I don't know how long we'd be stuck here while they investigated."

"Then let's not tell them now," she suggested.

Kevin nodded. "When we get back to Dublin, we'll tell Crowley what happened, and he can have the Limerick police pick up the car and go over it."

THE FOLLOWING MORNING, in a brief ceremony, Denis was laid to rest in the family vault. Teri and Kevin were both thankful the Irish rains had held off until they returned to the castle.

Those of Denis's well-heeled relatives who did attend departed shortly after they sampled the buffet served at the estate. Teri couldn't help but notice how relieved they all seemed to be that Kevin was assuming responsibility for Denis's son in Moira's absence. She was still in the hospital, her condition unchanged. Kevin had also tracked down Patrick's nanny and rehired her.

Teri dreaded the inquest, but she and Kevin stuck to their original story: they had come out of their rooms upon hearing the shots and had found Denis dead and Moira in a faint. They knew no more than that. The session proved short, and further inquiry was tabled, pending Moira's recovery.

Their farewell to Patrick early in the afternoon was difficult, particularly for Kevin, but he knew the boy would be in the loving and capable hands of his nanny and his grandparents, who had agreed to stay on and care for him until their daughter was well enough to return home.

As they drove away from the castle, Teri waved once more to Patrick, then looked over at Kevin. "It's hard to leave him, isn't it?" she asked, noting Kevin's troubled expression.

He nodded. "Patrick and I have so much lost time to make up for, but I've got to get this business with the Dublin police over with before I—" he glanced over at Teri and chuckled wryly "—before I sit him on my knee and say, 'Well, lad, guess what? I'm your father.'"

Teri knew Kevin was hurting, so she laid her hand on his thigh and said lightly, "I'm sure you'll come up with something more subtle than that."

"I wonder just how much I should tell him. When I was seven, I'm not sure I would have understood how adults could foul things up so much."

"Maybe things aren't as fouled up as you think. Patrick could do a lot worse than getting you for a father."

Looking straight ahead at the road, he said, "Or you for a mother."

"You're forgetting one little thing," Teri told him uneasily. "He already has a mother."

"I phoned the psychiatrist at the hospital before we left. He said that Moira has psychogenic amnesia, a disassociative reaction. He explained it as an unconscious flight from a situation of intolerable psychological stress."

"That's easy to believe, considering what happened. Who would want to remember something like that?"

Teri looked out at the rolling green hills, not really seeing anything. God, she thought, how people's lives could be changed in minutes. And the repercussions of the events of that terrible night had yet to be felt entirely. Looking back at Kevin, she said, "How do you think Maude and Ian will take the fact that you're Patrick's father? They're going to have to know."

"I hate to say it, but in one way I think they'll be relieved. I want to wait until Moira is feeling better, though, before I tell them. Right now she's running a fever, and they're keeping her pretty well medicated." Knowing the topic was difficult for Teri, Kevin changed the subject. "I'm also anxious to find out how Seamus is doing. With all that's been going on, I haven't given much thought to our other difficulties.''

Difficulties? Teri thought. *That's putting it mildly....*

They finally arrived in Dublin, their moods in deep contrast to the jovial ones of the city's inhabitants; Dublin was in the midst of its year-long millennium celebration.

The Street Carnival was in full swing; there was color everywhere. Traffic was stopped as the lord mayor's parade passed by, and on corner after corner, Teri saw young people and elders playing ancient and modern musical instruments while passersby and pub patrons came out onto the streets to sing Irish songs and dance to traditional Irish music.

When they at last reached Seamus's offices, they found that the moods there matched their own.

Wringing her hands, Fiona told them, ''The driver of the truck, the man who was in a coma...he died this morning. And this afternoon Seamus was called to police headquarters again.''

''Is that where he is now?'' Kevin asked.

''No. He phoned a few minutes ago to tell me he was going home.''

''That makes a fourth murder charge hanging over someone,'' Teri said quietly.

''But why Seamus?'' Fiona asked, focusing first on Kevin, then Teri, who offered her a look of sympathy. ''We've been trying to keep on here, to continue with the work, but no one's heart is in it. We're all too worried about him.''

Teri still wasn't convinced the police had the wrong man, but to calm Fiona she asked, ''Have the police checked out all the employees?''

"They haven't let us alone! Each and every box we ship now is gone over. If they ask me one more time about how long you and Kevin were in the mailing room alone, I think I'll scream. And poor Margaret! She has a heart condition, you know."

Kevin nodded. "I know. How is she?"

"Her doctor has her on tranquilizers. She sleeps quite a bit."

Teri remembered how sweet and gentle Seamus's wife had been the evening of Bonfire Night. Imagining what the woman must be going through started to tilt Teri's thinking toward Kevin's, and she dearly hoped Seamus wasn't the man in back of the smuggling operation.

Fiona crossed her arms and leaned back against her desk. "Seamus was so sure Denis Fitzgerald was involved somehow, but then we heard the news about his death."

Teri glanced over at Kevin, who had an arm propped on top of a file cabinet. His face was expressionless. Looking back at Fiona, she said tentatively, "That doesn't mean he wasn't involved...."

"I'm not so sure now," Kevin said slowly, causing Teri to turn her head in surprise. "He was very convincing when he accused me of trying to implicate him."

"Well, someone has to be responsible for this sordid business," Fiona said.

"Gary Dillon or Peter Quinn, maybe," Teri commented.

Fiona asked, "Who are they?"

After checking his watch, Kevin explained, "Dillon used to be the manager at the Fitzgerald turf plant. He was in charge of crating the hijacked artifacts. It might be coincidence, but the man just came into some money and bought property in Silvermines."

"And Peter Quinn?" Fiona asked.

"A horrible man," Teri said. "He actually tried to kill me, but he wound up killing himself."

Fiona turned pale. "Oh, my God!" Slowly she walked around her desk, sat down, then looked up at Teri with sharp and assessing eyes. "You've told the police, haven't you?"

"Not yet," Kevin said. "But I'm hoping they'll be able to establish a connection between the two men. And if the police can tie Quinn to Denis somehow, it should clear up a lot of things."

"Fiona," Teri inquired, "did Seamus ever get the message I left when I phoned from the Limerick Ryan?"

"Message?" she repeated, pausing as though trying to remember. "I left it on his desk when I finally had to leave. I assume he did."

"That reminds me," Kevin said. "May I use your phone?"

"Certainly." Fiona gestured toward the phone on her desk.

Kevin dialed police headquarters and asked for Officer Crowley, but was told the man had gone to Belfast on business and would be there for two more days. Kevin didn't leave his name but said he'd call back.

"That's one problem that's been postponed," he said to Teri with a grin, then told Fiona, "We've got to be going."

Fiona rose from behind her desk. "Teresa, your merchandise arrived from Cork. Would you like to see it before it's shipped?"

Teri laughed ruefully. "I think not."

"I can't say I blame you," Fiona admitted, "but I've gone over the items and so have the police. Everything is in excellent shape."

"Thank you. I appreciate your efforts."

"Oh," Fiona said quickly, "are you still at the Royal Dublin? In case I need to contact you regarding your shipments."

"No," Kevin told her, "Teri will be staying with me until this smuggling business is settled."

Fiona smiled pleasantly. "Good. Hotels can be so cold."

After saying their goodbyes, Teri and Kevin left the office. Seconds later, Fiona opened the door and peered out to see them start down the stairway. Quickly she went back to her desk, picked up the phone and dialed a number in Dublin, tapping the pad on her desk with a long fingernail as she waited.

"Gary," she said quietly, "Peter is dead, and we still have a problem . . . two to be exact."

CHAPTER FOURTEEN

ON THE WAY to the town house, Kevin and Teri stopped to pick up some groceries, and when they arrived home, he opened a few windows to air out the rooms, while Teri began to unpack.

"How does a boiled dinner sound?" he asked as she unzipped her garment bag and hung her clothes on the metal rack in the closet.

She looked over at him and smiled. "Boiled what?"

He leaned back against the dresser and watched her as she moved. "Corned beef and cabbage with parsley potatoes. We'll have some Guinness stout with it."

"Sounds good to me. Let me finish here, and I'll help."

"Uh-uh. You go ahead and shower if you like. I'll get things started. It's been a long day."

When she glanced over at Kevin, she guessed that he was thinking of Patrick again. She went to him and put her hands on his shoulders. "You've been through a lot in the past few days, haven't you?"

He slipped his arms around her waist and corrected her. "Haven't *we*?"

"Yes . . . we," she agreed softly, becoming more concerned when Kevin's smile waned and he went to the bed and sat down. She saw him lean forward, put his elbows on his knees and rest his forehead on his fingertips.

Sitting down beside him, she placed her hand on his shoulder. "You're worried about Patrick, aren't you?"

"Yes." He clasped his hands together and looked at her. "I hated to leave him this morning."

"Maude and Ian will take excellent care of him. They adore Patrick."

He nodded, then paused before saying, "Suddenly my whole life has been turned upside down. And to be honest, I don't know how I'm going to do as a father." He lay back on the bed and ran tense fingers over his brow. "I still don't know how to tell him the truth. I'm so damn scared of what his reaction will be."

Teri eased herself down next to him. "I'm guessing you'll be pleasantly surprised. Patrick loves you, Kevin, and with you he'll have a feeling of security that he's probably never had."

He looked at her hopefully. "You really think so?"

"I know so." She ran a gentle finger over his chin, and warmth echoed in her voice when she asked, "What's not to love about you?"

Grinning broadly, he told her, "You're just after my gourmet cooking."

"Among other things," she said, slowly trailing her finger down his throat.

"Don't do that," he warned, taking her finger and kissing it, "or I'll send you to bed without supper."

"See, you're getting the hang of being a parent already."

He reached around her, and when she put her cheek on his chest, he began to stroke her soft hair. "What do I do if he gets sick, or has an accident?"

"You call a doctor. Parents have been doing that for ages."

"How'd you get so smart about raising children?"

"I read a lot," she said playfully.

"Good, then I won't have to worry. You can take care of Patrick when he's sick."

Teri raised herself slightly and looked down at him. "Oh? What are you planning to do? Send him to Manhattan when he's not feeling well?"

Blue-green eyes searched her dark brown ones, then he said, "You know, you sound like a broken record sometimes."

"And sometimes you don't listen." She got up and started to move clothing from her suitcase to dresser drawers.

Kevin sat up. "That's because I don't want to hear what you say at times."

"Like, 'I'm going home'?"

"Exactly. I need you here. Patrick needs you here. This is where home is for you."

Teri looked into the mirror at Kevin's reflected image. With an aching heart, she told him, "Patrick needs a mother and a father, and he already has both." Immediately she busied herself, again remembering what Moira had told her: that she wanted Kevin, Patrick and herself to be the family they really were.

"I don't think about Moira the way I think about you. Doesn't that count?"

"You've got to think about what's best for Patrick."

"To the exclusion of everything else?"

She ignored his question. "Just as you said, he needs some stability in his life. Having his real father and his real mother will give it to him. The three of you are as *real* as a family can get."

"We're *real* in name only. You know that." He got up, moved behind her and put his arms around her waist. "A real home has love in it, and I love you. I've loved you ever since that week we spent together in New York, and we've got a lot of lost years to make up for."

"Just as you and Patrick do," Teri whispered, feeling Kevin caress her back. Not daring to meet his gaze in the mirror, she said, "And you're both going to have to give Moira a great deal of love and attention if she's ever to get well again."

Kevin didn't respond, but Teri felt his lips brush the side of her neck and his body press more firmly against her back. Automatically she crossed her arms, bemoaning the fact that although her words had sounded so noble, she didn't at all feel that way. She wanted a life with Kevin and with Patrick—but not at Moira's expense.

Teri had lain awake at night, fantasizing about marrying Kevin and building a life with Patrick and him. But the lovely dream had come crashing down around her when she thought of Moira recuperating from her illness, only to find that Teri had robbed her of her son and the man she loved and had killed for.

"Stay here and marry me," Kevin whispered. "Let's not let happiness get away from us a second time. Colleen told you she had everything under control at the shop, and Charlie's got a good job. You can visit your parents whenever you want. Maybe they'd like to spend half the year here in Ireland and have more time with their grandchildren."

Teri whirled around in his arms, her eyes wide and strained. "It all sounds so simple, so easy, doesn't it?"

She pushed his arms away and started toward the window, knowing she was becoming more upset than she had reason to. But she couldn't help it. Once more he was taking it for granted that she wanted to live in Ireland. And just as Moira had predicted, because Kevin felt duty-bound to his country, he expected Teri to feel the same way. That only confirmed where she remained on his list of priorities, and the realization stung bitterly.

Facing him, she blurted out, "You don't even listen to what I say sometimes. Why won't you believe that I'm not ready to cut my ties back home and move here? If you think your life has been turned upside down, what do you think would happen to mine if I did what you wanted? Sure, you'd have a ready-made family, but what about all the adjustments you're expecting me to make? Believe it or not, Kevin, I do have a life of my own in New York. I love the theaters, the museums, and I'm used to the excitement and the fast pace of life."

Kevin shoved his hands in his pockets and fixed hurt eyes on her. "Dublin isn't exactly the end of the world. It has the National Theatre, its own opera company, more museums than you'd have time to check out. And, if you've noticed, we have running water, too."

"Don't be snide," she murmured.

"I won't be if you'll stop seeing problems where there aren't any."

"'Aren't any'?" she repeated in disbelief. "What makes you so sure you're going to get custody of Patrick? Do you think Moira is going to happily hand her son over to another woman? Get real, Kevin!" She sank into the chair near the window and fidgeted with her fingers.

He could feel the heat rising on his neck, but he ordered himself to be calm, knowing that one of them had to be. Slowly he moved to the corner of the bed, nearer to her. "If there's going to be a custody battle, I'm certain the Irish courts will decide in my favor. Denis told me he couldn't father a child, and his medical records would prove it. And Moira's adultery would brand her an unfit mother in any court. Remember, Ireland is ninety-four percent Roman Catholic. Adultery is not taken lightly.''

Not believing Kevin had just said what he had, Teri stared blankly at him. There was anger in her voice when she asked, ''Would the courts think you a fit father? Would you expect them to believe that you were half-conscious at the time you helped conceive Patrick?''

The heat on his neck shot up to his scalp, and he squeezed the brass rail at the foot of the bed. ''You have a point,'' he admitted. ''But there's also the little matter of her facing a murder charge.''

Coming to Moira's defense again, Teri reminded him, ''She shot Denis to save your life.''

''Six times?''

Teri jumped up, stormed toward the bedroom door and asked, ''Oh, what's the use of dragging all that up?''

He was right behind her when she rushed downstairs. ''Because there are things we need to get settled!''

She said nothing, and he watched glumly as she sat down on the sofa. His hands on his hips, he said, ''There are things we need to get out in the open, things we need to talk about.''

Her eyes trained on the fireplace, she said, ''I don't feel like talking.''

''Wonderful! Women, the great communicators. You blast that premise all to hell.''

''All right! We'll talk!'' she shouted.

''Good!'' he bellowed back, then lowered his voice. ''Do you want a drink?''

''No.''

''Mind if I have one?''

''It's your home.''

"Thank you for not objecting." He started toward the bar cart across the room. "You do that so well, by the way."

"Do what?"

He glanced back at her over his shoulder. "Object to almost every damn thing I say, that's what."

"Not everything," she said quietly.

As he poured himself his drink—neat—he mumbled, "Just about everything." He took a healthy swallow, then began pacing in front of her. "I read somewhere that the main reason most marriages break up is a lack of communication. I'd like us to communicate... like adults, intelligently and calmly." She said nothing, so he asked, "Agreed?"

She lifted doubtful eyes to meet his, and she nodded.

"Great. Now I have a life here in Ireland and you have a life in America. I've already said I'd relocate there, and you dismissed that idea."

"Because it wouldn't work," she said flatly.

"Oh, I understand. You see the future, too."

"You'd be miserable, and you know it."

"Probably, but I'd be willing to give it a try. You won't even do that. What is it? Will Wall Street collapse and shock waves echo around the world if you spend six months here to see if life with me is bearable?"

She looked up again and grinned. "You said we were going to be adult about this."

His mouth twisted wryly, and after he took another swallow of Irish whiskey, he said, "All right. Now that I've communicated, it's your turn."

Teri just wanted to put her head under the pillow on her bed upstairs and go to sleep. She didn't need this aggravation, and she never realized that communicating could be so painful. Looking at Kevin, though, she saw that he was hurting, too. That made her feel even more miserable.

In a serious and quiet tone, she said, "I don't even know what role you would expect me to play as your wife. All of a sudden you want me to assume responsibility for Patrick. You'd probably also expect me to run the household while you were off on trips to the Orient and God knows where else. That wouldn't give me very much time for what I might want out of life. I don't even know if you'd really accept the fact that I have career ambitions."

"That's no—"

Immediately she raised a hand. "Wait, let me finish. I got the good ol' 'Sure, go ahead and have a career' from Angelo before we were married. But it was a totally different thing afterward. I don't want to go that route again. I'm just not prepared to."

As he sat down next to her, Kevin's expression softened. "Look, it's hard for me to admit that I don't have all the answers, but I don't. And you're right, there would be difficulties ahead of us. But we can work them out together. I'd give a little and you'd give a little. We would compromise."

Teri wasn't sure they could. What Kevin saw as "difficulties," she saw as insurmountable problems. She also realized that once she committed herself totally to him, there would be no turning back. And frankly, that scared the hell out of her.

"I don't know," she said, shaking her head. "I'm too confused and too tired even to think straight right now."

"I bet you're hungry, too." He flashed her an intimate smile that charmed and disarmed her at the same time. "That's why you've been jumping all over me like a bear.'' His eyes widened. "Dinner! Damn, I forgot all about it.'' He stood quickly and was just about to ask her to help, but instead said, "Go take that shower. It'll relax you. Not that you need relaxing,'' he was quick to add.

"Neither do you, of course.''

"See how agreeable we can be when we act like adults,'' he said. Then he blew her a kiss and headed for the kitchen.

When Teri came back downstairs, she was feeling a lot less tense. She had put on a comfortable pair of tan slacks and a bronze-colored sweater and had taken special care with her makeup. The aroma of corned beef and cabbage wafted through the living room. "Smells good,'' she complimented him at the kitchen doorway. "Maybe you do know what you're doing.''

"Got a problem,'' he told her. "I thought we had some stout. We don't. Watch that this doesn't boil over while I run to the store.''

"Do we have to have stout?''

"With this meal we do.'' Kevin handed her a pot holder, grabbed his car keys and dashed out of the town house.

He hadn't been gone for more than twenty minutes, but he returned to an apartment that smelled of scorched cabbage.

"Teri!'' he called as he went to the kitchen and turned the flame off under the pot.

He called out to her again, then charged up the stairs. She was gone. Taking two steps at a time, he returned to the living room and looked around. In the center of his desk he saw a piece of paper folded under the phone receiver. He picked it up and read it quickly.

Instant fear and anger shot through him as he reread the note informing him that if he wanted to see Teresa

Manzoni alive again, he would come alone to the abandoned lighthouse north of Howth, a suburb of Dublin.

His blood boiling at the thought of Teri in danger again, he rushed upstairs and changed into dark pants, a black turtleneck and sneakers. He knew the area well. The lighthouse, which could be found high on a cliff that jutted out into Dublin Bay, was near a small fishing village.

As he drove the nine miles to Howth, he thought of the kidnappers' threat that at any sign of police Teri would be a dead woman. But he also knew that if he walked in as instructed, he and Teri would both be dead in minutes.

Whoever they were, he decided, they had to be working for the person who had wanted them driven off the road and who nearly had Teri murdered at the turf plant. But why? What did he and Teri know that worried that person? Was it something he just wasn't seeing clearly?

It had to have started when they visited Dillon, but if Dillon had been one of the hijackers, someone had to have told him about the shipment schedule. Denis or Seamus were the logical choices, but Kevin just couldn't accept that Seamus could be involved. Who in his office could have had access to the dates of the shipment? No one, really. Except maybe—Fiona.

Fiona? But that was ridiculous, Kevin told himself as he parked near the boats moored to the long wharf.

Getting out of the car, he closed the door as quietly as possible. Dusk had set in, and luckily for him the sky was cloudy. The lighthouse was about a mile north of the wharf; he could see it from where he stood. He didn't know how many kidnappers there were, but he guessed there would have to be enough of them to post lookouts on the two roads leading down from the lighthouse to the village.

He scanned the area around him, then stepped into a rowboat and untied the line. Making as little noise as possible, he pushed away from the wharf and began to row out into Dublin Bay.

When he'd gone a good distance, he began a wide curve so that he could approach the lighthouse head-on from the sea, hopefully unseen. As he rowed, he couldn't get Fiona out of his mind. He stopped rowing, and the boat rocked in the water as he waited for it to get darker, his mind reviewing what Teri had told him so quickly at the estate.

He remembered her saying that she'd phoned Seamus from the Limerick Ryan, but that he hadn't been there, and she had left a message for him with—Fiona. A few hours later Quinn had arrived at the hotel. "Damn!" he said into the wind, which was picking up. "We weren't followed. Fiona knew exactly where Teri was."

Oars in hand again, he began to row against the current to keep the boat in line with the lighthouse. Now he also realized that Fiona was the only one who knew he and Teri were back in Dublin. He hadn't even given his name to the man who had answered the phone at the police station.

Kevin became angrier with himself by the second for not having thought it all through before. And Teri was paying for his inattention. But, Fiona? Why?

He glanced up at the dark clouds overhead and headed for shore.

As he neared it, he sized up the jagged sixty-foot cliff. He had climbed worse when he'd been in the army, he told himself firmly, and he had a damn better reason for doing it now. Upon reaching the rocky shore, he jumped out of the boat and pulled it up onto the narrow strip of sand and rocks. He looked up at the formidable cliff, rubbed his palms together and began the ascent.

The strong wind sent sprays of water over the rough limestone and he searched for secure handholds and footholds. The rock was rougher than sandpaper and dangerously slippery, but still he climbed higher and higher.

Halfway up, the pitted rock crumbled as he tried to wedge the toe of his sneaker into a crack. He almost lost his balance, but quickly he grasped the wet rock with strong fingers. Supporting his body with one foot, he searched blindly for another hole in the rock. When he thought he had found one, he tested it, then pushed himself up a little higher. The sharp wind blew his hair wildly and pushed him against the cliff, but he kept to his job and continued upward, not sure who he'd find at the top.

Grunting, pulling and pushing with his strong arms and legs, Kevin finally reached the top and grasped the ledge. Motionless, he listened, but he heard only the sounds of the howling wind and the churning water on the rocks below. He peeked over the ledge. There was no one in sight. He lifted his right foot high and gained a firm toehold, then waited for a brief lull in the wind. In one powerful motion he pushed with his foot, pulled with his hands and swung his body upward, turning in midair and falling backward onto the top of the ledge.

Quickly he rolled over and for moments he lay still, his alert eyes searching for any signs of movement. There were none. Crouching, he went from one large rock to another until he was at the back of the lighthouse. He took a few silent steps around it to see if the door was guarded. A man in the distance called toward the lighthouse, and Kevin flattened himself against the gray brick wall.

"How much longer are we going to wait for him?"

"Just get back down there like you were told!" another male voice yelled back.

Kevin looked up. The first window was about ten feet above him, and he saw that some of the outer layer of bricks had fallen loose. Thankfully, the wind made a noisy swooshing sound as it whirled around the base of the structure. He hoped it would cover the sounds of any bricks he might knock loose as he climbed to the window.

Up he went, his ascent easier this time. The glass was long gone from the window, and although it was a tight squeeze, he was able to ease himself inside and onto the curved stone steps.

One quiet step at a time, he moved stealthily up the worn steps, listening intently for any sound. As he neared the landing, he heard Teri's voice telling someone he wouldn't get away with it. "Let's hope you're right, luv," Kevin mumbled, and took the last step.

He moved to the side of the open door and recognized Gary Dillon's voice. The man was bragging about having melted down the gold artifacts to buy his property. Kevin wanted to rush in then and there, but concern for Teri stopped him.

He listened to their voices and mentally placed where each one was in the room, then he carefully tilted his head until he could peer inside. Dillon's back was to him, but he was holding a gun in his hand. Teri was tied to a chair next to a rickety table with a kerosene lamp on it. She saw Kevin, but looked away when he put a finger to his lips.

Thinking quickly, she said to Dillon, "My wrists feel as though they're bleeding. Would you just loosen the rope a little?"

He laughed at her. "You won't be tied up much longer. As soon as O'Shea gets here, you two are goin' to have another car accident, but you won't walk away from this—"

Instinctively Dillon dropped the gun and grabbed at the arm around his throat. Before he knew what had hit him, Kevin spun him around and rammed his head against the stone wall—once, twice, then a third time for good measure.

For seconds Kevin held the man to make sure he was unconscious, then he lowered him quietly to the floor. Again Kevin signaled Teri not to speak, and moments later she was free.

After feeling for a pulse, he bound and gagged Dillon, then cautiously led Teri back down the stairway to the window where he had entered. Whispering, he said, "We're only about ten feet off the ground. I'll go first. You follow. I'll make sure you have a good footing. Ready?" He turned to the window, but Teri tapped his shoulder. "What?"

"I love you," she said quietly.

"Same here. C'mon."

Kevin squeezed through the narrow space and started down the outside of the lighthouse. Teri stuck her head out, watching him. She didn't like the looks of the descent, but anything was better than being upstairs with Gary Dillon.

Halfway down Kevin motioned to her. A roll of thunder drew her attention skyward, but she held on to the top of the window frame as Kevin had, and worked her legs through the hole. It wasn't easy, but she managed to turn her body. Kevin grabbed hold of her foot and stuck it where a brick had once been. He did the same to her other foot, and soon they were both on the ground.

"Now what?" she asked, loudly enough for him to hear her over the wind that was almost gale force.

With his arm around her, he spoke close to her ear. "I came up the cliff, but there's no chance we'll both get down that way. There's a man around the front and others watching the roads, but we can't stay here." He pointed toward a large rock. "Over there . . . get behind it. You go first and stay low."

She dashed to the rock and he followed, wondering how they'd make it past the man he knew was standing at the front door—with a gun, most likely.

Kevin sniffed the air, then smiled when the heavens opened up and let loose a blinding torrent. "Thank God for the Irish rains! If the man out front has the sense of a snail, he'll get inside. Let's just hope he's not a fast stair climber. I don't know about the others, but I say we try to get out of here now."

Teri's hand securely in his, he skirted the lighthouse in as wide an arc as the boulderlike rocks would permit. His vision was limited by the rain enveloping them, and he had to wave his free hand in front of him to make sure he didn't guide her right off the promontory.

Teri followed Kevin for what seemed like an eternity. She was drenched to the skin and had trouble maintaining her footing on the slippery rocks. She stumbled, but felt strong hands pull her up, and she and Kevin continued moving away from the lighthouse as the cold, driving rain pelted their bodies.

It began to slacken a bit, and Kevin saw a line of trees not far from them. "We're home free if we can make it over there," he told her. He started for the safety of cover, pulling her with him.

Fifteen minutes later, standing in the steady rain and looking as though they had swum ashore, Kevin pounded on the door of a pub until an irate man in his pajamas opened it a crack.

"Do you have a phone?" he yelled.

The man nodded, and Kevin all but pushed his way in, pulling Teri inside with him. He promptly phoned the Dublin police, and after identifying himself, he suggested they pick up Fiona Riain and get to the lighthouse on the double.

RAYS OF MORNING SUN streamed through the kitchen window as Teri and Kevin sat in their robes, munching on ham and cheese sandwiches.

The police had made the nine-mile drive in record time and had surprised the men watching the two roads. As it turned out, instead of going upstairs, the man guarding the entrance had opted to run for his car when the rains came—to be near his bottle of Irish whiskey. It was the badly bruised Gary Dillon who finally told the police that what was left of the hijacked items were hidden in his barn at Silvermines.

"Fiona, Peter Quinn's sister-in-law," Teri said, shaking her head and taking another bite of her sandwich.

Kevin put his glass of milk down and shook his head, too. "Seamus said he'll never get over the fact that she, Dillon and Quinn had a smuggling operation going on under his nose for more than two years. They made a big mistake, though, when they branched out from shipping stolen valuables out of the country to hijacking and murder."

When Fiona and Dillon had been interrogated at police headquarters, neither one had wasted any time before accusing the other of being the "brains" behind the
operation. The reality was that both were in it up to
their necks, along with a few foreign postal clerks. The
clerks would wait for select boxes to come through for
delivery; once they had them, Fiona would phone the
customer and tell him or her the wrong box had been
shipped. Then Fiona would have a contact pick it up,
unopened. Fiona admitted she had been the one who
had put the artifacts in with Teri's merchandise soon
after she and Kevin had left the mailing room that Friday.

"Pretty neat little scheme they dreamed up," Teri
said. "But I think she was truly sorry when Seamus was
dragged into it. She should have realized he would be.
That was another mistake she made."

"If criminals didn't make mistakes, they'd never get
caught."

Teri smiled, but not with a great deal of happiness.
"At least I have my passport back," she said, averting
her eyes from Kevin's.

He watched her in silence, searching her features for
some sign that it would be difficult for her to leave him.
But he only saw determination to do what she had told
him time and again she would—return home.

Slowly he got up and began to take their dishes to the
sink.

"I'll do those," she said quickly.

"No, they won't run away. I'll just rinse them, then
let's catch a few hours' sleep. We both need it."

"Yes, I guess we do. It's been a long night."

She sat still while Kevin was busy at the sink. A few
hours' sleep, she thought, then it was goodbye Ireland,
goodbye Kevin—again. But this time *she* was leaving

him. That was the way it had to be, she told herself, feeling exhausted and emotionally drained.

"Ready?" he asked. When she nodded, he took her hand and led her upstairs.

At his bedroom door Teri stopped. "It's a strange time of day to be saying good-night, but—" her lips formed a curious smile "—my trip to Ireland has been a rather strange one, hasn't it?" Her soulful eyes clung to his a moment before she turned to go to her room.

"You're really going to leave, aren't you?" he asked quietly.

She looked back at him, and after swallowing the lump in her throat, she said, "Vacations have a way of coming to an end. It's back to work for me."

"Not yet. We still have a few hours," he pointed out, his tone pleading. "Spend them with me."

"Kevin, I don't think—"

"Please," he implored, "let me do the thinking for both of us right now."

Gently he drew her inside his bedroom, slipped her terry robe from her shoulders and let it fall to the carpet below. She closed her eyes and shivered when his warm fingers caressed her arms.

"You're cold," he murmured. Tenderly he turned back the spread and top sheet and held them while she slipped onto his bed.

After covering her, he went to the windows and closed the drapes to dim the bright morning sunlight. Then he gazed at her lying there, her face turned away from him. He shrugged out of his robe, dropped it onto the chair by the window and crept into bed beside her.

Leaning on his arm, he bent to kiss her shoulder. "You're trembling," he said quietly, and drew her up against his body to warm her.

"Kevin," she murmured.

"Yes, luv?"

"I'll always remember having found you again."

A deep pain filled his chest, but he said nothing.

"You do understand why I have to go, don't you?"

"No, not really," he said honestly.

Teri raised herself up and placed a gentle hand on his cheek. "You have a lot of decisions to make now, and my staying for even a short while longer will only make them more difficult for you."

"That's not true."

"It is. You have to decide what part Patrick will now play in your life, and like it or not you have a responsibility to his mother. Your Asian trip is coming up, and there's Mary Kate to think about. You don't need any other complications in your life right now."

His chest rose, then fell when he emitted a long sigh. "I could never think of you as a complication. Just the opposite. Without you I don't know if I can handle everything else. I'm not sure I want to even try."

"That's how you feel right now, but after I'm gone you'll see that I'm right."

He shook his head. "No, you're dead wrong. And why do you think you know what I feel better than I do? Yes, the next few months are going to be hell, but that's not what scares me. What scares me is trying to get through them without you by my side." His voice took on an urgent tone. "Teri, I can take on the whole world, cope with any problems, do anything if you're with me. Why won't you believe that?"

She didn't have a simple answer. Right now she couldn't even think straight, and her every instinct warned her not to make any important decisions in the emotional shape she was in.

Gazing down at him, she placed her fingers on his lips and whispered, "No more talk, darling. Time is rushing by so quickly."

Kevin pulled her to him and moved his body over hers, realizing this would be their last time together. Love and frustration clashed inside his brain, and he took her with a hungry passion he couldn't control, driving and driving, wanting to hear her cry out his name. But the cry he heard came from his lips, and it was her name that rang in his ears....

Afterward Teri lay quietly in Kevin's arms, breathing deeply. His kisses mingled with his tears as his lips moved over her closed eyes, her cheeks and along her throat. He wanted to implant the memory of her forever in his mind. Only after she fell asleep did he permit his own tired eyes to close.

Three hours later, Kevin reached over to shut off the alarm on the clock, but when his senses sharpened, he realized it was the phone ringing. Stretching, he reached for the receiver and mumbled, "Yes?"

The ringing had awakened Teri, too, and she turned toward him.

"What?" he asked. "When?"

Seeing an anxious look cloud his face, she raised herself up on her arm.

"Yes," Kevin said, "as soon as possible." Slowly he set the receiver back on its cradle.

"What is it?" she asked.

"That was Maude. Moira's very ill. She's asking for me."

CHAPTER FIFTEEN

AGAINST HER BETTER JUDGMENT Teri agreed to board her return flight home from Shannon Airport rather than Dublin after Kevin reminded her that doing so would give her a chance to say goodbye to Patrick. Kevin made a quick call to his secretary, and they headed for the airport to take a shuttle flight to Limerick.

When they arrived at the hospital, they found Moira's mother in tears. Her daughter now had bronchial pneumonia. Ian was just coming out of her room with Patrick.

"Kevin!" the boy yelled enthusiastically, running to him.

Kevin crouched and took him in his arms. After a warm hug he asked, "How is your mother?"

"She's real sick, Kevin." He looked up at Teri and asked, "She's going to get better, isn't she?"

When he held his little arms out, Teri stooped to welcome his embrace. "Of course she is," she assured him.

Ian took his grandson's hand and asked, "What say we go and have some strawberry ice cream?"

Patrick nodded enthusiastically, then looked up at Kevin. "You won't leave before I get back, will you?"

"No," he promised, "I won't."

Ian gestured to his wife to take the boy, and when Maude and Patrick started down the hospital corridor, he took Kevin aside and said quietly, "Moira remembers everything now...everything about the shooting." He turned away when a brief coughing spell hit him. After taking several deep and difficult breaths, he said, "She told Maude and me the truth about Patrick—that you're his father."

Kevin's gut wrenched, and he stroked the man's shoulder. "I'm sorry you had to find out that way, Ian. God, I'm sorry."

The older man nodded, and Kevin watched him shuffle down the hallway to catch up with his wife and grandson at the elevator.

Teri saw the tortured look on Kevin's face and went to him. "Ian sounds worse, doesn't he?" she said softly.

"He does." His eyes drifted to the door of Moira's room. "Well, shall we?"

Moira was lying in bed. Her head had been raised a little, and she was staring out the window. When the door opened, she turned. Teri smothered the gasp that caught in her throat. Moira was as white as the sheet on her bed, and dark gray shadows curved under her lifeless green eyes.

Upon seeing the woman in such a pitiful state and inhaling the strong odor of hospital antiseptics, Teri thought back to the time she and Moira had walked in her garden at the castle. Then the air had been filled with the sweet aroma of roses and gardenias, and Moira had looked radiant. But now—

"Kevin, Teri," Moira murmured in a weak voice.

At the side of her bed, Kevin smiled and asked softly, "How are you feeling?"

"Not much of anything. They're giving me some pills."

"Do whatever they say," Kevin told her. "Your doctor knows what you need right now."

Her eyes closed and she said quietly, "What I need right now is to be thirteen again." Opening her eyes, she raised her hand, and Kevin held it in his. "I was just remembering how we used to run through the moors to the ruins at the top of the hill near Glengarriff. Remember?" Smiling weakly, she looked at Teri, who was standing at the foot of the hospital bed. "I would pretend to be Beara, a medieval Spanish princess, and Kevin was Eogan, my handsome Irish warrior prince." She looked up at Kevin, and her smile dissipated, leaving a tired, wan expression on her face. Drawing her hand from his, she said sadly, "Those were happy days... but so long ago."

Kevin's troubled eyes sought Teri's, then he told Moira, "You need to rest now."

"'Rest,'" she repeated, and faced the window again. "There will be more than enough time for rest soon." Her watery, lifeless eyes drifted to his again. "You will take care of Patrick, won't you?"

He took hold of her hand once more. "You'll take care of him, just as soon as you're strong again. Until then, I will. You know that."

Moira looked at Teri. "Patrick likes you very much. He told me you have Indians as personal friends."

Teri's throat felt tight, but she managed to say, "He's a wonderful boy. I know you're very proud of him."

"That is the truth, isn't it... about the Indians?" she asked strangely. "You won't ever lie to him, will you?"

Teri glanced at Kevin, then said, "No, of course not, but I'm leaving for home today, Moira. I'm not sure when I'll see Patrick again."

With great difficulty, Moira raised herself up on her arms; her tangled red hair cascaded over the shoulders of her hospital gown. "But... you told me you loved Kevin."

"Moira," he said quickly, "we're going to leave and let you get some rest. I'll be with—"

"No," she said. Her head fell back onto the pillow. "We have to plan for Patrick's future. I want him to know you're his father. I've already told my parents and Dr. Butler."

"Moira," Teri suggested, "maybe you should wait until you're feeling better, until you're stronger."

"No, Patrick has to be told before they take me away."

Immediately Kevin asked, "Who's going to take you away?"

"The police," she said, her voice becoming even wearier. "They... were here this morning."

"Moira," Kevin said, "this is important. What did you tell them?"

"That I killed Denis."

Teri moved to the side of the bed opposite Kevin. "You had to in order to save Kevin's life," she insisted.

Lifting her hand, Moira ran trembling fingers over her forehead. "The first shot, perhaps."

Kevin sat down on the bed and smoothed several strands of hair back from her cheek. "You didn't know what you were doing."

She stared up at the ceiling, her expression strangely composed. "I remember every time I pulled the trigger. What bothers me is...that I'm not sorry about it."

"Good Lord, you didn't tell the police that, did you?" Kevin asked.

Weakly she said, "Yes, I did."

"Listen, don't even talk to them anymore. I have a barrister friend in Dublin. He'll come here and advise you."

"Kevin," she said, her voice becoming stronger, "it's Patrick I want to talk about. I have to know that he's going to be taken care of. I thought you and—" she turned her head to the other side of the bed "—Teri were going to be married. I thought—" A coughing fit cut her off.

Quickly Kevin told Teri, "See if you can find a nurse!"

She rushed from the room and went to the nurses' station; one of them hurried to Moira's room. Teri glanced down the corridor and saw several empty chairs. Slowly she walked over and sat down on one, fighting the queasiness in her stomach. Her heart went out to Moira, and Teri realized that more than ever, the woman now needed Kevin's support. Yes, she confirmed, she was doing the right thing by leaving.

And oh, how she longed for the simplicity of her life in Manhattan. Ever since she had arrived in Ireland, she'd experienced one catastrophic event after the other, and she didn't think she could take any more. If Kevin hadn't locked the rental car, she knew she would have run from the hospital as fast as she could, gotten her luggage and headed for the airport. *The coward's way out,* she said silently. Yes, she admitted, it was, but she had her breaking point, too, and it didn't seem far off.

From the corner of her eye she saw Kevin come out from Moira's room. Standing, Teri asked, "How is she?"

"Not good, I'm afraid. The nurse is calling her doctor in. I'm going to talk to him after he sees her."

Teri glanced at her watch. Her plane was scheduled to leave in less than two hours. "You stay," she told him. "I'll take a taxi to the airport. Would you mind unlocking the car so I can get my luggage?"

"You're still going to leave?"

"Yes, Kevin, I am. As soon as I get home, I'll have a lawyer take my statement about what happened . . . why Moira shot Denis. He can send it directly to the police in Limerick. If they need further information, they know where to contact me."

"You have it all worked out, don't you?" he said, slumping against the corridor wall. Then he smiled to himself. "I keep thinking things can't get any worse. Well, at least my boss is understanding and I still have a job. That's something."

Imposing an iron control on herself, Teri said, "Kevin, I know you're having an awful time right now, but Moira's parents are here, and you have friends who will help see you through this period."

"Sure," he said bitterly, "there are always friends."

Teri didn't know what else to say; she was as depressed as he was. Trying to be supportive, she told him, "You also have Patrick now. Day by day the two of you will grow closer. He's going to bring you so much happiness."

He looked at her with stony eyes. "Yes . . . Patrick. I wonder what he'll think when he learns you turned your back on us when we needed you most."

"That's not fair, Kevin," she said quietly, feeling a headache coming on.

Standing erect, he asked, "Are you being fair?"

"I'm trying to do what I think is best for everyone concerned, that's all."

"What's best for you, you mean."

Something blew inside her brain, and her voice turned sharp. "I suggest that you worry less about my motives and think of that poor woman in there and your son."

Her words struck him with the force of a sledgehammer. "Do you imagine for a second that I'm *not* thinking about them?" he said hotly. "I'm the one who's staying. You're the one who's running away."

"I'm not running," she insisted, her head throbbing now.

"Yes, you are. You're running just as I did twelve years ago, but at least I did it out of duty."

"'Duty'?" Her eyes widened, then narrowed. "Oh, yes, here it comes. Whenever you find yourself in a difficult situation, you fall back on 'duty.' It makes life much simpler for you, doesn't it? You can rationalize any choice you make. Well, I don't need excuses. I'm going home because I *want* to."

He nodded curtly. "Okay, Mrs. Manzoni, let's get your damn luggage and find you a taxi so you can run back home where it's comfortable and safe." He grabbed hold of her upper arm and started toward the elevator. "But remember this. One day you're going to have to be honest with yourself and face the fact that you don't have what it takes to make a real commitment to me, to Patrick or to anyone else. That could make for a very lonely life."

WHEN HE RETURNED to the hospital, Maude and Ian were sitting in the corridor outside their daughter's room. "Where's Patrick?" he asked.

Maude rose and put a hand on Kevin's arm. "He's inside with Moira. She wanted to talk to him alone."

Knowing why, Kevin said, "I'd better go in."

"No," she suggested. "Let her tell the boy in her own way."

Kevin searched her reddened eyes and put his hand over hers. "Maude, I want to take Patrick with me to Dublin until Moira is better."

"Good, I was hoping you would. A boy belongs with his father, and it's best he not stay in that house. It has too many bad memories for him." A sincere smile brightened her face a little. "Ian and I have always loved you, Kevin. If only Moira had had the sense to marry you, rather than—'' She didn't finish. Instead she said, "Well, maybe we can all comfort one another now.''

Kevin nodded his agreement, and began to pace the corridor, imagining his son's face and what he must be feeling at this very moment. He remembered telling Teri that his life had been turned upside down, and now he groaned inwardly at his selfishness. Second by second Patrick's world was being shattered, through no fault of his own.

"Teri," he murmured, regretting his final bitter words to her. He knew he had said them to hide the despair he had felt upon realizing he might never see her again. At the end of the hallway he sat down on a chair and asked himself why she couldn't have stayed just a little while longer. The answer came to him quickly enough. Her life had been hell ever since she had set foot in Ireland. He couldn't blame her for running; he would have, too, if he hadn't had so many damn things to cope with. Patrick was at the top of his list.

But the ache in his heart worsened, and the thought of spending a lifetime without Teri became unbearable. *Run, Teri,* he said to himself, *but you'll learn there's no place on earth you can hide without my finding you again.*

A movement down the corridor caught his eye, and he saw a solemn little boy come out of Moira's room. Slowly standing, Kevin trained fearful eyes on Patrick, desperately trying to sense his feelings as he stared back at him.

"Patrick," he said softly, but the boy didn't budge. Kevin could see the confusion in his eyes.

Kevin went to him and crouched. His hands moved to his son, but he stopped them in midair, not knowing how the boy would react to his touch now. Quietly he asked, "Is everything all right between us?"

"Yes, sir," Patrick said, lowering his eyes.

"'Sir'?" Kevin repeated, raising Patrick's chin with gentle fingers. In his clear, youthful eyes Kevin saw a disturbing mixture of fear and doubt. Now he took the boy's arms, but he held them lightly. "It's always been 'Kevin' before," he said, fighting the lump in his throat. "Why 'sir' now?"

"That's what I had to call my other father," Patrick mumbled.

Kevin took a long breath, trying to lift the heavy weight that seemed to crush his chest, then he said, "You've always had only one father...me. I wish I could explain everything to you in just a few words so you'd understand, but—" He ran a comforting hand over his son's blond hair. "Denis was never your father, not really."

"Why did he pretend he was?"

Lying for Patrick's sake, Kevin said, "Because he loved you very much."

Patrick thought about that, then shook his head slowly. "No, I don't think he did. I was afraid of him. He was always so mean to me."

Kevin blinked away the stinging in his eyes and glanced away momentarily. Looking back at Patrick, he smiled softly. "You won't ever be afraid of me, will you?"

Confusion still in his eyes and voice, Patrick said, "But you're my father now. Shouldn't I be?"

Shaking his head, Kevin drew his son closer and folded his arms around him. "No," he said, finding it difficult to speak. "I'll never give you any reason to be. I promise you that."

Patrick placed his small hands on Kevin's shoulders and pushed himself back a little. A tentative smile on his face, he asked, "Do you mean we can still be friends the way we used to be?"

Kevin wiped away the tear that trickled from the corner of his eye and he smiled, too. "Better than we used to be. From now on I'm the best friend you'll ever have."

"And I can still visit you in Dublin when you come back from your business trip?"

"No, I'm afraid not."

"Oh." Patrick's smile slipped away.

"Because you're coming to Dublin now...to live with me. If you want to, that is."

His face lit up. "You mean for good?"

"For good, if that's all right with you."

Patrick threw his arms around Kevin's neck. "I'll say it is!"

Kevin held his son tighter. Never in his life had he experienced such a feeling of elation, and suddenly the word "father" took on its true import. At that moment Kevin knew that things were going to be just fine between his son and him, and he felt a surge of protectiveness, joy and love.

Patrick pulled himself away and ran toward Maude and Ian. "Grandma, Grandad! I'm going to live with Kevin in Dublin!"

Kevin watched as his son excitedly told his beaming grandparents the news. Gazing at the boy with pride, memories of his own father flashed through his mind—the good and the not so good—and he promised himself he would do his damnedest to make Patrick feel like the most loved son in the world.

A nurse was checking Moira's intravenous tube when Kevin went in to see her. She was sleeping, but even in sleep she wheezed terribly. Kevin asked to speak to Dr. Butler, who told him that despite the antibiotics, Moira's pneumonia was worsening. The doctor said that everything possible was being done and he suggested that Kevin and the others go home and get some rest.

That night at the estate, after Kevin had tucked Patrick in, he lay down beside him on top of the covers and told his son about Mary Kate, his new grandmother, and about his own childhood in Glengarriff. He also talked about Padraig, telling Patrick that Moira had named him after his grandfather. When Kevin recounted stories of how he and friends would play on the moors after school and how his mother would bake them biscuits and spread homemade blackberry jam on them, Patrick asked if he had to return to boarding school. Only if he wanted to, Kevin assured him. Together they decided he wouldn't.

Long after Patrick fell asleep, Kevin remained there watching him. He still couldn't forget the bitter words he and Teri had exchanged at the hospital.

Carefully Kevin eased himself from the bed, went to the window and stared out at the inky darkness. He knew that both he and Teri had been exhausted and upset, yet her remarks about his sense of duty still troubled him.

Duty and honor, he thought as he slipped his hands into his pants pockets. They were qualities he wanted to pass on to Patrick just as his own father had passed them on to him. Why didn't Teri see the importance of a man having those qualities? Why didn't she understand that he'd had to leave her long ago? In regard to Moira, his honor had demanded his return, and his loyalty and duty to Ireland had necessitated it.

He glanced back at his sleeping son and realized that the boy was now the most important thing in his life. He was so small and needed protection. "Priorities," he murmured, recalling that Teri had accused him of placing her too low on his list. He'd never thought of it that way. Had he? Is that what Teri had wanted all along, for him to feel about her the way he now felt about his son?

As the dark clouds began to slip by, yellow-silver rays of moonlight washed over him. He stood there silently, trying to work through his confusion.

Leaning a shoulder against the window frame, he thought about the time he'd left her so long ago. He hadn't meant to hurt her. But he had. He shook his head, and for the first time he realized clearly that his sense of duty had been directed toward everyone and everything but Teri, the person he should have been most loyal to.

Hearing Patrick murmur in his sleep, Kevin returned to the bed, sat down and brushed back the boy's sleep-tousled hair. Softly he said, "Your father's got a lot to learn, son."

A gentle knock on the bedroom door drew his attention. He opened it and Liam told him he was wanted on the phone. It was Dr. Butler, calling from the hospital. Moira had just passed away. A priest had been present.

AGAIN KEVIN AND PATRICK made the dismal trip to the family vault, but this time the boy cried until he had no tears left. None of Denis's family bothered to attend Moira's funeral; the only others present were Maude, Ian, several of the servants and a priest.

As he held his son close, Kevin silently said his final farewell to Patrick's mother. In his heart he knew he would always remember Moira as the carefree Spanish princess with the long, shining red hair and laughing green eyes, running through the heather on the moor, calling to her Irish warrior prince.

COLLEEN OOHED AND AAHED as she and Teri un-packed the boxes that Seamus had mailed from Ire-land, and she complimented her partner on her selections, even the pins with the shamrocks on them.

As she admired the replica of the Ardagh Chalice, she glanced over at Teri's glum expression. "I don't under-stand you," she said. "If you're so miserable why won't you at least talk to Kevin when he phones?"

Placing a yellow sweater on a hanger, Teri said, "That's a part of my life that's behind me. I'd just as soon forget it."

"I can see you wanting to forget about nearly being killed a few times, but it's obvious to me you're in love with the man. Either that or you're coming down with something. I've never seen you drag yourself around the way you have been ever since you returned."

"Thanks," Teri said sarcastically. "That's just what I needed—a compliment on my posture."

"What you need is to have your head exam-ined...or your heart. I'm not sure which. Look at you, you're miserable."

Teri put the hanger on a rack, then leaned down on a display case nearby. "I am. I've been miserable ever since the plane took off from Shannon."

"Well, doesn't that give you a clue that something's wrong?"

"There's something wrong all right, something wrong with me," Teri admitted. "I always thought I was a strong woman emotionally, but I ran, Colleen. I ran because I was afraid. There was so much happening, and Kevin wanted to depend on me so much. I just didn't know if I could handle it."

Leaning on the other side of the display case, Colleen wrapped her hands around Teri's. "Look, don't put yourself down for being afraid. Don't you think I get frightened sometimes? Charlie's got a good job now, and everything is beautiful, but if he comes up against something he doesn't think he can handle, he might look to the bottle for help again. I know that, and it scares the hell out of me at times, but what we have together somehow gets me past the fear. Honey, there are no guarantees." After patting Teri's hands, she stood erect and squared her shoulders. "When fear strikes me, I just yell at it and tell it where it can go."

Colleen paused, then asked, "Aside from fear and Kevin's problems, were there any other reasons you decided to call it quits?"

Teri replaced the lid on the cardboard box they had just emptied. "Well, I did have to consider my parents. Even though they're in Florida and I'm here, I like to think they depend on me."

"They might be more content if they thought you were happily settled down."

"Maybe."

"Any other reasons?"

"Not really."

Over the years Colleen had gotten to know Teri pretty well, so she said lightly, "I hope you didn't think this place couldn't get along without you."

Teri's dark brows arched in surprise. "Thanks again. You're just full of compliments today."

Colleen smiled. "You know what I mean." In a more serious tone, she told her, "The Hansen Freiberg Agency has offices on the West Coast, and if they were to transfer Charlie there, I'd go with him. I might not like it, but I would."

"I'd expect you to," Teri said honestly, and suddenly she felt that some of the obligations she had confronted Kevin with were mere excuses.

Colleen picked up the cardboard box. "This was the last one. Let's call it a day. I'm beat and I'm starving."

"How's Charlie doing in the kitchen these days?" Teri asked as she followed Colleen to the back room.

"As long as the food's microwavable, he's doing great. Now if only he could breast-feed...."

"Pushy, aren't you?"

"Not really. Irishmen don't like to be pushed." She set the box down near the back door and faced Teri. "And the Irishman who's been phoning you sounds as though he's been pushed."

Teri leaned against one of the shelves on which inventory was stored and crossed her arms. "I still think I did the right thing. With me there, Kevin would never come to terms with his feelings for Moira. After all, she is the mother of his son. I had to give the three of them time together."

"Have you sent Patrick the sports magazines you bought last week?"

"Uh-uh, not yet. I'll mail them Saturday. It's the letter that goes with them that's giving me problems. I want to tell him how much I miss him and Kevin, but I keep thinking that maybe it's better if they don't know just how much."

Colleen ran her fingers through her tawny blond hair. "God, girl, when are you going to start thinking about what might be better for you? I hope you realize that you're just about throwing Kevin into Moira's arms."

"If he's content there, that's where he belongs, isn't it?"

"Well, it seems to me that you're expecting him to make all the effort while you do nothing but feel sorry for yourself."

At first the comment ruffled, but as Teri thought about it, she remembered what Kevin had asked her the night they had walked along the shore at Crosshaven: *"Are the barriers real, or are you erecting them because you think you need to?"* She hadn't wanted to admit it, but she had built barriers between her and Kevin. Had she wanted to see him knock them down as proof that he would never leave her as he had years ago?

"Give it some thought," Colleen said. Then the two women collected their things and closed up shop for another day.

Soon Teri was home, and just as she put the key in the lock of her apartment door, the phone started to ring. Her heart did a flip-flop as she grabbed the receiver.

"Oh," she said dully upon hearing the caller's voice. Then her tone became cheery. "Mom, how are you? Is everything all right?"

She settled down on the sofa and listened as her mother bubbled over with excitement, telling her daughter that she and Teri's father had just decided to take a trip to Italy to attend their niece's wedding. She hoped Teri wouldn't be too disappointed if they postponed their visit to New York.

"Of course not," Teri said, sincerely happy for her parents. But after their brief phone conversation ended, she groaned at the realization that Colleen had probably been right. This obligation had, no doubt, been born out of imagination, not reality.

She leaned forward and picked up a small porcelain sculpture from the coffee table. It was a miniature of two pink camellias with green foliage, one of the pieces she had selected in Ireland. A gift to herself, she had said upon bringing it home, but in her heart she knew that whenever she looked at it she would think of Kevin—just as she was doing now.

"Kevin," she murmured, and put the camellias back on the table. She rose and went into the bedroom, and as she removed her yellow suit jacket and laid it on the bed, she wondered just what she'd say to him if she phoned him. *Why, hello again!* she rehearsed silently, looking into the dresser mirror. "Brilliant," she said wryly, and began brushing her hair.

She stopped and stared into the mirror as Kevin's words assailed her again: *"One day you're going to have to be honest with yourself and face the fact that you don't have what it takes to make a real commitment to me, to Patrick or to anyone else. That could make for a very lonely life."*

Putting the brush down on the dresser, she admitted to herself that he had been right. She *was* lonely, and as Colleen had said, she was miserable, too. "'No guarantees,'" Teri murmured, repeating one of her partner's remarks.

Is that what I was hoping for? she asked herself as she turned and walked slowly back into the living room, where she sat down on one of the easy chairs. *A guarantee that Kevin would never leave me again? That he would marry me and magically arrange for Moira to let us have Patrick?*

Teri noticed a white speck of plastic packing material on the sleeve of her tan silk blouse and flicked it off. Her eyes drifted over to the phone, and she considered the time difference. It was seven o'clock in New York. That made it midnight in Ireland. Suddenly Teri knew she would be just as happy in Ireland as she was in New York—probably happier.

"Face it, girl," she told herself out loud. "You'd be happy anywhere on Earth as long as you were with Kevin."

She pushed herself up from the chair and was on her way to the kitchen to see what she could find for dinner, when the door buzzer sounded. Opening the door, her eyes widened, and her heart almost stopped.

CHAPTER SIXTEEN

ASTONISHMENT WAS WRITTEN all over her face as she exclaimed, "Kevin!"

"Well," he said, his hands shoved in his pants pockets, "you remembered my name. That's a start." Seeing that she was just standing there staring at him, he asked, "Are you going to invite me in?"

"Uh . . . why, of course." She stepped back, opened the door wider, then closed it after he picked up his suitcase and strode in.

Glancing around, he said, "Nice . . . bigger than your other apartment." He turned and examined her, from her tan pumps to her shining dark hair. "You're looking very well, more rested than the last time I saw you. Work must agree with you."

Every nerve end in her body rioting, Teri remained motionless. Out of the blue, she recalled how he had slammed the taxi door outside the hospital that day. Finally she said, "You look nice, too. Brown is your color."

"I'd forgotten how hot it gets in New York in July. Do you mind if I take off this wool jacket?"

"No, of course not. I'll turn up the air conditioner."

"Not necessary," he told her, setting his suitcase down.

After he'd draped his jacket over the back of a chair, Teri gestured toward the sofa. "Please, have a seat. Can

I fix you something to drink? I have some Irish whiskey."

Watching her, he wondered if she was nervous because she was happy to see him or if he was interfering with plans she had for the evening. "I'm not keeping you from anything?" he asked.

"No! I was just getting ready to fix something for dinner. Have you eaten?"

"On the plane. I just came from the airport."

"Oh." Her fingers went to the bow on the collar of her blouse, then she asked, "Ice with your drink?"

He shook his head, knowing she had never seen him put ice in a glass of whiskey.

"Yes," she said, smiling awkwardly, "I remember now." She hurried to the kitchen, still not able to believe that Kevin was actually in the next room.

She reached down into a cabinet and put the unopened bottle of whiskey on the countertop. She saw that her hands were shaking and she squeezed them together tightly, trying to steady her nerves. Wondering if he was in New York on business, she took two old-fashioned glasses from another cabinet and immediately put one back, reaching for a taller one for herself.

Distracted by her racing thoughts, she put ice cubes in both glasses, then dumped the ones from the smaller glass into the sink. She didn't bother to measure, but half filled his with whiskey and put an equal amount in hers. When she quickly poured the ginger ale into her glass, it fizzed up and spilled over the countertop.

"Calm down," she mumbled, wiping the glass and the counter with a towel. Then she grabbed two napkins, set the drinks on a tray and took a much needed breath.

"Thanks," Kevin said as she handed him the drink. Looking at hers as she sat down on a chair across from him, he remarked, "You're still putting ginger ale in good whiskey, I see."

She smiled, nodded and took a quick sip.

He did, too, his blue-green eyes never leaving hers. After placing his drink on the table next to him, he asked, "Are you surprised to see me?"

That's putting it mildly, she thought, but said only, "Yes...I am."

He leaned back, crossed his legs at the ankles and rested his hands on the arms of the chair. "Pleasantly surprised, I hope."

Teri wondered about the stern look on his face. "Yes, naturally I'm happy to see you again."

"You are," he said flatly.

"Certainly I am. Why would you even ask?"

"I wasn't sure you would be." Before she could say a word, he told her, "Colleen sounded very nice on the phone." He cocked his head. "She did tell you I called...several times?"

Teri nodded again and took another quick sip of her drink.

"It's a shame you were never there when I phoned. I left my number, but I guess she forgot to give it to you."

"How's Patrick?" she asked quickly.

"Just fine. He's living with me in Dublin now."

"In Dublin," she repeated inanely, envisioning his son's lively blue eyes and blond hair. Smiling, she said, "So, you're a full-time father now. How are you adjusting to it?"

"I like it. More importantly, Patrick likes it."

Looking at her glass, Teri said, "I knew he would."

"Yes, I remember someone saying to me, 'What's not to love about you?' That was you, wasn't it?"

Quietly she said, "You know it was."

"I guess you don't think that way anymore."

Becoming more uncomfortable by the second, Teri blurted out, "How are Seamus and Margaret?"

"Both doing wonderfully now. They send you their best."

"I'm happy to hear that." Attempting to mask her inner nervousness, Teri smiled and said, "I hope Moira is feeling better."

In a low monotone, Kevin said, "She's dead, Teri."

She only stared at him. His simple statement of the fact seemed so cold and unfeeling. She set her glass on the coffee table, rose slowly and went to the window. It had been less than two weeks since she had seen Moira in the hospital. Yes, she had been ill, but Teri had never thought her illness would be fatal. Poor Patrick, she thought; first the man he had called his father, then his mother. She turned, and her voice shook when she asked, "Why didn't you tell me?"

"I tried to, on the phone—eight times. I called you at the boutique and here."

"You could have written."

"You could have answered my calls," he said, standing and walking to the other side of the wide window. "Maude wanted to write, but I told her I'd be here before her letter."

Teri looked over at him. His left shoulder was braced against the wall, and in his face she now saw deep sorrow.

"She died the morning after you left," he explained. "Patrick took it hard, and so did Maude and Ian, naturally. There were so many things to take care of." For quiet moments his attention focused on a ship he saw moving on the river below, then his gaze drifted back to Teri. "I kept wishing you were there with me."

"If I'd thought for a moment that Moira was that ill, I would have stayed, believe me. Not just for your sake,

but for Patrick's.'' She saw his doubtful nod and she
lowered her eyes. ''Will there be any problems getting
custody of Patrick?'' she asked softly.

''No,'' he said, and Teri lifted her eyes. ''Moira told
several people and a priest that he was my son, and true
to form, Denis stated in his will that Patrick wasn't his
and left him nothing. Moira did better, though, and
Patrick will now have what's rightfully his. I'm having
a trust set up for him. My solicitor in Dublin is going to
see that I have the necessary court documents giving me
permanent custody.''

Teri breathed a sigh of relief. ''I'm so happy something has finally turned out well for you both.''

''And what about you? Are you happier now that
you're back home?''

She turned and walked slowly to a wing chair near the
sofa. Placing her hands on it, she said, ''Not really.''

Kevin came up behind her and put his arms around
her shoulders. ''Except for Patrick, I've been miserable ever since you left. I think about you day and
night . . . particularly at night, when I lie in the dark,
remembering how it was with us. Patrick misses you,
too. He said to give you a kiss for him.'' He leaned
down and kissed the side of her neck just under her ear.

She turned in his arms and cupped his face. ''Give
Patrick a kiss for me,'' she said softly, drawing his head
down and kissing his lips. When she drew her head
back, she saw a big smile light up Kevin's face.

''You left something in Ireland,'' he told her, and
reached into his pocket. Holding up the gold chain with
the little Celtic cross on it, he said, ''This is yours. It
always has been and always will be.'' He placed it
around her neck and fastened the clasp.

Teri fingered the cross and with shimmering eyes told him, "And if you still want me, I'm yours. I always have been and always will be. I love you, Kevin."

"God, I was afraid you didn't!" He pulled her to him and wrapped his arms around her. "And I love you—so much that it's driving me crazy." After kissing her hair, he gazed down at her and said, "I took a good look at my list of priorities, and I've done some rearranging. You're right up there on top."

His next words came out in a rush. "The minister has agreed to let me be attached to the Irish consulate here in New York for six months out of the year. Six months here and six months in Ireland. The moving back and forth will be a bit hard on Patrick, but I've talked it over with him, and he's enthusiastic if it means the three of us will be together."

Still in Kevin's arms, Teri thought her heart was going to burst with joy. She wasn't used to the carefree and wild sensations that were rippling through her; she felt buoyant, euphoric. Then, remembering that night twelve years ago, she drew back from Kevin, took hold of his hand and led him to her bedroom.

This time, though, she didn't avert her eyes as they undressed quickly; this time there were no doubts, no silent fears. Never again would she be separated from the man holding his arms out to her—never again. Whatever it took, whatever compromises she would have to make, she knew that her only happiness lay in being with him for the rest of her life.

She settled in his embrace and pressed her body against the warm firmness of his, letting him surround her with his love. When he swept her up in his arms, she circled his neck with her arms and kissed his cheek. He carried her to the bed, and without bothering to turn down the satiny spread, he gently laid her down, then kissed her lips as he positioned himself over her.

Leaning close, he whispered, "Take me into you, luv, right now. I need to be a part of you."

Teri did so eagerly, sighing with happiness as she felt the two of them become one again. When his chest pressed against her breasts, she moved her palms over his warm, smooth back, holding him securely, as if to tell him she would never let him go again.

Tangling his fingers in her silky hair, he murmured against her lips, *"Mo ghrá thú."* His soft lips traveled along her cheek to her ear and he said tenderly, "I need you, luv, and Patrick needs you."

As she trailed her fingers over his warm, velvety skin, she whispered back, "And I need both of you. Will you marry me, Kevin?"

Raising his head, he gazed down at her with adoring eyes and smiled. "You never stop amazing me, and I love you for it. Ask me again, though. I want to hear you say the words once more, so I know I'm not dreaming."

Teri took his face in her hands and said, "I love you, Kevin. Will you marry me and take me home to Ireland?"

"For good?"

"Yes, for always."

"What about all your obligations here?"

"I've rearranged my priorities, too. You and Patrick come first," she said, the words ringing true in her heart and soul. "Everything else we'll work out together."

"Then I'll marry you, Teresa Rosario, here, in Ireland or anywhere in the world, and you can build yourself any kind of career you want."

As she ran her fingers through his wavy blond hair, she told him, "I've been thinking about that. How do you suppose I'd do if I opened an American import boutique in Dublin?''

"You'd be a success no matter what you decided to do."

Wrapping his arms around her once more, he leaned back down and kissed her long and hard. Teri sighed, then murmured his name against his lips, and it was as though the heavens had opened up and were showering her with their most priceless gifts.

As Kevin nuzzled the side of her throat, he asked, "Are you sure you'll be happy in Ircland, luv?"

A brilliant light lingered in Teri's dark eyes, and she whispered, "As long as I'm with you, I'll be happy anywhere on Earth."

With a hint of mischief in his voice, he asked, "Even in a cottage in Glengarriff?"

Surprised, she asked, "What about your work in Dublin?"

He drew her even closer to him and placed her head on his shoulder. "We could build a summer vacation home in Glengarriff, on the hillside near the arbutus tree I planted for you. Would you like that?"

"Oh, Kevin, I would! And maybe we could spend Christmas there sometimes. That would be so lovely for Mary Kate and Patrick."

"We'll have to decide how many rooms we want, and you can furnish the cottage however you like."

Believing herself to be the happiest woman alive, Teri nestled against him, closed her eyes and said softly, "All I've ever really wanted was a place for us to bc together and a home filled with love."

Kevin smiled contentedly. "Any place where you and I are together, darling, will always be filled with love."

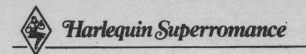

CALLOWAY CORNERS

Created by four outstanding Superromance authors, bonded by lifelong friendship and a love of their home state: Sandra Canfield, Tracy Hughes, Katherine Burton and Penny Richards.

CALLOWAY CORNERS

Home of four sisters as different as the seasons, as elusive as the elements; an undiscovered part of Louisiana where time stands still and passion lasts forever.

CALLOWAY CORNERS

Birthplace of the unforgettable Calloway women: *Mariah*, free as the wind, and untamed until she meets the preacher who claims her, body and soul; *Jo*, the fiery, feisty defender of lost causes who loses her heart to a rock and roll man; *Tess*, gentle as a placid lake but tormented by her longing for the town's bad boy and *Eden*, the earth mother who's been so busy giving love she doesn't know how much she needs it until she's awakened by a drifter's kiss...

CALLOWAY CORNERS

Coming from Superromance, in 1989:
Mariah, by Sandra Canfield, a January release
Jo, by Tracy Hughes, a February release
Tess, by Katherine Burton, a March release
Eden, by Penny Richards, an April release

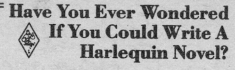

Have You Ever Wondered If You Could Write A Harlequin Novel?

Here's great news—Harlequin is offering a series of cassette tapes to help you do just that. Written by Harlequin editors, these tapes give practical advice on how to make your characters—and your story— come alive. There's a tape for each contemporary romance series Harlequin publishes.

Mail order only

All sales final

TEARS IN THE RAIN

STARRING
CHRISTOPHER CAVZENOVE AND
SHARON STONE

BASED ON A NOVEL BY
PAMELA WALLACE

PREMIERING IN NOVEMBER

TITR-1